A YEAR

A gentleman for every season

At the mercy of a ghostly matchmaker,
four gentlemen must perform a shocking task.
But claiming their inheritance may just lead them
to the women who will steal their hearts!

Don't miss this wonderful new quartet by

Harlequin® Historical author

Elizabeth Beacon

THE MARQUIS'S AWAKENING
December 2014

THE VISCOUNT'S FROZEN HEART
Already available

Author Note

Welcome to *The Marquis's Awakening*, and thank you for coming with me on my journey through A Year of Scandal.

As the season moves into spring, Tom Banburgh, Marquis of Mantaigne, finds more than he bargained for when he claims his once magnificent birthright at long last. I wanted Tom to have springtime as the season to have his life transformed by the most unlikely lady he's ever met, so I hope you enjoy the next adventures Lady Virginia left her four heroes in her will. After this it's summer and fall, but this is Tom's book, and I can imagine him reading it with a cynical grin on his face, telling me I got that bit wrong and should have made him less handsome and his lady even lovelier. But I would never have got this far if it had been left to him, so just for once I intend to ignore him...

Elizabeth Beacon

The Marquis's Awakening

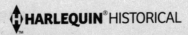
HARLEQUIN® HISTORICAL

Recycling programs
for this product may
not exist in your area.

ISBN-13: 978-0-373-30703-6

The Marquis's Awakening

Printed in U.S.A.

Available from Harlequin® Historical and ELIZABETH BEACON

Did you know that these novels are also available as ebooks? Visit www.Harlequin.com.

ELIZABETH BEACON

lives in the beautiful English West Country, and is finally putting her insatiable curiosity about the past to good use. Over the years Elizabeth has worked in her family's horticultural business, become a mature student, qualified as an English teacher, worked as a secretary and, briefly, tried to be a civil servant. She is now happily ensconced behind her computer, when not trying to exhaust her bouncy rescue dog with as many walks as the Inexhaustible Lurcher can finagle. Elizabeth can't bring herself to call researching the wonderfully diverse, scandalous Regency period and creating charismatic heroes and feisty heroines *work*, and she is waiting for someone to find out how much fun she is having and tell her to stop it.

Chapter One

Tom Banburgh, Marquis of Mantaigne, thought the polite world was about to be bitterly disappointed. If the wolfish glint in Luke Winterley's eye was anything to go by, he wouldn't be letting the former Lady Chloe Thessaly out of his bed long enough for her to go to town for a very long time, so the *ton* wouldn't be able to pass judgement on the new Viscountess Farenze until her new husband could spare her—some time in the next decade, if they were lucky.

'Can't this wait until after your wedding journey?' he asked with a sinking feeling in the pit of his stomach as Lady Chloe took a sealed missive from the neat reticule she was carrying. He should have been suspicious of that, since Luke was waiting to whisk her off on their bride trip and she hardly stood in need of whatever ladies carried in them when she had a husband all too eager to provide for her every need, and a few she probably didn't even know she had right now.

Feeling a fool for not remembering his godmother's

infamous will, even on this joyous day Virginia had done so much to bring about, he realised he'd stepped into the book room with the happy couple as naively as a débutante at her first grown-up party. As if they would have anything else to say to him before they left for Devon on their honeymoon but *here you are; you're next*.

'Here you are; you're next, I'm afraid, Tom,' Chloe said with a rueful smile to admit he wouldn't be pleased to take it and how could a few bits of expensive paper feel so heavy? 'Luke says we won't be back from Devon for weeks, and you must begin whatever you have to do for Lady Virginia before then if you're to get it done in the allotted three months.'

'Dash it all, though, it's the beginning of the Season,' Tom managed to utter after a heavy pause as he fought off a craven urge to throw the letter back at his best friend's new wife and refuse. 'Ah, well, suppose I might as well get it over with,' he said as lightly as he could while turning the letter over again, as if he might conjure it into someone else's hand if he put off reading it long enough.

'Look what my quarter of a year brought me,' Luke told him with a besotted smile Tom did his best to find nauseating.

'And can you see *me* neatly paired off at the end of whatever wild goose chase Virginia insists I carry out for her?' he demanded past a nasty little suspicion that was exactly what his wily godmother intended to happen, if Luke's adventures were anything to go by.

'One day you'll have to consider the succession,' Luke said half-seriously.

'I have and decided there's nothing very wonderful about the Banburghs, so who cares if there are no more of us?' Tom replied with a cynical smile that felt a lot better than the dread of being the next one on his godmother's list.

He ordered himself not to squirm under the sceptical mother's glance Chloe had perfected on her young niece. She and Luke would no doubt raise repellent quantities of brats in their joint images and be blissfully happy together for the rest of their lives, but he had no wish to follow in their footsteps and had managed without a family all his life.

'True,' Luke agreed with an impatient glance at the door. 'Why not leave him to read it in peace now, love? A very small part of me would like to stay and watch Mantaigne perform like a dancing bear in his turn, but the rest can't wait for us to begin our honeymoon.'

'I doubt your *best friend* relishes the task in front of him though, Luke,' she told her new husband sternly, then seemed to find it impossible to see anything but him once she'd turned her fascinated gaze his way.

'Have you any clue to what my quest could be, Lady Chloe?' Tom asked to remind the lovers he was still here, before it was he who needed to leave the book room in a hurry instead of them.

'Oh, that quest. No, I only hand out the letters,' Chloe said with a shrug that admitted she was so deep in love with Luke they were very poor company.

She flicked a glance at Tom's name and titles inscribed on his last message from his godmother and he was in danger of being ambushed by grief all over again. It was such a stark absence, having to acknowledge Virginia's wit, warmth and energy had left this world for the next. She and Virgil had lit up his life, and he felt the loneliness of losing both hit him anew.

'I had such plans, very seductive and beautiful ones they were as well,' he grumbled to hide his true feelings on such a joyful day.

'Rakehell.' Luke dismissed that objection with the wolfish good humour of a man about to have his own wildest fantasies come true. 'And where would be the fun in my great-aunt being predictable in death as she never was in life?'

'Fun for you, I suppose, Romeo, now your task is safely over.'

'True, watching you squirm is a pleasant side effect of standing at my own Lady Farenze's side while I watch three more idiots run about in their turn. If Virginia can see us from her place in heaven, I bet she's enjoying the view even more than I am right now.'

'Knowing her, it won't be some simple task easily got through and back to town before anyone misses me either.'

'Oh, I suspect those seductively beautiful plans of yours will, but we have to leave, and you need to discover whatever it is Virginia wants you to do in private,' the new Lady Farenze intervened.

'The fun's just starting—do we really have to go when it's getting interesting?' her lord said with the easy humour of a man whose task had come to a deeply satisfying conclusion.

'*We* do, Luke Winterley,' Chloe said with a severe look that only made him laugh.

Tom hadn't seen his friend and honorary brother this carefree since he was a dashing and hopeful youth, always game for a lark. The marriage his father arranged when Luke was barely twenty certainly knocked the youthful high spirits out of him far too young and he'd turned into a virtual hermit when the silly chit left him. After that Luke had locked himself away in his northern stronghold to raise their baby daughter and Tom blessed Virginia for managing to chip Luke out of frozen isolation, but he didn't want to be next the next victim on her list all the same.

'Well, we'll leave you to it then, Mantaigne. Try not to miss us too much, won't you?' Luke said with a mocking grin at Tom and a hot look at his lady that made her blush, then stride ahead of him, clearly in nearly as much of a hurry to begin married life as he was.

The door shut after them with a soft snick and Tom was left with the last letter he'd ever receive from his godmother, wishing she was here to tell him what maggot had got into her head this time herself. He'd spent the best years of his boyhood in this house and sometimes wondered if he had imagined his stark early childhood as the true lord of an ancient castle and vast estates, but master of nothing.

'Bonaparte's Imperial Guard could be marching about on the cliffs tonight and we wouldn't be any the wiser.'

Polly Trethayne shook her head, then remembered

her companion couldn't see her in the heavy darkness. 'I really think we would,' she whispered, wishing her friend and ally had stayed inside. 'If it *is* smugglers, we really need to be quiet.'

'Better for us *not* to know when they're out and about, if you ask me,' Lady Wakebourne grumbled a little more softly.

'I didn't and we can't simply sit back and let them use Castle Cove to land cargo whenever they fancy. The riding officers are sure to find out and report it, and the last thing we want is for the Marquis of Mantaigne to take an interest in Dayspring Castle for once in his life. He'll turn us out to tramp the roads again without a second thought and leave the poor old place to go to rack and ruin.'

'Even if he wants Dayspring to tumble down as the locals say, I'm sure he'd rather we stay than leave it empty for any passing rogue who wants a hiding place.'

'One or two may already be doing that and we are the rogues as far as the rest of the world is concerned. No, long may he stop away,' Polly argued.

Meeting Lady Wakebourne and finding this place abandoned on his lordship's orders was a small miracle and Polly had prayed every night for the last six and a half years for the man to stop away. Even the memory of how it felt to wander the world with a babe in her arms and two small boys at her heels for six long and terrifying months made her shudder.

'I doubt if anything would wrench him away from the delights of a London Season at this time of year, so I don't suppose we rogues need worry,' Lady Wakebourne whispered with an unlikely trace of regret.

Polly shook her head at the idea her practical and forthright friend secretly dreamed of playing loo and gossiping with the tabbies and dowagers of the *ton*, whilst the glitter and scandal of soirées and balls played out round them. Deciding she must be a freak to think the whole extravagant business sounded appalling, she wondered fleetingly how she'd have fared in that world if she had been obliged to make her come out in polite society. The idea was so far removed from her real life it made her want to laugh, but she bit it back and reminded herself this was serious.

'Surely you heard that?' she whispered urgently, listening to the night with the uneasy feeling it was listening back. 'I'd swear that was a window opening or closing on the landward side of the house.'

'The wind, perhaps?'

'There is no wind; nothing ought to be out here but foxes or owls.'

'Some poor creature could have got in and not been able to get back out, then,' Lady Wakebourne murmured.

'I refuse to believe bats and birds can unbar shutters or open windows,' Polly said as lightly as she could when this black darkness made her want to shout a challenge at whoever was out there.

'Tomorrow we'll go in and see for ourselves, but if you take another step in that direction now I'll scream at the top of my voice.'

'They will be long gone by then,' Polly argued, although she knew Lady Wakebourne was right and she couldn't afford to encounter an unknown foe in the unused parts of the castle.

Her three brothers had to grow up and be independent before she was free to have adventures, but it was so hard to fight her wild Trethayne urges to act now and think later. At least memory of her father's recklessness reminded her to leash her own though; she was all that stood between her brothers and life on the parish, if they were lucky, and she had no plans to leave any of them in the dire situation Papa's death had left her in as a very naive and unprepared seventeen-year-old.

'At least we'll find out if these felons of yours exist outside the pages of a Gothic novel. If they do we'll have to get them to believe there really are ghosts at Dayspring Castle and leave us in peace with them.'

'Perhaps I should cut my hair and borrow a fine coat, then ride up the drive and announce myself as the Marquis of Mantaigne come back to claim his own,' Polly suggested as the most absurd way of scaring anyone out of the old place she could think of.

'And perhaps you should stop reading those ridiculous Gothic novels the vicar's sister passes on to us when she knows them by heart.'

'Aye, they're about as likely to come true as the idea Lord Mantaigne will ever come here without being kidnapped and dragged up the drive bound and gagged first. So ghosts it will have to be then,' Polly agreed, reluctantly admitting there was nothing to be done tonight, and followed her fellow adventuress back to the castle keep and the closest thing she had to a home nowadays.

* * *

'I should have sent the butler and housekeeper from Tayne on ahead of us, Peters. At least they might have found a few rooms at Dayspring undamaged after all these years of neglect and managed to make them habitable for us by now.'

Tom halted his matched team of Welsh greys at the gatehouse and wished himself a hundred miles away. Dayspring Castle was puffed up as his most splendid country seat in the peerages and guides to the county, but he felt a clutch of sick dread in his belly at the mere sight of it ahead, wrapped round the clifftop like a beast of prey from his worst nightmares.

'They would have given notice,' his companion argued. 'It would need an army of servants to get such a place in any sort of order after lying empty so long.'

'True, but wouldn't that army need to be directed by my man of business?' Tom retaliated against a not very-well-disguised rebuke for neglecting the wretched place until it became the ruin he'd once sworn to make it.

'I like a challenge, my lord,' Peters said, and wasn't he a mystery of a lawyer now Tom came to think about it?

Nothing about this business was simple, though, and he supposed he'd have to admit the man had been useful to Luke in the part of the quest Virginia set him. According to James Winterley, who had a way of knowing things you didn't expect him to, Peters had helped a variety of aristocratic clients sort out the skeletons in their rosewood cupboards, including the Seaborne clan, whose shrewdness Tom would back against a corps of wily diplomats. So Tom had no choice but to trust this man to watch his back, even if the fellow saw too much of what lay below the surface of life for comfort.

'You're only here for three months, and heaven knows why Virginia thought I needed you by my side the entire time. Perhaps she expected you to force me up the drive at pistol-point if I lose my nerve.'

'The late Lady Farenze merely instructed me to meet you in Dorchester and accompany you here. I couldn't say what your godmother had in mind, my lord,' Peters said primly, but there was a world of disapproval in his gaze.

Perhaps the man was a Jacobin? Tom decided he didn't care if he was hell-bent on revolution, so long as they got on with this wretched business and left as soon as they found out what was wrong. 'I believe I mentioned my dislike of being "my lorded" at every turn when we first met,' he replied with a preoccupied frown at the neatly kept castle gatehouse.

'I'm supposed to be your temporary secretary here, not your equal, my lord.'

Tom found himself doubting that and how unlike him to look deeper into another man's life than he wanted him to. Lord Mantaigne had spent most of his adult life skimming over the surface of life like a pond-skater, and Tom shook his head at the picture of himself not caring about anything very much. He'd loved his godmother and Virgil, but they were both dead now, and at least he'd managed to keep the rest of the world at arm's length, except a voice whispered he'd let in Luke and his daughter and James. Now Lady Chloe and her spirited niece seemed to have chipped their way into a corner of what he'd thought was his cold heart, and how could he have been so careless as to let himself care about so many people without noticing?

He glared at a certain window high up in the ancient keep and stark memories rose up to whisper he was right not to come back until he had to. Virginia's last letter had told him one of her legion of friends had written to tell her something was amiss at Dayspring and he must go and find out what was so wrong with the place, but all he could see wrong with it right now was that it was still standing. Only for the woman who had taken in the feral little beast who had once existed in that keep and loved him anyway would he revisit the place despite all his resolutions not to.

'Whoever you intend to be, you'll have a poor time of it here,' he warned Peters as he slowed his greys to a walk.

'I expect I'll survive; I'm not faint-hearted.'

'Just as well. My last guardian only kept a few servants here once he took control of the estate for me, and I paid them off when I came of age,' Tom warned.

Peters shrugged as if he wanted to get on with his mission and leave, before he violated some lawyerly code and told a client exactly what he thought of his criminal neglect of such an historic property.

'I expect there will be a couple of rooms we can make habitable for the few days I intend to spend here,' Tom added glumly.

'Indeed, although the castle looks very well preserved to me, despite your orders it should not be.'

'And it's evidently a lot less empty than it ought to be,' Tom mused with a frown as he watched a plume of smoke waft lazily from a chimney in the oldest part of the castle.

The place had an air of being down at heel, but it wasn't the echoing ruin it ought to be after being left empty so long. There were deep ruts in the road leading down to Castle Cove that made him wonder even more who had stopped it falling into the sea. Virginia was right to make him come here to find out what was going on, and he pictured her impatiently telling him she'd told him so from her place in heaven. He had to suppress a grin at the idea of her regarding him with still very fine dark eyes and a puckish grin that told the world Lady Virginia Farenze was still ready to jump into any adventure going with both feet.

He missed her with an ache that made him feel numb at times and furious at others. Lord Mantaigne was a care-for-nobody, but he'd cared more for Virginia than he'd let himself know until he lost her. Still, one of his childhood resolutions was safe; he would never marry and risk leaving a son of his alone in a hostile world. The Winterley family might have trampled his boyhood vow never to care about anyone in the dust, but that one wasn't in any danger. He hadn't met a female he couldn't live without in all his years as one of the finest catches on the marriage mart, so he was hardly likely to find her in a dusty backwater like Dayspring Castle.

'Some traffic clearly passes this way,' Peters remarked with a nod at the uneven road in case Tom was too stupid or careless to notice.

Ordering Dayspring's ruin on what must seem a rich man's whim was one thing, but being judged stupid set Tom's teeth on edge. Was he vain about his intellect as well as finicky about personal cleanliness and a neat appearance? Probably, he decided ruefully. The last Marquis of Mantaigne already seemed to be learning more about himself than he really wanted to know, and his three months of servitude had barely begun.

'Heavy traffic as well,' he murmured, frowning at the spruce gatehouse and well-maintained gates and wondering if there was a link between those carts and whoever kept it so neatly.

'Perhaps we should follow in their hoof prints towards the stables? At least that way is well used, and the castle gates look sternly locked against all comers.'

'Since there are clearly more people here than there ought to be, I'll start as I mean to go on.' Tom replied.

'Maybe, but I don't have any skill with the yard of tin so I'm afraid I can't announce you in style.'

'I knew I should have brought my head groom with me and left you to follow on one of the carts, Peters. Hand it over and hold the ribbons while we see what this idle fool can do with it instead.'

'I never said you were a fool, my lord.'

'Only a wastrel?' Tom drawled as insufferably as he could manage, because being here prickled like a dozen wasp stings and why should he suffer alone?

'I don't suppose my opinion of anyone I work with during this year Lady Farenze decreed in her will matters to you.'

'I'm sure you underestimate yourself, Peters.'

'Do I, my lord? I wonder,' the man said with his usual grave reserve.

Tom wondered why Virginia had thought he needed someone to watch his back in what should be a straightforward ruin by now. Perhaps she was right, though, he decided with a shrug when he considered his non-ruin and the rutted lane down to the sea, but he still played down to Peters's poor opinion of him by raising an arrogant eyebrow and imperiously holding out a gloved hand for the yard of tin.

The greys accepted the change of driver with a calmness that surprised their owner as he produced an ear-splitting blast and, when there was still no sign of life, gave the series of emphatic demands for attention he'd learnt from Virgil's coachman as a boy. He was about to give in and drive in the wake of those carts when the door slammed open and an ageing bruiser stamped into view.

'Noise fit to wake the dead,' he complained bitterly. 'Yon castle's closed up. You won't find a welcome up there even if I was to let you in,' he said, squinting up at them against the afternoon sun.

'I don't expect one here, so kindly open up before I decide it was a mistake not to have the place razed to the ground.'

'*You're* the Marquis of Mantaigne?'

'So I'm told.'

'Himself is said to be a prancing town dandy who never sets foot outdoors in daylight and lives in the Prince of Wales's pocket, when he ain't too busy cavorting about London and Brighton with other men's wives and drinking like a fish, of course. You sure you want to be him?'

'Who else would admit it after such a glowing summary of my life, but, pray, who am I trying to convince I'm the fool you speak of so highly?'

'Partridge, my lord, and lord I suppose you must be, since you're right and nobody else would admit to being you in this part of the world.'

'What a nest of revolutionary fervour this must be. Now, if you'll open the gates I'd like to enter my own castle, if you please?' Tom said in the smooth but deadly tone he'd learnt from Virgil, when some idiot was fool enough to cross him.

'You'll do better to go in the back way, if go in you must. It's a tumbledown old place at the best of times, m'lord, and there's nobody to open the front door. These here gates ain't been opened in years.'

Tom eyed carefully oiled hinges and cobbles kept clear of grass both sides of the recently painted wrought-iron gates. 'I might look like a flat, Partridge, but I do have the occasional rational thought in my head,' he said with a nod at those well-kept gates the man claimed were so useless.

'A man has his pride and I'm no idler.'

'How laudable—now stop trying to bam me and open the gates.'

Partridge met Tom's eyes with a challenge that changed to grudging respect when he looked back without flinching. At last the man shrugged and went inside for the huge key to turn in the sturdy lock and Tom wasn't surprised to see the gates open as easily as if they'd been used this morning. He thanked Partridge with an ironic smile and, as the man clanged the gates behind the curricle, wondered who the old fox was doing his best to warn that an intruder was on his way even he couldn't repel.

'I'm still surprised such an old building isn't falling down after so many years of neglect,' Peters remarked as Tom drove his team up the ancient avenue and tried to look as if he hadn't a care in the world.

'Some misguided idiot must have disobeyed all my orders,' Tom said bitterly.

Memories of being dragged up here bruised and bleeding and begging to be let go before his guardian got hold of him haunted him, but he was master here now and thrust the memory of that ragged and terrified urchin to the back of his mind where he belonged.

'Anyway, if I intended to let the place fall down without having to give orders for it to be demolished, I seem to have been frustrated,' he managed to remark a little more calmly.

'And I wonder how you feel about that.'

'So do I,' Tom mused wryly.

He accepted there was no welcome to be had at the massive front door and drove to the stable yard, feeling he'd made his point, if only to Peters and the gatekeeper. He saw two sides of the square that formed the stable blocks and the imposing entrance and clock tower were closed up and empty, paint peeling and a cast-iron gutter, broken during some tempest, left to rust where it fell. The remaining block was neat and well kept, though, and two curious horses were peering out of their stables as if glad of company.

'More frustration for you,' Peters murmured.

'Never mind that, who the devil is living here? I ordered it empty as a pauper's pocket and they can't be any kin of mine because I don't have any.'

'How did you plan to look after your team when we got here then, let alone the carts and men following behind?'

'The boot is full of tack, oats and horse blankets, so it's your own comfort I'd be worrying myself about if I were you.'

'I will, once we have these lads safely stowed in the nice comfortable stable someone's left ready for them,' Peters said with a suspicious glance about the yard that told Tom they had the same idea about such empty but prepared stables and what they might be used for this close to the coast.

'Keep that pistol handy while we see to the horses,' he cautioned.

Chapter Two

It didn't take long to remove the harness and lead the now-placid team into four waiting stalls and rub them down. Once they were cool enough, Tom and Peters hefted the ready-filled water buckets so the horses could drink after their leisurely journey, then they left them to pull happily at the hay-net someone had left ready. Tom was enjoying the sights and sounds of contented horses when the shaft of mellow afternoon sunlight from the half-open door was blocked by a new arrival. Pretending to be cool as the proverbial cucumber, he cursed himself for leaving his coat and pistol out of reach and turned to face the newcomer with a challenge that rapidly turned to incredulity.

'Ye gods!' he exclaimed, stunned by the appearance of a shining goddess with no shame at all, at Dayspring of all places.

'Minerva or Hera?' he heard Peters murmur in the same bewildered tone and felt a glimmer of impatience that the man was ogling the woman he urgently wanted himself. He could hardly wait to wrap those endless feminine legs about his own flanks and be transported to the heights of Olympus as soon as he could get those scandalous breeches off her.

'You should at least get Greece and Rome sorted out in your head before you make such foolish comparisons in future,' the vision said crossly, proving she had acute hearing, as well as a classical education and the finest feminine legs Tom had ever seen, in or out of his bed-chamber, and he badly wanted this pair naked in one as soon as he could charm, persuade or just plain beg her to let him make love to her.

'I'll be happy in either so long as you're with me, Athene,' Tom recovered himself enough to offer with a courtly bow she should find flattering.

'And I have no time for such nonsense and nor do you, Mr Whoever-You-Might-Be. You're going to be far too busy reharnessing those fine horses of yours to that pretty little carriage and driving them back the way you came to indulge in such ridiculous fancies.'

'Why would I do that?'

'Because I demand you remove them from our stables immediately.'

'*Our* stables?' Tom's mind latched on to the possessive word among so many he could argue with and he wondered why it seemed so important she had no intimate other to pair herself with instead of him.

'Ours, mine, whatever you prefer. I'd certainly prefer you to go quickly and stop staring at my legs.'

'If you don't want them leered at, you should resume your petticoats. We males can't resist eyeing such fine feminine charms when they're so temptingly displayed without them.'

'A true gentleman wouldn't look,' she informed him, looking haughtily down a nose Hera or Minerva would have been justly proud of.

'Oh, but he would, wouldn't he, Peters? Peters is a proper gentleman, Athene, although I am only a nobleman myself,' Tom said, not at all sure he liked being looked at as if he was a caterpillar on a cabbage leaf.

'So you say,' she said sceptically.

Tom had often wished the world could see beyond the wealth and prestige he'd been born to and now he wanted an unlikely goddess to be impressed by them? Folly, he told himself, and goddesses didn't wear an odd mix of outdated clothes that looked as if they'd belonged to a few of his ancestors before they found a new glory on her.

'So I know,' he managed coolly enough.

'Prove it then.'

He laughed at the notion he needed to and at Dayspring of all places. Should he thank her for distracting him from the ordeal he'd thought this homecoming would be without her? 'Do you expect me to produce a letter of introduction from the patronesses of Almack's, or an invitation to Carlton House? Perhaps the record of my birth in the local parish church might do the trick—what would you advise, Peters?'

'Any one might be a fraud,' she argued before Peters could open his mouth.

'And I'm not prepared to prove myself on my own

property, madam,' Tom said, deciding it was time to bring the game to an end.

'Everyone in the neighbourhood knows the Marquis of Mantaigne never sets foot beyond the clubs of St James's or the ballrooms of Mayfair during this season of the year and has sworn not to come here as long as he lives. You need to think your story out better if you plan to masquerade as that idle fool.'

'You think me more useful and less vain than Lord Mantaigne? Hasn't anyone told you appearances are deceptive?'

'Not as badly as yours would have to be,' she said as if it was a *coup de grâce*.

Stray curls of russet-brown hair had worked free from the impressive plait hanging down her back to dance about her brow and distract Tom from a subject that kept slipping away from him as he wondered why she was so irresistibly female when her dress and manner were anything but.

'Blue,' he mused out loud as he met the smoky mystery of her eyes under long dark lashes. Her unusually marked eyebrows made her frown seem exaggerated and her smile a delicious flight of mischief, or at least he thought it might be, if she ever smiled at him, which currently seemed unlikely. Just as well really, he supposed hazily; if she ever gave up frowning he might walk straight into the promises and secrets in her unique eyes and fall under her witchy spell for ever.

'No, they might be grey,' he muttered as he tried to disentangle smoke and mystery from reality. 'Or perhaps even a little bit green.'

He saw shock in the bluey-grey marvel of her eyes, with those intriguing rays of green in their fascinating depths when she widened them, as if suddenly realising they were staring at each other. She shot Peters a questioning look, as if Tom might be a lunatic and the lawyer his unlucky keeper.

'I am the sixth Marquis of Mantaigne and have been so for most of my life,' Tom informed her testily, 'but who the devil are you?'

'None of your business,' she snapped back.

'How ironic that I've come back after all these years and nobody seems to believe I have the right to, don't you think, Peters?' Tom mused to play for time whilst he gathered his senses.

'Much about life is ironic, my lord,' Peters said unhelpfully.

'Aye,' Tom drawled with an emphatic look at his reluctant hostess that should make her blush and run to fetch whoever tried to lend her countenance.

Not that she had any idea of her own looks, he decided with a frown. She must be close to six feet tall to meet his eyes so easily, especially when looking down her haughty Roman nose as if he was the source of an unpleasant smell she hadn't been able to track down until now. Most of her inches were made up of leg and he almost wished he carried a quizzing glass so he could infuriate her all the more. Not that she didn't have a superb body to match those long and slender feminine legs of hers; dressed in form-fitting breeches, flowing shirt and a tight spencer jacket as she was, he'd be a fool *not* to notice she had a fine collection of feminine curves to go with them.

The wonder was she could roam round Dayspring in such a guise without a pack of wolves hunting her as such beasts usually did any unprotected female. She must be able to go about unmolested, though, since she hadn't stopped doing it, and that made him take her more seriously than he wanted to. If ever he'd met a feminine disaster waiting to happen it was this argumentative young goddess and he hadn't time or energy to cope with the challenge she presented just now.

'You don't look like any of the portraits of past Lord Mantaignes scattered about the castle,' she informed him with the sort of infuriated glare he hadn't been subjected to since he last annoyed Virginia.

'I doubt if one of my father survived my former guardian's rule here, but I'm told I take after him,' Tom said, wondering why it mattered.

'Don't you know?'

'I don't remember either of my parents.'

'That's as may be, but none of the pictures look like you,' she said accusingly.

He sighed in his best impression of a bored society beau and hoped she found it as superior and annoying as he meant her to. She took a long look at his dusty but perfectly fitted boots, then her gaze flicked dismissively over the coat Weston would no longer be quite so proud to admit was his handiwork lying nearby, but he saw the odd giveaway sign she wasn't as confident of his nonentity as she wanted him to believe. Her breathing came a little short and there was a hint of desperation in those fine eyes, as if the truth was too much to cope with and she wanted to fend it off as long as possible.

'I dare say you know the State Rooms better than I do. My guardian never let me explore that part of the house when I lived here,' he admitted, trying to shrug off the feeling he'd revealed too much.

'The villagers do say Lord Mantaigne's guardian was a cruel man,' she conceded, thinking about rearranging her prejudices, but not yet ready to turn them on their head.

'How tactful of them,' he said with a bitter smile.

Why the devil had he let Virginia bullock him into coming here? Tom wanted to be out of this intimate stable in the fresh air. With hints of fish and brine, seaweed and wide oceans on the breeze from the sea, at least that was something his guardian had never been able to take from him. How could he have forgotten that and all the other things he loved about this place, despite the neglect and cruelty he'd endured? He'd never wanted to set eyes on this place, but the scent of the sea settled a strange sort of longing in him for home that he hadn't even known he had until he got here.

He used to risk his life creeping down the hoary old stones of the North Tower as soon as his bare feet were big enough to cling to the bumps and cracks in the rock. Grably was too much of a coward to kill the 'spawn of the devil', he had called Tom when no outsiders were listening, but he wouldn't have shed a tear if Tom had fallen to his death and saved him the stain of murder on his mean and twisted soul.

'I suppose you could be him,' a very different

keeper of Dayspring Castle admitted begrudgingly and wrenched his thoughts back to the present. 'You're the right age, but Maggie said his little lordship looked an angel fallen out of Heaven and you don't look angelic to me.'

'You know my one-time nurse then?' he said, sounding far too eager. That reminder of the one constant in his life after his father had died, until his guardian sent her away, caught him unawares.

'I knew Lord Mantaigne's childhood nurse before she died,' she said, eyeing him as if unsure his word could be trusted or not.

Not, Tom concluded, at least not if she was aware of her own allure as she stood in the shadowed gloom of the stables and stared at him as if she could read his sooty soul. Not, if she was possibly the most unlikely virgin lady he had ever met, with her mannish garments, unmanly figure and a mass of unruly hair barely held by the tail she'd plaited it into some time during the last week.

An unforgivably urgent desire to see the heavy weight of it about her naked shoulders like rumpled silk taunted his body and his senses. Half hiding and half enhancing a figure he knew would be as perfect in real human flesh as any classical statue of a two-thousand-year-old goddess carved in ancient Greece, he could picture it rippling over the fine skin he suspected was creamy and satin smooth where the sun hadn't reached her not-quite-redhead's skin and tinted it pale gold.

Considering nothing about her seemed quite sure how to be, she was a very definite snare for a man who liked his ladies bold and confident of their own charms. Her hair wasn't quite red, brown or blonde and he'd already had that silly discussion with himself about her eyes. He could feel Peters's cool gaze on him as he realised what the unwary goddess wouldn't let herself see—that she was in the presence of a lone wolf and could be very unsafe indeed. If not for where they were and what he'd been sent here to do, she would be in more danger than Peters realised, but Tom couldn't afford distractions until he got to the bottom of a very odd barrel of fish.

'*Knew* her?' he asked after he'd racked his brains to recall what they were talking about before he got distracted again.

'She died five years ago,' his mystery snapped.

'I have no resident agent here,' he said stiffly. 'Nor have I kept in contact with anyone in the villages.'

'Something they know all too well,' she condemned, and he suddenly felt impatient of his would-be judge and jury.

'Something they can now complain about directly to me, if I ever manage to leave these stables and meet any of them,' he said wearily.

'Is he really the Marquis of Mantaigne?' she asked Peters, as if unable to trust his word, and Tom bit back an impatient curse.

'Ask yourself if he could be anyone else, ma'am, and I suspect you'll have your answer. I'm his employee, so you can't trust me to tell the truth. Lord Mantaigne could terminate my employment if I was to argue against him.'

'As if I would dare,' Tom allowed himself to drawl

and felt he'd almost won back the detachment he prided himself on.

'He looks useless enough to be a marquis, or he might if he was wearing that dandified coat,' she allowed with a nod of contempt at a once-exquisite example of Weston's fine work.

'Do you think there might be a compliment hiding somewhere in that sentence if I look hard enough for it, Peters?' Tom asked as if they needed a translator.

'I wouldn't bet your rent rolls on it, my lord.'

'Paulina! Oh, Polly! Wherever are you hiding yourself this time?' a brisk soprano voice called before being drowned out by what sounded like a pack of large and hungry dogs barking as if they were eager to sink their teeth into any passing stranger—be he a marquis or a commoner.

Tom's guardian used to hunt him down with his pack when he thought he'd had his freedom for too long. Remembered fear made him cast a swift glance in the direction of the hunt kennels his guardian had built far enough away for their howls not to keep him awake at nights. Luckily his companions were too busy to see it and he clamped adult self-control on childhood fears and reminded himself he'd learnt to like and trust dogs since then.

'I know you're in the stables because these misbegotten hounds insist you are, so who does the curricle belong to?' that brisk voice added from much nearer at hand.

'Which question would you prefer me to answer first, Lady W.?' the goddess shouted over the hubbub.

Paulina-whoever-she-was sounded as calmly unruffled as any woman could with such a commotion going on in her stable yard, but shouldn't that be his stable yard? And why did he feel a need to claim the property he'd been tempted to destroy all his adult life?'

'How many times have I told you not to call me by that repellent nickname?' the newcomer demanded.

'So many I wonder you still bother,' Paulina replied as Tom peered over her shoulders and managed to meet the lady's shrewd blue eyes. 'He claims he's the Marquis of Mantaigne and this is Lady Wakebourne,' Paulina said as if not quite sure how to introduce a possible impostor.

'Lady Wakebourne,' he said, searching his memory for clues to how the lady fitted into the complex patchwork of the *ton*.

He dredged up the tale of a certain Sir Greville Wakebourne, who had bankrupted a great many people before putting a bullet in his brain several years ago. This lady, who had evidently been a true beauty in her youth, was probably his widow, but it was impossible to tell if she mourned the swindler or not. She didn't look as if she dwelt on him or anything else in the past, so vivid and vital was her presence in the here and now.

'Lord Mantaigne,' she greeted him with such superb assurance he was in mid-bow before his brain reminded him he was the host here and not the other way about, but he carried on anyway.

'Weren't you one of my godmother's coven of regular correspondents, my lady?' he asked and felt Polly-Paulina's gaze fix accusingly on him, as if he'd been trying to deceive her about his identity instead of trying to convince her he really was rightfully lord and master here.

'Please accept my condolences on her death and desist from using such terms in future,' Lady Wakebourne told him with a firmness that told him she was every bit as stubborn as the goddess.

'Is he really the Marquis of Mantaigne?' Polly-Paulina asked, sounding so disgruntled she must be taking him seriously.

'Of course he is—why would anyone else admit to being a notorious rake and dandy?' Lady Wakebourne replied before he could say a word, stern disapproval of his chosen way of life plain on her striking countenance.

'They would if it meant getting his possessions along with his reputation,' Paulina-whoever-she-was muttered.

Outraged barking had waned to a few vague snuffles and the odd whine as the owners of those formidable canine voices sniffed about the curricle for concealed villains. Now two huge paws hit the bottom half of the door and a shaggy head joined Lady Wakebourne's attempts at blocking out daylight. The creature appeared comical until its panting revealed a set of strong white teeth the hounds of hell could be justly proud of.

'Get down, sir,' Lady Wakebourne ordered the enormous animal irritably. 'If you must take in any stray lucky enough to cross your path, Polly, I wish you would train them not to dog my footsteps as if I actually like them.'

'But you do,' Polly said, seeing through Lady Wakebourne's frown as easily as the large hound seemed to, given he was now watching her with dogged adoration.

An impatient bark from lower down said the hell-hound was blocking the view, so he sank back to sit next to a busy-looking terrier with a thousand battle scars and a cynical look in the one eye he had left. He met Tom's gaze in a man-to-man sizing up that was almost human, and if a dog could snigger this one did in a crooked aside. An elderly greyhound with an aloof look that said *I don't get involved, so don't blame me* and a lolloping puppy with some spaniel and a great deal of amiable idiot completed the canine quartet. Even Tom couldn't bring himself to blame them for the sins of the pack of half-starved beasts his guardian had once used to terrorise the neighbourhood and his small charge.

'Not in the house, I don't,' Lady Wakebourne asserted, as if it was her house to be pernickety over if she chose.

Tom frowned as he searched his mind for a reason why the widow of a disgraced baronet was living in his house without his knowledge. 'I expect several carts and their teams before dark, my lady. Can anyone help us make more of the stabling usable?' he asked the simplest of the questions that came into his mind.

It felt strange to be so ignorant of his household, especially when there wasn't supposed to be one. Two coachmen, several stalwart grooms and three footmen were on their way with supplies to make camping in a ruin bearable and they would need somewhere to bed down as well. It would be too dark to do much more than sleep by the time they arrived, but he'd often sought the warmth of the horses at night as a boy and one more night in the stables wouldn't hurt him.

'No, but the northern range is better than the west. It takes less battering from the winds that come in from the sea,' Polly-Paulina said with a sly glance at Tom's riding breeches, shining top-boots, snowy white shirt and grey-silk waistcoat. He wasn't dressed for heavy labour, but she seemed happy about the idea of him doing some anyway.

He had no old clothes here and wouldn't don them now if he had, so he hoped there was a copper of hot water over the fire betrayed by its smoking chimney. Tom met the girl's hostile gaze, determined not to prove as useless as she clearly thought him.

'We'll need pitchforks and a wheelbarrow, buckets and a couple of decent brooms. You will have to re-mind me where the well is,' he prompted as she stayed stubbornly silent.

'The boys can come in from the gardens this late in the day to help, Paulina. They are probably disgrace-fully dirty by now anyway,' Lady Wakebourne said with a caution in her voice to remind her fellow interloper some tact was needed when dealing with the owner of a house you were living in without his knowledge or permission.

For a long moment Paulina the Amazon glared at Tom, as if quite ready to lay aside any pretence of civil-ity and risk expulsion. He raised one eyebrow to ques-tion her right to be furious with him, but she seemed unimpressed.

'Very well,' she finally agreed without taking her eyes off him, as if he might steal the silver if she did so.

He couldn't help the mocking smile that kicked up his mouth, because it was his silver, or it would be if it hadn't been taken away years ago.

'Lunar, go and fetch Toby,' she told the huge beast, as if he would understand. 'Go on, boy, go fetch him in,' she added when the bigger-than-a-wolf dog put his head on one side and eyed Tom and Peters as if not sure it was safe to leave them here.

'Maybe he'd feel better if we went with him?' Tom suggested lightly.

'The boys would run away from such a dandy,' Paulina-Polly muttered darkly, shooting him a look that said she wouldn't blame them.

'Perhaps it would be better if you went yourself then,' he said blandly.

The hound sat on his mighty haunches and eyed first him, then his younger mistress, as if awaiting his cue to protect her to the last breath in his amiable body.

'Or you could make it a clear to your mixed pack of hell-hounds we're not going to rip each other to pieces when their backs are turned?' he added.

'I would have to be certain myself,' he thought he heard her mutter under her breath, but then she seemed to make a huge effort to be civil and held out her hand as a sign to their canine audience that peace reigned.

Tom took it, wondering at the state a lady could get her hand in and not care. A glance at her short nails and tanned skin, nicked and scarred here and there from her labours, did nothing to warn him how it would feel in his broad, well-manicured palm. *Ah, here she is, at last*, an inner voice he ordered not to be so foolish whispered. He felt emotions he didn't want to examine stir and threaten something impossible at the feel of work-hardened calluses on her slender fingers and finely made palm.

She shouldn't have to work at anything more strenuous than pleasing herself and me, his inner idiot whispered in his ear. A shock of something hot and significant he'd never felt before shot through him like a fiery itch. It was too much of an effort to shake her slender hand then let it go as if she was just a new acquaintance.

'I'm honoured to meet you, Miss Paulina,' he said as lightly as if they had met in a Mayfair ballroom or, heaven forbid, Almack's Club. He'd long ago resolved never to venture there again for fear of the tenacious matchmaking mamas and their formidably willing daughters.

'Trethayne,' Lady Wakebourne said abruptly. 'Her name is Miss Trethayne and since she has no elder sister that is all you are required to know.'

Tom felt the girl's hand tug insistently in his, realised he was still holding it like a mooncalf and relaxed his grip with unflattering haste. No wonder she was glaring at him now, and the vast hound was growling under his breath, rather than running off to fetch Toby from the garden as he was bid, whoever Toby might be.

'Three tired teams and their drivers will be arriving here in the next couple of hours, so I suggest we put aside questions of what a Trethayne and you,

Lady Wakebourne, are doing here under my less-than-comfortable roof and get on with preparing the stables to lodge them as best we can.'

'Something you should have thought about when you set out,' Miss Trethayne informed him, and Tom bit back an urge to defend his right to visit his own house if he wanted to, or even if he didn't.

'And if you expect me to put off examining your presence here, perhaps you should lay aside your hostility,' he suggested coldly.

Part of him wanted to trade words with her until the sun went down, for the sheer pleasure of gazing at her scandalously displayed form and extraordinary face, but the rest knew better. She had fascinating eyes and then there was that strong nose that should make her a character, not a beauty, but didn't. Her mouth was too wide to fit an accredited beauty as well, but it was as full of unstudied allure as the rest of her. There, hadn't he just ordered himself *not* to catalogue her graces? Fully recognising his desire to kiss her deeply and urgently would be folly; best not think of such fiery needs when dressed in tight buckskin breeches—for all they concealed of his errant masculine urges he might as well stand here buck naked.

'You'd best get on with cleansing the Augean Stables before it's pitch dark and you can't see what you're doing, then,' she said with a shrug, opening the stable doors with a glance of contempt at his once-spotless linen and expensive tailoring.

He was glad to see it contained none of the cynicism in Lady Wakebourne's gaze as she silently challenged him to keep any lustful thoughts he might harbour about Miss Polly Trethayne strictly to himself. Bracing himself to meet the assorted hounds at closer quarters with suitably manly composure, Tom stepped out in Miss Trethayne's wake and blinked in the late-afternoon sunshine. The four dogs sat to attention at a stern word from Lady Wakebourne, looking more comical than threatening as they watched her as if they knew they'd violated the laws of hospitality by being uncivil to guests.

'Lunar, Zounds, Ariel and Cherubim, otherwise known as Cherry,' the lady introduced them. 'Lunar, give a paw,' she commanded the great hound, who was clearly reserving the option to bite Tom if he misbehaved.

The terrier, Zounds, let out a gruff bark; Ariel looked regally indifferent, and Cherry rolled onto her back and waved all four feet in the air in a frantic plea for attention.

'Hussy,' Lady Wakebourne said with a sad shake of her head that didn't deceive anyone, and the half-grown spaniel-cross waved her paws to tell her mistress she still wanted her belly scratched, hussy or no.

Chapter Three

Polly watched the castle's official reception committee behave in character and sighed. It was too much to hope the man would be scared of Lunar's mighty build and need to protect them to his last breath. She had sensed fear in the tall figure at her side and tried to convince herself it made him less of a man, but then he'd sauntered out of the stables in her wake as if he hadn't a care in the world and confounded her again. How could she not admire a man who confronted his fears with such style, even if she didn't want to like anything about him?

Cherry decided a pantomime of what she wanted wasn't doing the trick and yipped a command in his lordship's direction, so he bent to give the pup a full belly rub she enjoyed so much she let out a little moan of delight and threatened to surge to her feet and jump at him in an excess of joy.

'No!' Lady Wakebourne ordered firmly, so Cherry simply demanded more fuss, and Polly felt the rich echoes of his laugh prickle like a warning along her spine.

'Misbegotten hound,' Lady Wakebourne said, and Cherry wagged her tail as if it was a huge compliment.

'Go get the boys,' Polly ordered Lunar and Zounds, and they bounded off, or at least Lunar bounded. Zounds skittered after him as fast as his uneven gait would allow, and Ariel weighed his options and decided he would like a run, so he streaked after them like the wind. Cherry saw she was being left behind, gave Lord Mantaigne an apologetic lick and dashed off as well.

'The pump?' his lordship asked Polly with one of those exceptionally irritating eyebrows of his quirked in an imperious question.

'There is no pump, only a bucket on a rope,' she said to him with a nod at the most deeply shadowed corner of the yard.

This was no time to soften towards him and join in the mighty clean it would take before the empty stable block was at all usable. Polly fetched the giant key to the tack room on the other side of the quadrangle, daring him to complain at the decay he'd caused in the first place. They'd fought his wilful neglect since the first day they happened on the castle, so he could see for himself how hard that struggle was for an hour of his soft life.

He didn't look soft as he turned the key in the ancient lock without apparent effort. It was beyond her strength to move it without both hands and much cursing and swearing, and Polly told herself it was wrong to ogle his magnificently displayed physique as blatantly as he had done hers and sighed under her breath. His coming here would change everything, and all the wishing him away in the world wouldn't alter the fact he was home at last. An untamed part of her was intrigued and even a little bit triumphant about the fact he'd been well worth waiting for.

Well, he didn't know about the Polly she kept well hidden, and she certainly wasn't going to tell him. Nor was he going to lord it over them; not after neglecting this wonderful old place so shamefully a battalion of thieves could have hidden here without any risk of being challenged. She recalled her father telling her nobody could make her feel small and insignificant unless she let them and bit back a smile as she wondered what her adventurous parent would make of his tall and all-too-significant daughter now.

Not a great deal, a sneaky voice whispered in her ear, but she hid her self-doubts behind the mask of confidence Papa had taught her to use to outface her enemies. Except she couldn't afford to be headlong and reckless and arrogant as he'd been the first to admit a true Trethayne was by nature and intent. He had lost every penny they ever had, and a good few they didn't; then he died during an insane midnight race across the moors to try to recoup his losses with a mad bet on his favourite horse.

Claire, her stepmother, had died when her smallest brother was born, so seven years on from Stephen Trethayne's reckless and untimely death Polly and her little brothers lived on whatever they could grow or make at Dayspring Castle, which went to show what happened when Trethaynes refused to rein in their wilder impulses. At times she had longed for a life of passion and adventure instead of hard work and loneliness, but Polly only had to recall how it felt to be seventeen with three little boys to raise on nothing and the urgency faded.

Yet a dart of something deep and dangerous had shot through her at first sight of this handsome golden-haired Adonis, staring back at her as if she was water in a desert. It still sang somewhere deep down inside her as if he'd branded her with warm lightning. She shivered at what might be, if she wasn't four and twenty and father, mother and every other relative they had never had to three little brothers, and if Lord Mantaigne wasn't one of the richest and most powerful aristocrats in the land.

She shook her head at the ridiculous idea of him wanting her as other than a passing fancy she was not willing to be. Trying to distract herself, she wondered how many horses and servants were on their way with the luxuries he would demand as his right. She could imagine him a great lord or prince in medieval times on a grand progress about the land with a huge entourage of brightly arrayed courtiers and an army of servants to answer his every need along the way. If Dayspring Castle was once capable of housing such a household, it certainly wasn't now. She scaled down his retinue to a couple of carriages and a few carts laden with boxes of superbly cut clothes to deck him out in style.

He would need a valet to keep such splendour band-box fresh and wasn't it lucky the thought of him mincing down Bond Street carrying such an item after a visit to the milliner made her want to laugh? Whatever she thought of him, and she wasn't sure she wanted to know what that was; even she couldn't accuse him of being effete.

She would like to, of course, but she couldn't delude herself so badly. Not with his powerful breadth of shoulder and heavily muscled arms on show when he stood there in his shirtsleeves ready to begin his Herculean task. He had narrow flanks and long and sleekly muscled legs, finishing in those damned boots of his that made him look more like a tidied-up pirate than the mincing marquis her imagination had painted him.

His hair might have started out the day in neatly ranked waves or even the artful disorder some of the dandies affected, but now his golden locks were in such disarray he must be as impatient of a hat on such a fine spring day as she was herself. Which didn't mean they had anything in common. The fine cut of his immaculate waistcoat; the stark whiteness of his linen shirt and beautifully tied neckcloth all argued the Marquis of Mantaigne was used to the finest money could buy. Miss Paulina Trethayne had long ago resigned herself to life shorn of all her kind took for granted and sniffed, as if doubtful he could lift a pitchfork, let alone wield one.

'You'll get very dirty,' she warned, as if he couldn't see the dust and smell the unused staleness of the air inside long-neglected stables for himself.

'I'll wash,' he said indifferently, letting her implied insult pass as he surveyed the dust of ages in front of him. 'We'll need those buckets and something to scrub with as well as more hay and straw, if it can all be got at short notice.'

'Enough of both are in the barn and there's more in the rickyard,' she said, and he raised his annoying eyebrows again, as if surprised they were so organised. He might not be so pleased when he realised animals and crops came ahead of people in their household and there would not be enough to feed him in style.

'Good, we'd best get on with it then, if you'll tell us where a couple of decent brooms and buckets are, then leave us to our labours, Miss Trethayne?' he said, as if he swept and washed down stables every day dressed in Bond Street's finest and with that fallen-angel smile never wavering for a second.

Mr Peters eyed the blanket of stale dust and detritus overlaying everything and looked as if he had better places to be. Moved by his mournful look at his neatly made coat as he took it off, as if he was bidding goodbye to his sober raiment and tidy appearance for ever, Polly went to make sure fires were lit under the vast coppers in the laundry to provide baths for the lord as well as his man. If there was only water for one, doubtless the marquis would take it all and let his fastidious aide sleep in his dirt, so there was no point trying to make him even more eager to leave by skimping on such necessities after their hard labour.

Tom and Peters were almost unrecognisable as the lord of this ancient pile and his supposed secretary by the time all four cartloads of luggage and provisions rolled down the rutted drive. It was dusk and on the edge of true darkness by then and the grooms and stable lads seemed delighted to be at journey's end, even if it didn't promise more than a roof over their heads against the coming night. Their calls to each other and exclamations at the state of the roads and their new lodgings made the yard livelier than it must have been for decades. Tom shook his head as if he was Lunar trying to dislodge a persistent fly and dust and old cobwebs threatened their handiwork with a new sprinkling of ancient history.

'Hercules had the River Styx handy to divert through the Augean Stables,' Peters remarked gloomily as he swept up the dislodged dust and followed his broom outside into the fading daylight, before Tom could make more work.

'And the nice warm Aegean to bathe in when he was done,' Tom said with a grin at his once-pristine companion. 'You look as if you've been pulled through a hedge backwards, rolled in the dust and trampled by a herd of wild horses.'

'I feel filthy,' Peters said disgustedly, and Tom laughed.

'Ah, but you must admit the place is full of surprises,' he said.

'Aye, it's confounded us so far,' the man said as if that wasn't a good thing, but hard work had settled some of the tension of the past few days, and Tom didn't intend to fall into a gloom again.

'At least there's not much chance of being bored for the next few weeks.'

'Boredom can be a good thing, given the alternative,' Peters said with a sigh, but Tom turned to greet his head groom and managed to ignore him.

'There's good news and bad, Dacre,' he informed the man cheerfully once Dacre reported a smooth journey and they had compared notes on the roads and the state of the horses after the easy run they'd had today.

'I can see the bad part of it, milord, so what's to be happy about?'

'Mr Peters and I have swept and scrubbed the unused stables as best we can, so we can house the horses in reasonable comfort and safety. If your lads go and fetch bedding and feed from the barns over yonder, I dare say the nags will be as happy as we can make them, even if I don't hold much hope for the rest of us. I trust you didn't push the teams so hard we can't water them when you find a few more buckets?'

'Not I, but it's as well we brought plenty with us, my lord,' Dacre said with a disapproving look at their handiwork.

Tom's head groom always disdained anything he hadn't ordered himself on principle, but, since Amazonian Miss Trethayne had sent her three young brothers and other assorted urchins to 'help', Tom knew they had achieved a lot. Luckily the lads had soon grown bored with sweeping up choking clouds of ancient dust and cleaning windows and melted away to find more amusing things to do.

'Never mind, Dacre. Barnabas will be here with the riding horses any moment, he can help you restore order in the morning,' Tom said.

'I'll try to be grateful for small mercies then, my lord.'

'For now the horses need your attention and I hope

you find all their gear on the wagons in the dark. A few moth-eaten brushes and a curry-comb with every other tooth missing won't do the job after their journey.'

'Very true, my lord. Now you leave the beasts to me while you go and turn yourself back into a gentleman.'

'Of course. Why else would I pay you so handsomely? Even when you think it's your duty to set me down like a scrubby schoolboy with every other word.'

'Somebody has to do it, my lord,' Dacre replied dourly. 'Her ladyship trusted me with the job when you was a lad, and I'm not done hoping you'll toe the line one day quite yet.'

'Do let me know when you consider me mature enough to run my own life, won't you?' Tom said cheerfully.

Knowing he could relax and leave his horses and men in good hands now, he wondered if he and Peters would have to make do with a very quick dip in the still not-very-warm April sea he could hear whispering against the foreshore of the cove below the castle. There was no chance of him getting a wink of sleep if he tried to bed down in all this dirt, even if it was in a stable, so the sea it would have to be and what else had he expected of the wreck he'd made of his former home?

'Polly said we were to bring lanterns to light you and Mr Peters inside,' little Joshua Trethayne's childish voice piped up as the glow of them softened the fast falling darkness in the stable yard. 'But you're to be careful because the whole place will go up like a tinder box if you let one fall, or so Lady W. says. Oh, and you're not to be late for supper if you have to scrape the dirt off to be in time.'

'Bagpipe,' Master Henry Trethayne condemned his little brother in his halfway between child-and-man voice. 'Lady Wakebourne said we're to say there's enough hot water for two baths in the coppers, but you'll have to take them in the laundry house, because there's nobody to carry water up and down stairs for you.'

'And there's the biggest pie we ever saw ready for dinner and we're starved,' the boy Tom thought was called Joe said from behind the three brothers.

'We'd best hurry, Peters,' Tom told his filthy companion, wondering if he had that much dust and dirt on his once-immaculate person as well. 'Do you know if there's any soap to spare, boys? Or must I search the wagons before we come in?'

'I sincerely hope not, my lord,' Peters said as if he'd experienced quite enough misplaced optimism for one day, 'you would get dust and dirt on everything.'

'Aye, there's soap all right,' one of the skinny urchins Tom thought more at home on a London street than rural Dorset said gloomily, 'more of it than a body should have to put up with in a whole lifetime, if you asks me.'

'That's because you're a mudlark,' Henry Trethayne said cheerfully.

'Then at least I ain't a pretty little gentleman.'

'D'you still think I'm pretty now?' Henry asked as he lunged for his friend and wrestled him to the ground.

'Please ignore them, my lord,' his elder brother said loftily, but Tom's night vision was good enough to see him eyeing the pair with the wistfulness of an adult looking back on the pleasures of his youth. 'They know no better, I'm afraid.'

'Clearly,' he said as solemnly as he could. 'Now, about that soap and water? Could you point us in the direction of it so we're rid of our dirt before the ladies see us? We'll get a fine scolding if we venture inside looking like this.'

'Hmm? Oh, yes, Josh will take you, won't you, Josh?' the boy said absently, weighing up how best to intervene as a third boy launched himself into the fray and maturity felt less important than evening the odds.

'Come on then, Mr Lord,' the youngest Trethayne ordered cheerfully.

'You don't want to join in?' Tom couldn't help asking as they walked towards the castle with the noises of battle fading behind them.

'I'm the smallest and weakest. It would be foolish *and* painful to do so,' the boy informed him as if he was the grown up.

'True,' Peters said with a heartfelt sigh.

'Younger son?' Tom couldn't help asking.

'Something like that,' his companion replied in his usual guarded tone when Tom tried to learn more about this enigma of a man than the enigma really wanted him to know.

Tom forgot his companions and everything else when Dayspring Castle loomed ever closer out of the half-dark. Its air of down-at-heel raffishness was hidden by the coming night and the feeling of malevolent power he recalled all too well from his childhood was in command once more. Then it had seemed to have a real, beating heart tucked away somewhere, hellbent on showing him he was as nothing compared to the grand history of Dayspring and its warrior lords.

His breath shortened and his heartbeat began to race, as if he was on the edge of the same panic he'd felt every time he was dragged back here from an attempt to run away as a boy. Back then he'd usually betrayed his terror by being physically sick or, on one terrible occasion, losing control of all his bodily functions as his guardian and that terrifying pack of dogs bayed at him from the castle steps and he felt the snap of savage jaws held just far enough off not to actually bite, but close enough to be a boy's worst nightmare come horribly true. Thank Heaven Peters knew nothing of that awful moment of weakness as he remarked what a fine place it was and how he might envy its owner, if it wasn't close to ruin.

'It's not a ruin,' Joshua Trethayne said as if he loved it. 'The North Tower is dangerous and Poll says we're not to go there, even if someone could *die* if we don't. Jago says it's haunted, so I don't want to go up there anyway and Toby can say I'm a coward as often as he likes, but I really don't want to know who the ghost is.'

'Quite right,' Tom said dourly. 'He's not worth meeting.'

'I would consider meeting any ghost a memorable experience, even if their very existence is beyond the realms of logic to me,' Peters argued.

Tom was tempted to growl something disagreeable and stump off towards the laundry house he remembered as a warm, if damp, hiding place when he escaped his prison in the North Tower to roam about the countryside. Frightened of the smugglers and other unpredictable creatures of the night, he would come back here to sleep in the outbuildings and feed on scraps of food carelessly left out by the laundresses and grooms. With adult perception Tom realised that was done deliberately and felt a lot better about being back here all of a sudden. At least some of the people who once lived and worked here had cared enough about the ragged little marquis to leave him the means to stay free and safe for a little longer.

'I was kept in that tower for several years by my wicked guardian, Master Trethayne. So, no, there are no ghosts up there I can assure you. I'd have been glad of their company, feral boy as I was back then.'

'That's what Poll said Jago was when Lady W. found him: a feral boy,' Josh Trethayne said, and Tom could have kicked himself for saying too much about his past in front of this acute young gentleman, although there had to be rumours still flying about the area of shocking goings on up at the castle before Tom was taken away to be brought up by a very different guardian to the one he'd begun his career as an orphan with.

'I dare say he and I would have got on well if we had met when I was young, then,' Tom made himself say cheerfully as he tried to dismiss the past. 'Right now I'm sharp set and filthy. Do you think your sister and Lady Wakebourne will mind if I eat in my dirt?' he asked to divert the lad from what he'd revealed about his early life, lest he have nightmares of that long-lost boy shut up in the tower alone.

'Yes, her ladyship says she has her standards, however low she's fallen in life, and cleanliness costs only a bar of soap and some hot water, which is just as well since she can't afford much more. We told her we'd be happy to save on the soap part to help out, but Poll insists it's a price worth paying.'

'Bad luck,' Tom said sympathetically, recalling earnest arguments with Virginia on the same subject he'd been secretly relieved not to win when he looked back with a shudder on being filthy and on the brink of starvation at Dayspring Castle, before his life took an unexpected turn for the better with her arrival in it.

Polly stood up from stoking the fire in the communal room they'd made from the great parlour of long-ago lords of Dayspring Castle. It had been little more than a huge lumber room until they came, but now the oak-panelled walls and mix of ancient furniture gathered from other neglected chambers shone with beeswax.

Richly coloured cushions made even awkward old oak chairs comfortable enough to sit and doze in on a winter evening. The fact they were made from the good bits of brocade or velvet curtains too old or damaged to repair probably wouldn't go down well with the owner of this faded splendour, but she really didn't care. No doubt Lord Mantaigne would condemn them for making a home here and turn them out tomorrow anyway, but today they had more right to be here than he did. Given the neglect he'd inflicted on his splendid birthright, if there was any justice he'd have no rights here at all.

'Ah, there you are,' the man observed from the doorway and she turned to make some sarcastic comment on his acute powers of observation.

'Heavens,' she said lamely instead and felt her mouth fall open at the sight of a very different Lord Mantaigne to the man polite society fawned on like fools.

'I believe "Lawks" was how your cook put it,' he said, and drat the man, but his grin was pure charm, and suddenly she understood all that fawning after all.

'Prue's not *my* cook, she's a friend,' she argued, but there was no bite in her tone as she gazed at perhaps the dirtiest nobleman she'd ever laid eyes on.

He shrugged, and a clump of grey dust-covered cobweb fell from of his once-burnished curls and drifted softly to the threadbare but spotlessly clean Turkey carpet. 'Whoever she is, she is a wonderful cook if the delicious smells coming from her kitchen are anything to go by.'

'She is, and they are,' Polly agreed lamely.

'She has invited me to eat with you all, once I've dislodged the dust of ages from my person and can sit down to it like a civilised human being.'

'That sounds like her,' she said, still trying to enmesh her image of the wicked and sophisticated aristocrat she'd hated for so long with this rueful, sweaty and filthy man who seemed very ready to admit the joke was on him.

'I offered to marry her, but she says she's already spoken for,' he added, and she refused to like him— yes, that was it, she simply refused to be charmed. He wasn't going to subvert Paulina Trethayne with his easy, intimate smiles, or the glitter of mischief in those intensely blue eyes that invited her to laugh with him and bid goodbye to the wary distrust she wanted to keep between them like a shield.

'It will take you until midnight to get yourself clean enough for that,' she blurted out, and he laughed as if at a brilliant witticism. She felt it as if he'd reached inside her and jarred her whole being with that one rumble of masculine enjoyment. 'And I refuse to wait here like a waxwork while you preen and primp and peacock yourself back into a state of suitable splendour and the rest of us go hungry, so you'd best hurry up.'

'You thought me splendid before I acquired all this dirt then, Miss Trethayne?' he asked with an ironic bow that lost some of its effect when a twig from some ancient bird's nest fell on the carpet at his dusty feet and he had to stoop down even further to pick it up.

It would be silly to find it admirable in him to consider whoever had to keep this place clean. Of course she didn't think he was anything of the kind and reinforced her disapproval with a glower that might be a little overdone. The sight of it certainly seemed to cheer the contrary man for some reason, and he clicked his heels in a mock-military salute, then stood as upright as a soldier on parade.

'I can quite see why your brothers are terrified of your wrath, Miss Trethayne. You must set very high standards of cleanliness and good behaviour.'

'They are *not* terrified of me,' she told him with the feeling of having been caught kicking puppies, making her meet those blue, blue eyes of his with shock and reproach in her own before she remembered he was a master of manipulating those about him and glared full at him, since he was so determined to get her attention.

'No? And they seem such well-behaved and sensible lads,' he lied with a straight face.

Dote on them though she might, she had no illusions about any of her lively and headstrong brothers and nobody had ever accused them of being less than a handful, even when they were on their best behaviour.

'You know very well they're nothing of the sort,' she said dourly.

How had he tricked her into saying any such thing within such a short time of his arrival? She would have sworn to any other outsider that her brothers were the best boys she had ever come across if they even tried to tell her the Trethayne brothers were a touch wild and ought to be confined to the care of a strict schoolmaster until they learned some manners. Now she was admitting they were a trio of noisy and argumentative urchins to her worst enemy and he was her worst enemy, wasn't he?

'I like them,' he claimed, and that was just plain unfair of him.

'So do I,' she replied repressively and stared pointedly at the spider about to drop off his elbow onto Lady Wakebourne's favourite chair. 'If you don't go away and take your livestock with you, there won't be any dinner left for you to devour when you get back from restoring yourself to your usual state of dandified magnificence in an hour or two,' she told him nastily, but this man brought out the worst in her and that was that.

'Scared of spiders, Miss Trethayne?'

'No, only marquises, my lord.'

'Very sensible, you really wouldn't want one of us in your hair,' he said as lightly as if she hadn't just shot a dart past his armour, but somehow she knew she had and felt a twinge of shame twist in her belly that she refused to consider more closely until he'd gone. She wasn't scared of him so much as her own reactions to him and neither of them needed to know that just now.

'Go away,' she said dourly, and the wretch did with one last, thoughtful look back at her that said he wondered exactly why she wanted him gone so badly. 'Why were you looking for me?' she called after him, feeling as if he'd taken some of the air and all the excitement out of the room with him and contrarily wanting it back.

I bet lots of women can't help themselves whenever he's around, a bleak, repressive inner voice whispered, but she ignored it as best she could.

'Because Lady Wakebourne thought you would know where my valise has gone. If you will excuse me, poor Peters is very likely shivering himself into an early grave out in the laundry room right now, since he refuses to enter the castle in a state of nature after his much-needed ablutions. I, of course, have no such gentlemanly scruples and will be perfectly happy to run about the place stark naked as soon as I've washed the dust and dirt of the last century or so away and feel restored to my rude self again.'

'Sam Barker took it up to the South Tower. That's where all the men sleep,' she said in a strangled voice she hardly recognised as her own.

'I must remember to thank him for such a kindness,

but I don't think he'd want me searching the place from top to toe and getting dust everywhere right now, do you?'

'I'll find him and ask him to bring it out to you,' she said in a loud voice she told herself wasn't in the least bit squeaky with panic as the idea of this particular man appearing in the hall of his ancestors and naked as the day he was born sent a shudder through her that had nothing at all to do with her being cold.

'My thanks, Miss Trethayne,' he said as smoothly as if they'd been discussing the weather, then he sauntered away to join poor Mr Peters in the laundry as if he would never dream of wondering how it would feel if they happened to be naked at the same time.

Chapter Four

Polly was glad to be alone as the very idea made her clamp her legs together against a hot rush of wanton excitement at her feminine core that felt sinful and delicious in equal measure. 'Oh, heavens,' she husked on a long, expelled breath that felt as if it had come on a very long journey all the way from her boots.

The most appalling images of a naked, sweat-streaked and vital Lord Mantaigne were cavorting about in her head like seductively potent demons now. He was disgusting, she told herself, and in more ways than one. He was certainly physically filthy, and she ought not to find that the least bit appealing in the man. There had even been a streak of ancient grey dust right across the front of his disgracefully open shirt and, come to think of it, that garment had clung to him as if it loved him as well. She could recall exactly how the dust darkened across the bare torso visible under that once-pristine linen and the powdery stuff had clung to the sweat on his tanned and glistening skin like a fond lover.

If she had dared let even a hint of her fascination with his work-mussed person show, he would have played on it as shamelessly as an actor in a melodrama, but even willpower couldn't control the physical response of her body to his now he'd gone and her wicked imagination had taken over. Of course it was folly to wonder how it would feel to be his equal in sophistication and passion and flirt right back at him, to risk the shame and scandal of being a fallen woman for the absolute pleasure of being such a devastatingly masculine yet civilised and urbane man's lover. He was an accomplished breaker of women's hearts and it was good that she was nothing like the females such finicky men of the world chose as their paramours.

She brushed a hesitant, wondering hand tentatively over her breeches and up to her slender waist with the feeling she was leaving stardust in its wake, then she gasped as she realised where her too-vivid imagination was taking her again. So horribly conscious of her own body that she suddenly felt as if it had a life and demands independent of the rest of her, she slammed a door on the image of lordly Lord Mantaigne luxuriating in the make-shift bathing room they'd made in one of the laundries. It would be steamy, the air warm from the fire Dotty would have lit for the comfort of the weary labourers as they got rid of all their dirt, because Dotty had a soft heart under her gruff manner and she openly admitted making men comfortable had been the mission of her youth.

Thank goodness the self-appointed castle laundress was middle-aged and didn't continue with her life's work in quite the same way nowadays. The image of his lordship in his tub with a very willing and gleeful female seemed utterly disgusting somehow, as the one of him in it with the likes of her that hesitated on the edge of her thoughts never could be, even though her everyday self wished it was.

'Oh, no, the valise!' she yelped and ran out of the room to find Sam Barker before there was the slightest risk of the marquis carrying out his implied threat to parade about the castle naked if someone didn't produce his clothes in time. 'Useless dandy,' she grumbled as soon as she'd run Sam to earth in the kitchen and met his amused gaze as he reassured her the master of the house had already been safely reunited with his clothes and there was nothing for her to panic about.

'That's what he thinks,' she mumbled to herself as she went back upstairs to put out a few of their precious store of wax candles in honour of their unwanted guest.

'So, what do you think?' Tom asked his supposed secretary-cum-agent-cum-lawyer half an hour later.

'Nobody would think you even knew what a broom looked like now, let alone how to use one,' Peters told him distractedly as he did his best to shave by the light of a flickering candle.

'That's not what I meant,' Tom told him grumpily, wondering why the world thought him such a peacock. 'I was asking your ideas about the self-appointed keepers of my castle.'

'From what I've seen so far, they seem a very mixed bag.'

'True, but I'm ready to defer to your superior knowledge of the criminal classes. Do you think any are active law-breakers?'

Peters seemed to consider that question more seriously as he wiped the last of his whiskers from the blade of his razor and was himself again, whoever that might be. 'I doubt it,' he said, as if the fact surprised him as well.

'So do I,' Tom said with a preoccupied frown as he used the square of mirror his confederate had vacated to brush his hair back into gleaming order. 'I suspect Lady Wakebourne would have them marched out of here faster than the cat could lick her ear if she had the slightest suspicion any had gone back to their old ways.'

'It's not just that. They respect her and Miss Trethayne. Even that battered old rogue in the gatehouse seemed more concerned about them than his own doubtful claim to employment and a roof over his head.'

'So why are two ladies living in what should be an abandoned barrack with a pack of reformed rogues and criminals?' Tom mused as he decided he was ready to face the world outside the castle laundry once again.

'Some don't seem the type to have ever been out-and-out rogues, so maybe they were all victims of an unlucky fate.'

'Maybe, but what sort of circumstances would set two ladies so far apart from their kind? They must have been dire to leave them squatting in such a bleak old barn of a place, scratching a living from whatever they have managed to find here to sustain some sort of life on.'

'Dire ones indeed,' Peters said starkly, confirming Tom's own conclusions.

He frowned at his now-immaculate reflection and came to terms with the idea he couldn't simply come here, take a look round and walk away again as he had half-hoped when he was given Virginia's letter ordering him to come here, find out what was amiss, then make up his mind if he wanted to demolish the castle or accept the duties and responsibilities that went with being born the heir of Dayspring Castle.

'Dire indeed if I meant to bring in a full staff and live here, since they would then have to leave the place.'

'And you don't?'

'Of course not, man. Would I have avoided it like the plague all these years if I had the slightest desire to settle in and play lord of all I survey here?'

'I really couldn't say, my lord,' the supposedly quiet and unassuming Mr Peters said, as if he had his own opinion about Tom's feelings for the place but was keeping it to himself.

'Good,' Tom drawled, squaring his shoulders at the suspicion the man might be right.

'Is Lord Mantaigne's bedchamber ready yet?' Lady Wakebourne asked Polly from the doorway of the great parlour.

'It would take an army to make that echoing barrack room ready for him,' Polly snapped back and felt the new tension in the air now the rightful owner was back in his castle. 'They can both sleep in the South Tower with the rest of the men,' she added, knowing all the same that nothing here was ever going to be the same again. 'We can't get them into the staterooms fast enough for my taste, but lodging the man in a musty and bat-ridden chamber in the empty part of the house won't endear us to him in any way.'

'And we don't want him to feel more uncomfortable than he has to here.'

'No, indeed,' Polly agreed with a weary sigh.

'Nor should we allow him the chance to form any wrong ideas about a lady residing under his roof, my dear. You must resume your petticoats in the daytime as well as at nights now, Paulina, whether you like them or not.'

'I don't. They're confoundedly restricting and make it well-nigh impossible to for me to do any work,' Polly complained, knowing her ladyship was right.

Casting a last glance round the comfortable room at the odd family they had made out of a pack of rootless strangers used of an evening, she wondered how many would stay in their own quarters tonight to avoid the puzzle of how the sweepings of the King's Highway dined with a marquis. Biting back a wistful sigh for yesterday, when they had no idea the impossible was about to happen, she nodded her agreement and bit her lip against a furious protest against the darker whims of fate.

'Never mind, my dear, it won't be for long. The boy must loathe the place, given the terrible things the locals whisper about what he endured here as a boy, and this is the first time he's been near Dayspring in twenty years. He probably won't be back for another twenty, once he's done whatever it is he came here to do.'

'And whatever that might be, he certainly didn't expect to find us here,' Polly answered glumly. 'I can't imagine why you wrote to his godmother about whatever is going on here. You must have done that months ago, since the old lady has been dead three months,' she said sharply, as all those nights when she had lain awake worrying about whoever was making incursions into the castle at night reminded her Lady Wakebourne was a devious woman.

'He is the only person who can tell them to go, my dear. I wasn't going to risk you losing your temper one day and confronting them, then maybe leaving those boys of yours even more alone in the world than they are already.'

'Oh, then I suppose I can see your point,' Polly conceded reluctantly, knowing she had a tendency to act first and think later, although of course a measured risk was perfectly acceptable and she had weighed that one up already and decided she needed more information before taking it.

'And I am very fond of you, my dear. I want you to be safe and happy as much as any of us.'

'Thank you, I am very fond of you to,' Polly admitted.

'Then there is no harm done between us?' The lady actually sounded anxious about that and Polly had to nod and admit it.

'No, but I now know you are a splendid actress and will be very wary of you in future.'

'I don't think I'll take to the stage to repair my fortunes even so. Now run along upstairs and put some petticoats on, my dear, if only for my sake.'

'Very well, but I still hate them.'

Going back across the courtyard to the women's quarters, she climbed the stairs to her lofty room and washed hastily. Trying not to give herself time to think too much, she bundled herself into the patched and fraying quilted petticoat, wide overskirt and unfashionably long bodice she wore when she absolutely had to. It felt ancient and impractical, and she hated the corsets she had to wear to make the bodice fit and the curb the heavy skirt put on her long stride so she must mince along or hold them so high they were indecent and defeated the purpose of wearing them in the first place. Without the hoops and panniers the gown was designed for, it hung limply about her long legs, but it was the only gown she'd found that wasn't so short on her it was more revealing than her breeches, so what couldn't be cured must be endured.

Until she had come here and discovered the liberty of breeches and boots she must have spent her waking life enduring the wretched things, she supposed with a sigh. As she lifted her skirts to descend the stairs without tumbling down them, she wondered how she'd borne it for so long. She minced impatiently into the housekeeper's kitchen they used instead of the vast castle kitchens and tried hard not to knock anything over now she felt several feet wider than usual.

'Oh, for goodness' sake, girl, you'd look a fright even without the sad state of your hair,' Lady Wakebourne exclaimed as she turned from stirring a saucepan for Prue with a look of despair at Polly's unfashionable array.

'What's wrong with me now?' Polly replied defensively.

'It looks as if you last ran a comb through it about six months ago.'

Polly raised a hand to feel if she was right and realised the hasty plait she'd twisted it into first thing this morning had gone sadly awry and she might as well be wearing a bird's nest on her head. She felt herself blush at the spectacle she must have made when Lord Mantaigne first laid eyes on her. She wasn't surprised he'd let his gaze linger on her long legs and what curves she had to her name so impudently now. No, she was, she had to be. His preoccupation with her long limbs proved to her that any reasonably formed female body would do for him to bed a woman, she reminded herself militantly.

'I'm not primping and preening for any man, let alone him,' she said, even as the idea of sharing a meal with that finicky, arrogant aristocrat looking as if she had been left out in a tempest for a day made something deep inside her cringe.

'Don't worry, I think we would know that, even if you did the rest of us the courtesy of taking a brush and comb to that wild mess now and again.'

'I'm not going all the way back to my room to try and turn myself into a sweet and docile lady for the marquis's benefit.'

'Not much risk of you ever being one of those, Miss Polly.' The girl stooping over the fire to turn the spit for her sister Prue straightened up as far as she could to eye Polly critically. 'If you wouldn't mind watching this for me, your ladyship, I could take Miss Polly along

to my room and tame that tangle into something closer
to how it ought to look.'

'Of course, Jane dear. Far be it from me to stand
in the way of such a noble undertaking,' Lady Wakebourne said cheerfully and took over the task with an
ease her former friends might find a little distasteful if
they could see her. Since they had turned their backs
when she found out her husband had gambled away
his fortune, Lady Wakebourne's dowry and a whole
lot more before he shot himself, Polly was very glad to
have missed out on knowing them.

'You have such beautiful hair, Miss Polly,' Jane said
when she finally persuaded Polly to sit still on a three-
legged stool in her bedchamber on the other side of their
makeshift kitchen from the men's sleeping quarters,
where the heat of the fires at least warded off the chill
from the southwest winds and ancient walls left too long
without enough fires powerful enough to warm them.

'It gets in a mess as soon as I've finish tying it back
every morning.'

'That's because it needs thinning here and there and
if you'll let me take a few inches off the ends, I'm sure
you won't find it so hard to manage,' Jane said shyly as
she undid the heavy mass, then brushed and combed it
into a crackling and vital cloak about Polly shoulders.

Even her hair seemed imbued with some of her impatience with being primped until suitable for the lord
of Dayspring to set his noble eyes on so he wouldn't be
put off his dinner. Polly wondered how long Jane had
wanted to be a lady's maid and it was a hope unlikely

to ever come true, given society's prejudices, so if playing one for a night made her feel better, Polly found she could keep still after all.

'Do what you like with it then,' she said with a restless shrug.

'Only if you promise to sit quiet,' Jane chided, then produced a pair of sharp scissors and began snipping at Polly's hair as if shaping it was a work of art. 'Sit there while I fetch a branch of candles. I can't see well enough to do this properly,' Jane said just as Polly was beginning to hope she'd finished.

So Polly had time to sit and wonder why she was doing this. Surely she didn't want that popinjay to admire her as he might have if their eyes met across a crowded ballroom? She squirmed at the idea of being sized up as the other party in a wild and fleeting affair by a society rake and told herself it was because her seat was too low and rather hard, not because the very thought of Lord Mantaigne made her feel as if a crucial part of her insides might be melting. She despised unprincipled dandies and who could doubt he was one of those when he wore that ridiculously elegant get up as if he was about to take a stroll across Mayfair instead of camp out in a dusty and crumbling castle?

If she'd first seen him sauntering down Bond Street in that exquisitely cut coat, tightly fitting pantaloons and gleaming Hessians she would have shot him a scornful look, then forgotten him as a man of straw. If he'd raised his perfect top hat from his gleaming golden curls and bowed as if he knew her, she would have given him the cold stare of a lady dealing with an overfamiliar gentleman and moved on with a dismissive nod. How she wished she had seen him like that, in his natural orbit and revealed for what he was under the cool light of a London Season.

Except she had only ever heard about such beings in Lady Wakebourne's tales of former glory. Miss Paulina Trethayne had no youthful rites of passage to look back on; she had never stood on the verge of womanhood, waiting nervously to meet a hopeful youth who might marry her and make her and her children secure for the rest of her life, or might gamble and whore his way through every penny of his fortune and her dowry. She never would now and, since she was already a woman who knew the best way to feel secure in life was to rely on herself; that was just as well. If she came across the Marquis of Mantaigne outside the castle walls it would be as his unequal in every way and she refused to regret it.

So why *did* a part of her she didn't like to admit existed long to dance with him at grand society balls and drift about the dance floor of Almack's Club during a dazzlingly intimate evening of gossip and dancing? The flighty Paulina Trethayne she might have been, if things had been very different, stopped twiddling her thumbs in boredom with the mundane life she had been forced to live beyond the playgrounds of the *haut ton* and livened up at the idea of dancing with such a man, intimately or not.

Polly wondered how much of the wilful and contrary young girl she had once been was left in her soul, breathlessly green and curious as ever. It felt as if she was on the edge of something life changing and potentially wonderful and nothing could be further from the truth. She looked sideways into the square of mirror Jane and her sister had rescued from somewhere and saw a beanpole dressed in a jumble of hand-me-down clothes with a rough cloth draped over her shoulders to collect stray hairs. What was worse, the lanky creature was staring back from that pane of silvered glass all soft-eyed and dreamy with a silly smile on her face.

Idiot, she condemned her inner fool. *You know exactly what happens to such romantic dreamers.* With impatient revulsion she turned her head sharply away and was about to get up and ruin Jane's day when the girl came bustling back into the room as rapidly as her twisted limbs allowed.

'Sit down and have a bit of patience for once in your life, Miss Polly,' she ordered, and Polly folded her long legs back on to her perch and meekly did as she was bid. Just because dreams stopped being rosy when reality broke in, it didn't mean Jane's secret ambition deserved to be pushed aside as if it didn't matter.

'There's so much to do,' she protested half-heartedly, but Jane frowned with the air of an expert interrupted in a vital task. 'And that mincing fop wouldn't care if I sat down to dinner wearing a sack.'

'But you should,' Jane reproved her gently, and Polly felt ashamed for not caring she had straight limbs and an acceptable, if lanky, female form when Jane must long for such luxury every time her legs refused to obey her.

'It's been years since I needed to,' Polly admitted softly and they were both silent for a while, Jane busy with her self-appointed task and Polly wondering how her life might have been, if Papa hadn't been so feckless and the boys so very young and dependent on her when he died.

'There, I've finished,' her companion said at last. Polly sighed with relief and got ready to get up and go about her interrupted evening without another thought for her reflection in that unforgiving mirror. 'No, you don't. You have to at least take a look at yourself now I've done all I can at short notice,' Jane protested.

'I'm still me,' she argued, snatching a glance in the mirror to pacify Jane. 'It looks a little wild for my tastes,' she said, eyeing her newly barbered and carefully arranged hair dubiously.

'Not wild; cut and dressed to frame your face properly. You have beautiful hair, Miss Polly. It's a crime to bundle it up as best you can and hack bits off it when you get impatient with the weight of it like you do. Come to me whenever it gets in your way and I'll soon have it looking lovely again.'

'You can't make a silk purse out of a sow's ear, Jane, but since you enjoy cutting hair you might as well practise on me as anyone else.'

'You're a fine-looking lady, Miss Polly, and it's high time you realised it,' Jane said with a militant nod. 'His lordship won't be able to take his eyes off you tonight.'

'Flatterer. You know perfectly well I'm a quiz at my last prayers and I don't care a jot what that lordly fribble thinks of me,' Polly said as she left the room and walked straight into a wall.

Blinking at the odd fact it was a warm and very well-dressed wall that smelt of Lady Wakebourne's best herbal soap and clean linen, she groaned very quietly as she replayed her own words in her head.

'Forgive me,' Lord Mantaigne said with meticulous politeness as he set her at arm's length and stood back. 'I seem to have got sadly lost in my own castle.'

'I'm sorry too, Lord Mantaigne,' she said stiffly as she pulled back from the impact he had on her senses as if he'd stung her. 'I didn't see you out here.'

'Little wonder, you'd have a job to see a shooting star in all this gloom,' he grumbled rather dourly.

'What did you expect after so many years of doing your best to let this poor old place fall down, a diorama put on in your honour?'

'Even I am not that unreasonable or deluded. No, I expected a great deal worse than this and should thank you all rather than complaining about shortcomings I caused in the first place,' he admitted. She refused to find the sight of him running a distracted hand through his now wildly curling golden locks endearing. 'I expected we would have to camp out in an outhouse or sleep in one of the barns. Hence all those wagons and so many provisions for the horses until we could buy more.'

'I'm relieved to know the space was not entirely taken up by your clothes,' she said before good manners could catch up with her tongue.

'What a very high opinion of me you do have, Miss Trethayne,' he said so smoothly she wondered if anything touched the real man under the gloss and glamour. She must have imagined her scathing opinion of him had hurt, for there was nothing in his eyes but mockery of them both for standing here trading insults whilst their dinner was waiting and they were sharp set.

'This is a fine and noble heritage, my lord, and I don't approve of your wilful destruction of it,' she said dourly. There seemed little point trying to be sweet and polite when he was about to put her family out of the only home they had.

'Some things are better left to rot,' she thought she heard him mutter.

'People harm other people. Buildings merely endure our faults and caprices, as this one testifies all too well, but they have no feelings about us.'

'Thus speaks the voice of experience?' he asked with too much perception for the empty-headed Bond Street Beau she so badly wanted him to be.

'Of course, none of us would be here if we had anywhere else to go,' she replied with a shrug meant to deflect more questions.

'And I suspect you think I have no right to ask,' he said with a look in his deceptive blue eyes that promised he would find out anyway.

'Since you're sure to turn us all out now you have turned up, you have no right to know anything about us.'

'And if I don't?'

'You will, once you are properly settled here you won't be able to help it. What could Lord Mantaigne have in common with a ragtag band of beggars?'

'I'm surprised you haven't listened to the tales of my childhood that must be raked up when someone wonders why I don't cherish it as my forefathers did.'

'For some strange reason I admit I can't fathom, your people are loyal to you. We were told you disliked your guardian and he went mad, but they don't give out details to newcomers, and you must know we'd still be those if we'd been here decades.'

Polly caught a flash of emotion in his watchful gaze, then it was gone as if he didn't allow himself such luxuries. He was touched his people felt something for him; she could have sworn it in the brief moment he left himself unguarded. It shouldn't matter to her if he felt endless sonnets of overblown emotions or none at all, but if she wasn't careful she could find this contrary and deeply irritating man fascinating and that would lead her to places Polly Trethayne could not afford to go.

'Such loyalty is beyond me,' he admitted with a rueful shrug.

'Indeed?' she made herself say as if it was a puzzle she didn't care to enquire any further into. 'It must have been as long a day for you and Mr Peters as for the rest of us, my lord. Perhaps we should agree to eat and sleep before we resume arguing how your arrival will change Dayspring Castle in the morning.'

'We might as well, but tonight I can say thank-you for saving my house from dereliction and my staff from an uncomfortable night in an abandoned wreck and a cold supper, Miss Trethayne. I'm sure you would say that was all I deserve, but you must admit Peters and my servants are not to blame for my misdeeds.'

'They are welcome to share what little we have and I didn't do it on my own,' she said, but could tell from the twitch of a smile at the corner of his mouth that he'd noticed her side-step his share of their hospitality.

'Then let's agree there will be time enough for a report on all you and your friends have managed to save from my neglect another day,' he allowed, but there was a steely purpose under the limpid blue of his eyes now that ought not to surprise her. He'd already proved a very different marquis from the one she'd despised for the past six and a half years, so it was little wonder he kept surprising her.

Managing a half-hearted smile of greeting for her friends and Mr Peters when they finally reached the Great Parlour together, Polly did her best to fade into the background when Lady Wakebourne greeted his lordship like the Prodigal Son. Even those who ought to know better seemed dazzled by the presence and glamour of a real live lord in their midst. She tried to tell herself he was really a wolf in very handsome camouflage, but even to her the fact of him outdid the image.

If only she could have held on to her first impression of him as a man of fashion; spoilt, idle and self-obsessed as the Regent himself was reputed to be. Hating him would be so much simpler if that cliché was nearer the truth than this complicated rogue. She slanted a glance at him being polite to his guests as if they were the noblest gathering in Europe and frowned at him for not being high enough in the instep to put her off feeling this unwanted connection between them.

And she couldn't fool herself into thinking he was a soft and dandified gentleman who loafed about Mayfair raking, gambling and doing whatever else idle young lords did to relieve their boredom any longer either. She was in a very good position to affirm there wasn't a spare ounce of fat on Lord Mantaigne's lean but powerful frame and he didn't get like that by going to bed with the dawn and rising too late to see more than a glimpse of daylight. This afternoon his grey-silk waistcoat had clung so lovingly to his muscular torso and narrow waist she suspected many otherwise respectable women would be eager to examine the fit and quality of it for themselves if he gave them the chance.

Luckily she had already given herself a stern lecture on the differences between such women and Polly Trethayne and she trampled down any lingering spell her first sight of him had cast and told herself she would now be immune. There had been a sharp moment of *Ah, here he is* before she felt the heat of those bluest of blue eyes linger on her long limbs and remind her she had given up all hope of respectable marriage the day her father died and left nothing but a mountain of debt behind him.

She had dared all she had in her to keep the boys with her, but that was dare enough for one lifetime. She couldn't consider the dishonourable intentions of a rake, or dream of might have been if things were different. The boys were not yet grown and she wasn't free to meet any rash promises those hot blue eyes of his had made her, even if she wanted to and of course she didn't want anything of the sort.

Yet still his magnificent physical presence was still emphasised by the long-tailed dark coat of a fashionable gentleman dining with friends, and she was still a sentient female with the use of her eyes. How could she *not* look at him and be reluctantly impressed, despite all her resolutions not to be? Clearly no Cumberland corset was necessary to give him a nipped-in waist and even the idea of his tailor having added buckram to pad out those muscular shoulders was laughable. She wondered what the fine ladies and gentlemen of the *ton* would make of the Marquis of Mantaigne sweeping his own stables, then spreading straw for his horses and waiting until they were fed and tended before taking himself off for a much-needed bath in the castle laundry.

The gentlemen might laugh up their sleeves while they secretly envied him his fitness and cheerful good humour as he got very dirty indeed, but the ladies would be too busy with less straightforward thoughts and impulses to listen to jokes at his expense. Polly knew that because she'd experienced a terrible urge to watch him at his labours this afternoon and had almost peeped through a knot hole in a shutter at the back of the building in an effort to do so. Somehow she found the strength to turn away, but considering he'd found her in his sweat-and-dust-covered glory afterwards anyway she might just as well have indulged herself to the full.

Now she squirmed in her seat as she waited for the men to sit once the women were in their accustomed places at the table, despite the marquis being a lord and most of them of far lower rank than any ladies he was accustomed to dining with. The heat that ran through her at her shameful thoughts of him sweaty and dishevelled and naked before jumping into his bath told her she found this particular lord far too desirable for her own good. She was suddenly very glad their precious beeswax candles were placed sparsely and flickered now and again in the draught from an ancient window. At least nobody would know she was blushing at such a scandalous idea in this mellow and uncertain light.

Chapter Five

For a while it was quiet in the room while they ate hungrily after a hard day of toil and travel. The silence was testament to Prue's fine cooking, Polly told herself as she slanted a look at Lord Mantaigne every now and again to make sure he was duly impressed. If he kept Prue on to cook for him, she and Jane would be safe. A plan to point out the skills and talents of her fellow interlopers took shape in her head as she tried to distract herself from his all-too-vivid presence next to her as everyone else had insisted, as if she was chatelaine and he the lord. He might employ them as a skeleton staff or caretakers if she convinced him how loyal and hardworking they were, despite the odd quirk that led to them being rootless in the first place.

'Were you and Mr Peters on the road for long today, Lord Mantaigne?' Lady Wakebourne asked politely.

'Peters joined me at Dorchester, but the rest of us took the journey from Derbyshire slowly to pace my team and let the wagons catch up every day.'

'They look fine beasts and your team are highsteppers, aren't they? I don't suppose they enjoyed being held back like a string of donkeys,' Tobias declared, and Polly glared at her eldest brother for breaking his absorbed silence. How typical that the only thing to divert him from his dinner was the team of perfectly matched greys now happily settled in their stables.

'The dray horses were bred for strength and not speed and can't match the pace of my greys, so we made slow progress by the standards of a true whip, but it was an easy enough journey at this time of year,' Lord Mantaigne said with a ready smile, and Polly had to stifle an urge to tell her brothers to be quiet and eat their dinner so it might be over with sooner.

They had little chance to converse with gentlemen, isolated as they were from local society by their poverty and dubious status as unofficial residents of Dayspring Castle. One day she must face the puzzle of finding suitably gentlemanly occupations for three quick and energetic boys who no longer enjoyed the privileges they'd been born to. For now she supposed it would do them good to see how easily a true gentleman conducted himself in company, but she hoped they didn't learn any of the idle, rakish and expensive ways this one could afford to indulge in along the way.

She loved her little brothers fiercely and would never be without them, but it was hard to be father, mother and everyone else to them. The burden felt especially heavy now they must make a new life out of nothing again. Dayspring had given them a life of peace and usefulness after their lives became a wasteland. If they hadn't stumbled on Lady Wakebourne in as sad a case as they were and this place so temptingly empty and forsaken, they would not have had it, though, and Polly sighed at the idea of taking to the roads again, in search of some other place to live until someone claimed it back. She fought a deep-down weariness at this constant struggle to keep her family happy, healthy and hopeful and told herself to count the blessing of a roof over their head and good food in their bellies for one more night.

'Your sighs could rival the gusts even the shutters can't keep out tonight, Miss Trethayne,' Lord Mantaigne remarked.

'It's been a long day, my lord. I suppose I must be weary of it,' she replied, refusing to squirm at the disapproving look Lady Wakebourne shot her to say she should remember her manners and make polite conversation.

'I suppose you must be,' he said blandly. 'I could be a little tired of it myself if I let the idea take root.'

'Aye, your lads from the wagons was worn to a thread. We took their share of stew and what bread we could spare to the stables so they didn't have to wash and shave until morning,' Dotty Hunslow said cheerfully.

Polly smiled a 'thank you' for that attempt to lighten the tension she'd caused with her edgy feeling they were walking on eggshells. By not being able to put her fear out her head that they were about to be homeless, she'd probably made it more likely they would be ejected than not.

'My thanks for making Dacre and my stable lads comfortable, ma'am,' Lord Mantaigne said as politely as if Dotty was a patroness of Almack's Club. Polly had to admire his manners, even if they highlighted her poor ones. 'I warned them not to expect much at the end of their journey, but you have made a liar out of me.'

'Even though you hate the place?' Sam Barker, the one-legged sailor who arrived here without a penny in the pocket of his ragged breeches, said from his seat with its back to the window where the worst of the draughts came in.

'Even so,' Mantaigne replied with a straight look. Sam met it with a challenge, then a nod, as if admitting this lord had backbone, despite his sins.

'And who can blame you for that, my boy? Now, we're at dinner, not the local assizes, Sam Barker. Let us talk of matters conducive to good digestion rather than past sins,' Lady Wakebourne said gently, and Polly was almost ashamed of her own determination not to see good in the man. It would be dangerous to like the spoilt aristocrat at her side and that was that.

'This is far too delicious a meal to mar with mine at any rate,' Lord Mantaigne agreed, 'but where has the artist who produced this fine meal hidden herself away?'

'She's not an artist, she's Prue,' Polly's littlest brother, Josh, informed him with a nod to where the sisters were sitting, flushed with pleasure at such praise.

'Then thank you, Mrs Prue. If the Prince of Wales gets word of your culinary skills, you'll be gracing his kitchens at Carlton House as fast as he can carry you off.'

'Oh, I wouldn't like that,' Prue said shyly, and Jane nodded wisely by her side.

'I'll be grateful if you continue here then. Tomorrow I'll find you a couple of assistants, though, as my arrival has doubled the number of people you cook for and more will have to be found if the old place is to be put in any sort of order.'

Lord Mantaigne offered such help so lightly Polly frowned, certain he meant his offer to have a limit. It sounded like a 'for now', until he decided what to do with this unwanted part of his splendid inheritance. Even if he ordered repairs to stop the castle from falling down, he would order it closed up again afterwards.

'What about the rest of us?' she blurted out and instantly regretted it.

Her sharp query arose from a stab of intense envy. He had so much while they could live on a small portion of it—if only he'd stay away. The others were shocked she had raised such a topic at the dinner table, gasped at her temerity, or sat in their seats, fearing they'd be turned out now she'd asked what no one else dared.

'Well, really, Polly!' Lady Wakebourne exclaimed.

'Coo, Miss Poll, you ain't half got a big mouth,' Jago said admiringly.

'A good question, but perhaps not an aid to good digestion,' Mr Peters said wryly.

'Do you ride, Miss Trethayne?' Lord Mantaigne asked coolly when the murmurs of agreement or dissent had died down.

'Of course I do,' she said scornfully, before she remembered she always did so astride and had no ladylike habit, or even an old-fashioned and not particularly ladylike one such as this shabby and decades-out-of-date evening gown.

'Then meet me in the stable yard after breakfast tomorrow and show me what you've been doing here. Once I know that, I shall be in a better position to decide what comes next.'

'You can't ride about the place dressed as a young man now his lordship is here, child,' Lady Wakebourne put in with genuine distress in her voice. 'You won't have a reputation left to whistle down the wind if you gallop about the countryside alone with such a gentleman looking like some heathen amazon.'

'Nonsense, ma'am, we shall take Peters with us. He's more of a proper gentleman than I shall ever be, so nobody will dare to think ill of us in his sober presence. My consequence is much improved since he entered my employ; I preen myself on the appearance of virtue without the effort of reform.'

'I am, of course, suitably grateful for your good opinion,' Mr Peters said in his usual quietly ironic fashion.

Polly wondered at the steel under his words. Who was Mr Peters to dare challenge a man of rank and power, even if he did it so subtly it took sharp ears to notice it?

'You need not fear for Miss Trethayne's reputation in such company, Lady Wakebourne,' Lord Mantaigne finished with an air of settling the question.

'Since I don't ride, I must be content with your word as a gentleman you will chaperon Miss Trethayne as effectively as I would, Mr Peters?'

Polly was touched by Lady Wakebourne's concern for a reputation already in shreds, given her unusual mode of dress and the life she had lived these past few years.

'Of course, my lady, it will be my pleasure,' the enigmatic secretary agreed with the deference he refused his powerful employer.

'Should I be feeling sadly cast down by your lack of faith in my gentlemanly instincts?' the marquis mused with a smile in his eyes Polly mustn't find disarming.

'Probably,' she replied and lowered her gaze to her plate in the hope Prue's cooking would put tomorrow to the back of her mind.

'You are about as easily cast down as a distant planet, young man,' Lady Wakebourne muttered into her soup.

'How well you seem to know me, ma'am—were you a long-standing friend of my godmother?'

'Oh, no, she belonged to a more sophisticated set than I aspired to. My maiden aunt was one of her bosom bows, but she's been dead for fifteen years or more now and I doubt you remember her.'

'Virginia had a variety of terrifying friends who would interrogate me about my morals and intentions in life and the shameful state of my neck and hands when I was a grubby schoolboy. I dare say your relative was a sweet little lady with a doting fondness for small boys and would not dream of such an inquisition?'

'I never found her heart of gold if she possessed one, which I doubt.'

'Oh, dear, who was your particular tartar in petticoats, then?'

'Miss Euphemia Badlerstone,' Lady Wakebourne said with a shudder Lord Mantaigne echoed, and Polly felt it set off a twinge of heat and dangerous fellow feeling stir deep within her once more.

'I remember her only too well: a lady of great perception, little patience and a devastatingly frank tongue.'

'I would think less of you if you pretended she was sweet, gentle or charitable,' Lady Wakebourne said indulgently.

Polly only just bit back a groan at the thought her friend was about to adopt another lone boy. This one was certainly not in any need of her fierce protection and frustrated maternal love. Lord Mantaigne was clearly able to take care of himself, and Polly couldn't imagine how any woman would see his all-too-evident strength and boldness and feel in the least bit motherly, because she certainly didn't.

Something told her he was even more complex than she'd first thought under his shell of indifference, so she tried to let his genial small talk wash over her as she ate her dinner. Then she went through the plans she had for tomorrow in her head in order to put them off for a day that might never come now he was here. This was the true business of her life: ensuring there was enough to eat and a safe place for her family to sleep. Things she grew up taking for granted were a vague memory for Toby and Harry and a myth to Josh and she was all that stood between them and destitution. She would keep standing there, though, and this feral attraction to a marquis could not be allowed to get in the way.

Heaven forbid her boys ever looked like Jago, Joe and Benjie did when Lady Wakebourne lifted them down from the cart she had driven back from London. None of them could blame their new friend for snatching three little exhausted climbing boys from their master one night as he lay drunk in the gutter on their earnings, but for a long time they lived in dread of someone connecting Lady Wakebourne's last desperate appearance in polite society with their disappearance. She had gone to see if anything was left from the disaster her husband had wrought to add to what they could grow or make from a mouldering castle and its neglected gardens.

It was a reminder Polly must still fight to make sure her boys were never dependent on cold charity. Thank heavens all but Josh were too big for such a trade now, but it took months for the sores on Jago, Joe and Ben's poor burnt and soot-encrusted feet to heal, longer for their shocked eyes to spark with mischief and to this day Jago had nightmares about being trapped in dark and ever narrowing chimneys. He was still only twelve years old, and Polly caught herself glaring at Lord Mantaigne for having so many chimneys in need of small climbing boys to clean them.

She had no right to judge him, she reminded herself. How would she have been by now if she had lived the life of a lady of quality? Ladies were not supposed to question the grand order of things and even the thought of such a little life made her yawn. Lady Wakebourne misread it as weariness and rose to her feet as if she had been waiting for someone else to wilt so she could too. Gathering her female troops about her, she was gracious as the men sprang to their feet.

'I think we might as well retire, ladies,' she remarked. 'There is a great deal to do in the morning and no point wasting candles if we're only going to nod over our needlework.'

'Until the morning then, Lady Wakebourne; Miss Trethayne; ladies,' Lord Mantaigne said with a bow that made no differences between them.

'Boys, you might consider yourselves quite grown up and able to sit up half the night plaguing your elders, but I do not. Bedtime, my lads,' Lady Wakebourne ordered.

'Will he let us stay, Poll?' Toby asked her quietly as soon as his younger brothers were asleep.

'I doubt it,' she had to admit because he was too old to be fobbed off with a shrug or a diversionary tactic.

'We'll come about somehow, though, Sis, don't you worry,' he said with a grave look that ought to be beyond a boy born to comfort and privilege, even if there was little of either in his life now.

Toby was the only one of her half-brothers old enough to fully remember how it felt to wander the world with nowhere to go and an ever-dwindling supply of money to do it on. Polly had tried so hard to make their new life an adventure; to encourage him to look forward to every day as full of hope and possibility instead of fear. She had felt enough of that for both of them and memory of it made her heart thump.

'We shall be together, that's all that matters,' she replied with an attempt at light-heartedness he met with a brave smile.

'I'm a man this time, Poll,' he told her sleepily.

'You are, love, but men still need sleep, and you've had a long day, so let tomorrow take care of itself.'

'You will discuss anything important with me, won't you?' he asked, and yet again she had to face the reality her brothers were growing up without much more prospects in life than Jago, Benjie and Joe.

'Of course, and we're the bold and bad Trethayne family, don't forget.'

'Aye, of course we are,' he mumbled with a sleepy sigh and slept as suddenly and completely as a boy must after a day of action and excitement.

'Oh, love, may you dream of better things,' she whispered softly, dousing the candle before tiptoeing out by memory.

'Are they asleep?' Lady Wakebourne murmured when Polly shut the door as softly as ancient oak and a heavy latch allowed.

'Yes, it would take an army marching about the courtyard to wake them now.'

'Then come to my chamber and talk while we take some of that claret Barker found in the inner cellar. I dare say you'll get no sleep without it, despite what I said when we left the great room tonight.'

Polly and Lady Wakebourne crossed the courtyard to the women's quarters together. No doubt Lord Mantaigne would find it amusing such barriers existed in such a ramshackle household, but it was a matter of pride to confound those who called them vagabonds and misfits—not that many villagers dared say so after they met Lady Wakebourne. Polly bore the lantern to light them to the stout door of the inner courtyard and a suite of rooms that once belonged to the castle steward.

'Hold still, girl,' her companion demanded, using both hands to try to raise the latch holding the ancient studded oak door firmly shut. 'What's the point of being half a foot taller than you should be if you can't act the footman once in a while?'

'None at all I dare say,' Polly replied placidly, wondering why the lady's blunt comments didn't set her teeth on edge as any slight criticism by Lord Mantaigne did. 'Would you like me to try?'

'No, keep that light steady and I'll do well enough.'

'May *I* open it for you then, my lady?' the marquis's deep, amused voice asked out of the gloom.

Polly wondered why instinct hadn't made her nerves jump the moment they stepped out of the tower door into the darkness, since he was obviously strolling about the inner court, making what he could of his domain in the pitch dark.

'Of course you can, Mantaigne, it's your door.'

'I apologise for its intransigence,' he replied as if he'd escorted them home from the play and conducted them to their door as a proper gentleman should. He shifted the heavy iron latch the other side of the wrought handle with one hand and gently pushed open the door.

'Well done, my boy,' Lady Wakebourne said as if he had just achieved some hugely difficult quest and took advantage of the lamp left burning low in the little hallway to sail upstairs before Polly could follow her.

'I suspect we're being left to settle our differences and stop making her uncomfortable, Miss Trethayne,' he said as she frowned after her so-called friend.

Differences could be good. Particularly if they kept you from having silly daydreams of what might be for her and this potent and infuriating lord if life had only been different. She would still be nigh six foot tall and he would be as armoured against her in a Mayfair ballroom as he was in the starlit darkness of a Dorset night. Any other reasonably young and not unattractive lady might tempt him to test her virtue once they were alone with the sea whispering on the shore and spring seeming to soften the very air around them, but Polly Trethayne was in no danger.

'I don't think we'll ever be bosom bows, my lord. We have neither interests nor acquaintances in common,' she said as distantly as she could when her foolish inner self wanted to rail about his immunity to her as every move he made seemed of unique interest to her.

'We should give each other the benefit of the doubt until we know better, but if you'd like to confide your dearest secrets in me I'll try not to broadcast them,' he said so blandly she felt her palm itch to slap the smile off his face.

'I would sooner tell them to a town crier,' she muttered darkly.

It simply wasn't acceptable to find his answering chuckle disarming. They had moved away from the circle of light cast by the lamp he'd hung on a hook by the old door to light her way back. Now it felt too intimate in the shadowy courtyard for her peace of mind.

'Yet we must rub along over the next few weeks if I'm to do what I set out to here. If you and your friends remain here, we must reach some sort of truce and make it obvious Lady Wakebourne is your very strict chaperon. There is no other way we can live under the same roof without scandal, and I'm not the one gossip will reflect on most. This isn't a fair world, Miss Trethayne, and we have to pretend we respect each other if we're to stay at Dayspring with any appearance of respectability,' he said soberly, and drat him for being right.

'I suppose so,' she admitted reluctantly, and that won her another soft masculine laugh that made her shiver with warmth and feel the natural order of things had been upended.

'And I'm really not such a bad fellow if you ignore my shortcomings,' he said as if he was coaxing a wary dog to like him.

Ridiculously offended he showed none of the caution he would have used toward any other lady of her age and single status, she squirmed at the prickly discomfort of being close to him. He was so oblivious to her as woman he'd hardly noticed she was one since that first heady moment when he seemed to see it very clearly indeed, but how stupid to feel piqued by his indifference now.

'I'm sure your friends hang on your every word and deed, Lord Mantaigne, so you hardly need me to join in. I am squatting in your grand castle with my friends and family and your coming must change that, so you can hardly expect me to welcome you with open arms. You'll turn us back into beggars and vagabonds sooner or later, however nicely you try to wrap it up in ifs and maybes.'

'You're not like any vagrants I ever came across,' he muttered, as if his inability to slot them into convenient places troubled him.

'I suspect they're not like them either, if you can see past rags and desperation to the person underneath. I've had all the sneers and slights most beggars get thrown at them over the years, my lord, but words only sting for a while and blows are much harder to shrug off.'

'Someone hit you?' he asked indignantly as if it was an affront he would dash off on his charger to avenge in blood.

'Of course, and attempted worse when I said them nay. I was a beggar woman with a babe in her arms and two children clutching at her skirts. Why else do you think I stopped wearing them in the end, my lord?'

'For ease and to fit the hard labour you undertake, I suppose,' he admitted with a shrug she could feel rather than see. 'Maybe you're right and I am only a man of fashion and not a deep thinker,' he added.

'If you truly believe that, you really are a fool,' she said impatiently.

'You are a very forthright female, Miss Trethayne.'

'And you're a cunning opponent, Lord Mantaigne. You deflect difficult questions so ably I don't suppose your foes recall asking them in the first place.'

'Yet you have an uncomfortable knack of clinging to them whatever hares I put up to divert you, but I really didn't set out to be your enemy.'

'Since you own this place and I've been living in it without your permission for nearly seven years, that makes us enemies whatever you set out to be.'

'First I'd have to care about Dayspring and I'll never do that. If you and your friends living here means I need never come back, you can all stay until doomsday as far as I'm concerned.'

'For a man who doesn't care you're almost passionate about your birthplace, my lord,' she pointed out slyly.

Polly saw him flinch now her eyes were accustomed to the faint starlight even in this dark corner of the court-yard. The idea she might have caused him pain gave her no satisfaction at all and sparked a little echo of his hurt in her own gut. It was worrying to feel such connection to a man far outside her reach and experience. She retreated into the darkest pool of shadows lest he could read her too easily back.

Tom caught the faint movement even as he tried to defend himself against her curiosity. No, that was harsh; he couldn't accuse her of so simple a human failing. This odd mix of a woman now trying to hide her thoughts in darkness as she wouldn't let him had lived her life shorn of the pretences, as well as the comforts, of her kind. No wonder she was impatient of the strategies he used to fend off anyone who wanted to know the Tom under his wealth, fashionable clothes and titles.

He felt a nigh overwhelming urge to let her find him and couldn't recall feeling such connection with a stranger since the day Virginia had marched into his life and changed it for ever. His mouth quirked in a reluctant smile as he recalled how little he'd liked his godmother for breaching his defiant hatred of the world that could treat him as this one had so far. Virginia took no notice of his barricades either; she marched straight over them with one impatient shake of her still-handsome head and informed him he was to live with her from now on and everything would be different, beginning with a hair-cut and a bath. Even that threat didn't stop something hard and brittle at the heart of him from cracking open to let a new Tom step out.

The man who grew out of that boy sighed for the awkward and mistrustful urchin he'd been and almost wished himself other than who he was now. Once he was gone Polly Trethayne could do what she wanted with Dayspring and he mustn't wish he could be at her side, wanting it too.

Chapter Six

'What the devil was that?' Tom demanded as the echo of a distant thud carried through the still night.

'Damned if I know,' she whispered, sounding more gruffly impatient than he was. 'Someone has been getting into the closed-up wings of the house at night and we don't know what they want or how they get in.'

'Smugglers?' he suggested grimly, knowing there was a risk the local rogues were emboldened by his hatred of the place to use it for their own ends.

'You must know better than that, my lord. You spent your earliest years here, even if you now live as far away from the sea as a body can get.'

'Aye, too much starlight,' he agreed as he listened for any other signs they were not alone out here in the night and felt the prickle of her so closeness shiver against his skin in the intimate dark.

Confound it, but even listening for what shouldn't be in the night wasn't enough to divert him from this ridiculous consciousness of her so close and feminine and even more goddess-like than ever in her shabby and ill-fitting gown and old-fashioned petticoats.

'News will have got about that you're here by now as well,' she warned, and he supposed she was right, given the network of gossip and intrigue that operated so effectively in any areas where the free-traders ran their illicit cargoes.

'Maybe that's what spurred them into action,' he wondered out loud.

'Then what brought them here last week or the one before?'

'When did it begin, then?'

'I felt there was something wrong before the turn of the year, but I wasn't sure until a couple of weeks ago. Now I need to know how they get in and out and why they seem to be looking for something, rather than hiding it or fetching it away as you would expect the free-traders to do. Everyone knows the castle is all but empty and anything left behind is so heavy or useless it has no value, or it would have been taken away for safe keeping when the castle was closed up. Either they are curious youths hell-bent on some sort of secret carouse, or your second guardian did not clear out the newer parts of the castle as well as he did the older one where we live. I can vouch for the fact he did a very good job indeed on our quarters.'

'Virgil Winterley was an efficient man. When he and my godmother decided to do something they always did it to the best of their ability—they took me on when anyone else would have blenched and run away at first sight of the sullen brat I was then.'

'I find that difficult to believe, my lord.'

'That I was sullen or a brat?

'You are almost too much in control of your temper and I can't visualise you as the furious and defiant urchin even my littlest brother can turn into at times.'

'Oh, visualise it and multiply it by a dozen, Miss Trethayne,' Tom told her softly, his thoughts in the past with the resentful, terrified boy he had been for the three years of his early life between five and eight when his first guardian controlled his young life with sadistic thoroughness. 'I'm astonished Virgil didn't bundle me up, drive halfway across the country and leave me on the madhouse doorstep for my old guardian to take back, however few wits he had left.'

'So old Maggie was wrong about you being so angelic, then?'

'You should have listened a little harder. She might have said I *looked* like an angel as a child, not that I ever behaved like one. From what little I recall before Philip Grably turned her off, my old nurse was far too honest to tell anyone her former charge was aught but a spoilt and hasty-tempered urchin.'

'She did say you'd have turned out as proud as a turkey cock if that devil hadn't tried to break your spirit, but she truly loved you, my lord. She was still mourning her inability to defy the man and stay with you last time we spoke.'

'I don't remember anything much of my life before my father died. It feels as if someone built a wall between before and after.'

'You were very young, so little wonder that you can't recall much.'

'For all I know I could be my father's bastard smuggled into the nurseries one night when his wife wasn't looking, as my guardian told me I was on one memorable occasion.'

'I think that unlikely.'

'Aye, but a great deal about my life seems unlikely now I'm back here.'

'Us included?'

'You especially. You're the most unexpected surprise of all.'

'And not a very welcome one either, I suspect.'

'Oh, no, you have rarely been more wrong. It's not every day a man meets a goddess in breeches, and I wouldn't have missed the experience for all my castles and unearned wealth put together.'

Tom felt her start at his clumsy reminder he was a vigorous and lusty man under all his fine plumage and she was a magnificent and very desirable female under her rag-bag of a wardrobe. He'd been doing so well until that moment as well and he cursed his normally glib tongue for failing him with a woman who felt a lot more important than any of the impeccably bred young ladies trailed under his nose by their hopeful mamas had ever been to him, try how they might to catch themselves a marquis. He felt as if every word they said had a significance that was almost terrifying as they whispered of the past out here in the now and listened for intruders into an empty and echoing mansion nobody wanted to live in. If he'd read about himself and his odd mix of feelings in a book he wouldn't have believed a word of it, but here he was, senses more alert than he ever recalled them and every male cell in his body awake and alert towards the very female puzzle at his side.

'We weren't talking about me, my lord. I would like your help tracking down whoever is here under cover of darkness, but if you're going to be facetious I'll find out alone.'

'That you won't,' he muttered as he cast his mind back to that first soft and distant thud as another fainter one carried across the yard on the clear night air.

'Smugglers trying to remove a cargo before I can look closely at the place or employ a proper staff?' he suggested as her tension told him there was no point pretending he hadn't heard.

'There have been lights on the upper floors now and again as well,' she admitted reluctantly, as if she suspected local rumour would reach him sooner or later and he would wonder why she hadn't told him about them.

'Seen by those out in the night who should not be, I suppose?' he asked laconically, remembering his own nodding acquaintance with the night-hawks from his childhood. 'The local poachers didn't betray me to my guardian although he'd have winked at their sins if they did; so why would I hand them over to the local magistrates now?'

'Because you're no longer a child and hold our fates in your hand?' she said bitterly, and once again he felt the pull of connection between them as he saw how hard her life must have been these past few years and cared that she had suffered so much for the boys she obviously loved more than her own comfort.

The Marquis of Mantaigne famously cared for nobody and here he was teetering on the edge of worrying about a pack of strangers and one in particular. It wouldn't do. He must find out what was going on here as Virginia asked and leave without a backward look. He might leave an echoing, half-empty barrack behind him, but it would be a well-run one if Peters had a say in the matter.

'I'm just a man like any other, Miss Trethayne,' he defended himself against her scorn and wondered why.

'And you're making too much noise,' she muttered distractedly.

Her preoccupation with whoever was invading his castle in the dark clearly overcame any faint interest she might have had in him until someone trumped it. He felt piqued that she could so easily dismiss this wild curiosity to know more. He'd been so sure it was mutual, but perhaps he flattered himself. Maybe she was immune; his warmth and scent and the sound of his voice didn't do anything spectacular to her senses, now her sight was blunted by darkness, as hers did for him.

He wanted to employ every sense he had to learn all about her, but could he really feel such strong attraction to a woman who only wanted him to keep quiet or go away? Unless he chanced a rebuff and violated the laws of hospitality by kissing a guest under his roof to find out, he'd never know. Now the idea was in his head it was the devil of a job to ignore the temptation to do just that and risk an Arctic reception to find out if she was as indifferent to him as she wanted to be. No, only a rogue would do that and he wasn't quite one of those yet, so he exerted his brain and came up with an answer that almost made him groan out loud.

'Surely you don't intend to go and see for yourself?' he asked incredulously and could have sworn he saw her bite her lip and silently curse that lucky guess. He hadn't thought even she was that wild and reckless until that giveaway silence told him he'd hit a nail on the head.

'Not if you won't be quiet I don't,' she managed with a snap that wouldn't carry on the night air.

'And do what?' he gritted as softly as he could between his teeth, shaken by the thought of her confronting some villain in the dark.

'Find out,' she muttered impatiently, as if it was so obvious she couldn't imagine why he had to ask.

'Not on your own you don't,' he was surprised into arguing as she took things into her own hands and stole away as silently as if part of the shadows herself.

He grabbed her hand and felt her start and get ready to demand he unhand her, as if she was royalty and he was committing treason by touching without permission. He smiled grimly into the darkness as he felt the firmness of her long, slender hand in his, the work-worn toughness of her skin and the realness of a woman who made her own way in the direst of circumstances. It felt right there, as if it belonged, and that would never do. A sharp bolt of awareness shot through him as it had at first contact with this warm, all too live woman against his skin back in the stable yard. Drat it, but he wanted her as he couldn't recall wanting a woman so

urgently since he was a desperate and callow youth and
there wasn't a hope of having her and being able to look
himself in the face next day when he shaved.

You're playing with fire, Mantaigne, he warned himself sternly, but he kept hold of her hand through her resistance, then silent acceptance he wouldn't let her flit
off into the night and tackle who knew what invaders
on her own. Recalling all those illicit adventures he'd
risked in the darkness of this very place when he crept
down from his tower and evaded capture for a day or
two, he felt as if a cold place in his heart had warmed
as he set out with her.

*You're not alone at Dayspring this time then, Man-
taigne?* Virginia's voice seemed to whisper out of the
night as he crept along the darkest part of the courtyard
and through the elaborate arch that gave access to the
newer parts of the castle.

*No, it seems the nights here are full of things that
ought not to be*, he replied in his head as he might if
his beloved godmama were witnessing this unlikely
adventure.

Good point, he almost heard her say, and his sense
that Virginia was here vanished as he felt Polly Trethayne's hand tense in his and the very alive woman at
his side took up all his attention once more.

He sensed her impatience with him even as he felt
her draw an arrow on his skin. Biting down on a gasp
when it felt as sensuous as half-a-dozen nights in his
current mistress's bed, he reminded himself it was only
her way of directing him in the dark. Anyway, it wasn't
right to lust after a lady he had only met today and who

lived under his roof. It wouldn't be right to lust after her if she'd been his best friend since childhood, he reminded himself with a wry quirk of his lips, but knowing it didn't seem to stop him. Allowing himself be led for once, he peered through the shadows at the firmly closed side door he knew led into the grand wing.

Glad she couldn't follow any stealthy intruders inside, he soon found out he'd misjudged her. He muffled a curse as she tried once again to wriggle her hand out of the grip he was having the devil of a job to make firm but not painful. Somehow he managed it and heard a soft grunt of frustration before she surprised him by dipping down to delve in a nigh invisible nook in the carved archway with her other hand to extract a key. All sorts of question about the keys to Dayspring Castle that were supposed to be lying in Peters's trunk in the ancient castle armoury flitted through his mind. Best not to ask how she got this one, he supposed, as she bit off an annoyed hiss at his continued grip on her left hand and fitted the key in the lock with her right.

Tom did his best to put aside the thought of the fine pair of Manton's best duelling pistols sitting uselessly in his own trunk. He supposed there was a faint hope Miss Trethayne might have a pistol concealed in the pocket of her ridiculously ancient gown, but he was probably giving the bird-witted female too much credit for common sense. She really needed to carry one if she intended to delve every mystery Dayspring held, but something told him she was as unarmed as he was.

Now she was silently turning the key in the modern lock his lawyers had probably ordered fitted when he abandoned this place to its ghosts. It must have been oiled, and he revised his opinion of her foresight up a notch as his anger at her for being even more reckless than he'd thought her went up several more. He was tempted to shout a challenge and hope it sent her quarry scurrying down whatever rat-hole they'd come from. He would do it if he sensed a threat the rat would turn and bite, then track the vermin another day, when she was busy interfering in someone else's life. No, this was her life, more than it ever would be his, and now they were in here it behoved him to pay attention. The ifs and maybes of feeling some sort of connection with this wretched female that neither of them wanted might go away if he ignored them hard enough, except the low hum of excitement in his body as her hand tightened in warning on his told him that was very unlikely.

She nudged him to help her close the door as silently as she had opened it, then tried to push the key into his hand to let him know she wanted it locked again so she could flit off alone into the profound darkness in this part of the castle he hated most. He silently refused to take it. Hearing her huff an annoyed sigh, then turn it herself, he frustrated her as she tried to brush him aside again. She couldn't afford to demand out loud he let her go so she could run her head into any reckless adventure that came her way uninhibited by his presence.

His senses reached past the exploration his baser instincts were urging him to make of this warm and reckless female, and he told himself any distraction must be welcome. He was almost rigid with need in this heavy darkness as parts of his imagination he couldn't seem to control any more demanded an intimacy they should never have. If she felt even a tithe of the same affliction, she would never admit it. For all her outrageous attire, air of confidence and what he judged to be mature years for a single lady, there was a curious innocence about her. She had done all she could to keep the wary barrier of strangers between them.

Now they were here, he suddenly didn't want that barrier there any more. It made him feel lost in this sense-stealing darkness. He had spent most of his life avoiding this place and now he was wilfully courting the worst parts of his nightmares with the most unlikely siren he'd ever encountered at his side. Any moment now she might find out what a coward he was at heart and somehow it mattered far more than it should what this penniless and vagrant female thought.

No, that was quite enough worrying about Miss Trethayne's all-too-obvious contempt for the Marquis of Mantaigne; they were here now and might as well find out what they could. Apart from her, he scented only dust and disuse, and the droppings of generations of bats and mice on the air. For a moment he wished he'd brought his best spaniel with him to track the intruders, but a housebreaker would hear Rupert coming long before the eager animal could corner him. Tom tried not to miss Rupert's eager good humour and liking for his master anyway, telling himself he hadn't set out to endear himself to anyone who loved Dayspring Castle so could hardly be surprised Miss Trethayne only held his hand now because he refused to let her go.

He swallowed a curse as his knee connected sharply

with the carved newel post and he held his breath as
even that soft thud echoed in the empty hall. As it died
away he only just stopped himself whispering an excuse, then tried to put his memories of the layout between them and the silent blackness inside this echoing
barn. Shutters kept even the faint starlight out and it felt
as if the house was listening. Fanciful nonsense, but
anything could be lurking in those shadows and Tom's
heart thumped, then raced; remembered fear snapping
at his heels as they crept up the steps. It felt for a moment as if his guardian might leap out of the night to
shout out half-mad accusations and taunts, then try to
beat him senseless again. Tom licked suddenly dry lips
and forced his old fears aside. He was more than big
enough now to knock the weedy little tyrant down these
stairs and into Hades, if he wasn't there already.

Lord Mantaigne boxed and fenced with the best; rode
the finest horses as hard as if the devil was on his heels
when the mood took him and famously drove to an inch.
He was a Corinthian and, if he cared enough to lead
anyone, he could lead his chosen pack wherever he decreed they should go. Reminding himself of his usual
light-hearted indifference to the world, he still felt the
warmth of Polly Trethayne's hand in his as they stole
up the marble stairway together and was grateful not
to be alone here this time all over again. Over the smell
of long years of neglect he caught traces of soap and
woman and fresh air, as if she had brought the scent of
the spring itself here with her.

With his other hand he trailed an exploring finger
through twenty years of dust and found finely tooled

mahogany under his fingertips. It felt smooth and oddly warm under his hand, as if the old place was wistfully welcoming him home despite all he'd had done to it since he came of age.

On the top step they paused to gauge the silence. Tom felt her brace as if ready to rush into whatever trouble might be waiting, but he tried to convey the fact he was listening intently and they needed to gauge the dangers ahead before they dashed towards them. There; he heard a faint creak of distant movement on the other side of the state rooms from where they stood. He frowned into the darkness, knowing from bitter experience it was impossible to creep down the oak-boarded enfilade undetected.

'The back stairs are made of stone,' he murmured, as close to her ear as he could get so nobody could overhear.

He felt her nod, the whisper of a fine curl against his skin, and could picture her as vividly as if she was lit by half-a-dozen flambeaux. Despite the old clothes and her impatience with all things feminine she would look magnificent in her outmoded gown, but he was the Marquis of Mantaigne and she was a beggar-maid. He would have to fight his blazing attraction to a reluctant goddess and get on with whatever he had to do here, then leave.

Knowing his way by the uncomfortable memory of all the times he'd crept in and out of the servants' hidden passageways about the house, he pulled her away from a board that always creaked and wasn't sure if he was glad or disappointed when the door to the servants' stair swung silently on its hinges.

'We'll have to go down to come back up,' he warned her, so close to temptation he could easily breach the fractions of an inch between them and kiss her, if he wasn't such a noble man and didn't know he'd get his face slapped if he did.

'Hurry up, then, we'll die of old age before we get there at this rate.'

Fighting the seductive feel of her breath so near to his own ear, he could sense her lush mouth close enough to set about a sensory exploration. He'd not dreamed how much he'd like his lover to embark on such an intimacy until tonight and ordered himself to forget it again. He went down the steps in front of her, to stop her dashing into any trouble she found at the bottom of them and leaving him behind.

They were at the foot of them now and in the dark and echoing passage, built broad enough to get a horse and cart through to the vast kitchens and storerooms a great household once needed. Miss Trethayne gave a small sound of impatience and softly muttered, 'Shame on you', as their steps were softened by years of dust and detritus. His feet seemed to slide out from under him as he turned to listen to her in the darkness and whatever he'd slipped on shifted and tumbled him in a heap with Miss Polly Trethayne dragged on top of him by their linked hands.

'Oof!' he barked involuntarily and managed to shift her weight slightly as he got his breath back, hoping she wasn't aware how delightful he found the feel of her curves against his winded body.

Not even the listening silence all around them could divert him from the delicious feel of nigh six feet of Miss Polly Trethayne lying prone on his torso. For a long moment it seemed as if she felt it too; a breath-stealing anticipation; an odd belief she was uniquely right in his arms. He heard an unsteady sigh, felt her heartbeat thud against his own ribcage. He reached for her, cupped her head with reverent hands and drew her down until their lips met in a breath-stealing, open-mouthed kiss that made his world shift and left him desperate for more when she raised her head and made a soft sound halfway between a mew of protest and a regretful moan for more, then she was wriggling frantically to get up and he must act the gentleman again, somehow.

Her mouth had been so wondering and curious, then eager on his in those few moment that he felt a new world open up, then be snatched away. 'Be still for a moment,' he murmured, certain he'd embarrass them both by acting on this foolish urge to keep her here if she kept thrashing like a captured mermaid in his arms.

'No, let me go,' she demanded breathlessly, and he hastily opened his arms as soon as he caught a note of fear in her whispered voice, shame rising in a mortified flush he was glad neither of them could see in this musty gloom.

'Precious little point in us going on now, I suppose,' he observed as carelessly as he could while counting his bruises as he tried to calm his errant body.

'Thanks to your clumsiness,' she informed him crossly.

'Indeed, I'm sorry my foot slipped in the dark. You would have done better without me,' he admitted grumpily, wishing she seemed as deeply affected by that hasty kiss in the dark as he had been, and frustration thrummed through him like a fierce gale.

'Nobody else knows this place as you do,' she said as if she had to give the devil his due, even when she didn't want to.

'A misspent youth,' he replied as lightly as he could. In truth, he used to creep down in the dead of night to sneak food, hoping his guardian's lackeys were too drunk to drag him upstairs for a beating.

'I heard you were just a boy when you left, so you hardly had time to indulge in one here,' she argued softly.

He really didn't want to talk about this when he already felt so vulnerable to her, as if he'd had a layer of skin peeled off him and had let her too close after that unwary kiss to fend off her questions as he'd like to.

'I was eight,' he admitted flatly.

'Poor little boy,' she murmured.

'Not as poor as Lady Wakebourne's waifs or even your own brothers would be without their fierce protectors. Do they know how lucky they are?'

'When we march them to their lessons every day and they have to do without the ponies they want to pay for them? What do you think?' she whispered.

It seemed education came before riding for boys lucky enough to live under this roof nowadays and yet he didn't hear a hint of self-pity in her tone. Tom felt something heavy threaten to move in his chest and re-make him. Simply being here had threatened to un-dam a torrent of feelings he'd kept to himself since leaving twenty years ago and now this.

Appalled by the idea this woman might come to mean far too much if he let her, he did his best to wall that wild notion up behind my lord's facade of careless man about town, for her benefit as much as his. She was the oddest sort of lady he'd ever come across, but didn't deserve to be shackled to a fool like him if they were discovered lurking in the dark. He scrambled to his feet, brushing down his once-fashionable attire and wrinkling his nose at the feel and smell of dust and dirt under his touch once again.

'Dashed midden,' he muttered grumpily, then tensed as stealthy footsteps sounded on the stairs from the other side of the building. Grabbing Polly's hand out of sheer instinct and a worrying urge to protect her at any cost, he dragged her behind one of the great pil-lars that held the weight of the cantilevered stairs above and whispered to her to keep quiet. He felt her fury at his presumption and squeezed her hand in what he hoped felt like an apology as well as a plea to do as he asked for once. His pulse raced at the contact of her skin against his once more, even as he wondered at himself for not feeling on edge with apprehension instead of frustrated desire.

'I tell thee I heard a noise down here,' a strongly ac-cented voice echoed down to them. Tom wondered how many felons were infesting a place no self-respecting burglar would walk half-a-dozen steps out of his way to break into.

'It's only rats,' a more-educated voice informed him, and Tom shivered at a register in it he couldn't quite place and didn't like one little bit, then felt her fingers tighten about his as if she was trying to reassure him and that pulse of wanting turned into something far more dangerous.

'They're the biggest rats I ever did hear then, Guv'nor,' the first man muttered as if not sure why he bothered arguing.

'This whole place is an infernal rat-hole; what else would it be?'

'One of them band of gypsies as lives here. I'm sure they heard us last time we was here, but still you keep coming back. They'll inform on us if you ain't careful.'

'Not they—if they do they'll be out of here faster than the cat can lick her ear. No magistrate will listen to a pack of vagrants.'

'You're lucky they're only squatting here, then. I'd sooner be on the streets than live here myself, what with all them ghosts and witches they whispers about in the taproom of the Raven late at night.'

'They're nothing but a pack of smugglers, you superstitious fool, of course they tell tall stories to keep strangers away from the coast on dark nights so they can carry out their trade undisturbed,' the other man said contemptuously.

Tom hesitated between a need to challenge him and a deeper one to keep Polly as far from this dark business as he could get her. From the tension in her fingers it felt as if she might be able to read his mind and that was a danger he really didn't want to think about, so he worried about his castle instead. Reminding himself he didn't care what happened to the place didn't ring quite true now he was actually here. Perhaps he cared more than he wanted to, but if it wasn't for this idiot he wouldn't have had to come here and find out Dayspring meant something after all.

'Tall tales or no, I can't abide the place.'

'Fool,' the leader said with contempt that set Tom's teeth on edge.

'I ain't the one spending every night you think the gentleman ain't at work searching this old ruin for a pot of fairy gold, though, am I?'

'It's real, I tell you. The old fool raved about his treasury, insisted I get him in here so he could die with his riches around him.'

'Shame he stuck his spoon in the wall before you did then, weren't it?'

Tom stiffened as their whispered conversation sank in and he decided they were fools to discuss their mission where they could be overheard. His one-time guardian was put in a lunatic asylum once Virgil challenged his fitness to be anyone's mentor. The man had ruled Dayspring for three years, though, and could have done what he liked here for all the trustees cared. Tom listed his larger assets in his head, but there was nothing important missing, so what had Grably convinced the more educated idiot was hidden in a house stripped of valuables when Virgil closed it?

'Mind your tongue,' the man said, and suddenly Tom

knew why he'd shivered at the sound of his voice. Snapping orders like that, he sounded so like Tom's guardian they must be related in some way.

'Can you see aught?' his reluctant companion asked, as if he sensed them in the shadows or thought some ghost the locals had scared him with was waiting to haunt him if he came closer.

'No, there's naught to see. You're nervous as a spinster.'

Tom felt Miss Trethayne's hand tighten involuntarily, as if it was a personal insult. He supposed she was unlikely to marry, penniless and responsible for her three brothers as she was. She might be at her last prayers by the time the last one flew the nest, but any woman less like the proverbial spinster he found hard to imagine. He was touched by her plight and wished he could see a way to offer her a respectable way out of it.

If he tried to settle a competence on her, she might find a suitor besotted enough to take on her three brothers, of course, but she wouldn't accept it and they were not related so he couldn't even suggest it. Paying a man like Peters to wed her stuck in his craw, even if he agreed to do it. Then there was this fierce desire he'd been struggling with since he set eyes on her in those outrageous, disreputable breeches of hers. Tom reminded himself his biggest ally in his fight to keep his hands off her was the lady herself, then remembered to listen to these housebreakers instead of worrying about things he couldn't change just in time to catch their next bad-tempered exchange.

'We've tramped up and down too often to see if anyone else has been down here,' the second housebreaker was saying resentfully.

'If I'd known we'd need to check this filth for footprints, I'd have flown across it like a bat. It was rats, I tell you, now get up here and help me search the state rooms before one of that ragtag band really comes to see what we're up to.'

'I don't like the look in the old bruiser's eye and he ain't past milling either of us down, if you ask me.'

'Fortunately I'm not that foolish.'

Chapter Seven

The housebreakers' voices faded as they went back up the stair arguing. Tom felt Miss Trethayne tense as if getting ready to creep after them and wondered if the wretched female had some sort of death wish.

'Let them go,' he murmured as urgently as he dared.

'Coward,' she accused in a bitter little whisper, and he was surprised how sharply the accusation stung.

'If you were a man, you'd meet me for that,' he replied gruffly.

'Then go after them before they can get away,' she said, quite unimpressed by his offended dignity, and this time he had to muffle a startled laugh.

'And do what?' he demanded laconically.

'Find out what they are doing here.'

'Oh, why didn't I think of that? Let's just go and ask the nice housebreakers why they're searching an empty house in the middle of the night and how they got in to do it in the first place then, shall we?'

'I admit they won't want to tell us, but I'm sure you can awe them into it.'

'And what will you do while I'm busy?'

'I could hold your sword if only you'd thought to bring one,' she mumbled crossly, as if seeing the foolishness of her scheme, but still refusing to admit it.

'How remiss of me,' he murmured as he stifled the fantasy of impressing her by confronting two villains with bare fists and the few wits she'd left him.

'Yes, it was,' she agreed and surely that wasn't a huff of suppressed laughter?

'Next time we embark on one of your nocturnal adventures, I'll make sure I'm armed to the teeth,' he said solemnly, and her hand relaxed in his as they fumbled their way back the way they'd come. 'First we'll plan it a little better,' he added when they were by the side door again, and she fumbled for the key.

'I want to know how they get in and out.'

'Patience, Miss Trethayne, we need to know who our enemies are before we let them know we've smoked them out at the time that suits us best.'

'Why not catch them first and ask questions after?'

'At least I know now that the legendary impulsiveness of the Trethaynes hasn't been exaggerated,' he murmured, determined not to admit he was unwilling to let her risk injury and worse at the hands of an unknown foe. Nothing was more likely to send her smashing recklessly back into the house to confront danger than knowing she was being kept out of it for her own good.

'They made me angry,' she admitted with a shrug once they were on the other side of the door, and he slid the key back in his pocket before she could appropriate it again. 'We may be beggars, but we don't scavenge in the dark, stealing whatever we can lay our hands on. They come and go as they please while we stay out of the way of the magistrate as if we're in the wrong. What right do they have to look down on us when we work every hour God sends not to be a charge on the parish?'

'If I tell the authorities you have my permission to live at Dayspring, nobody will be able to tramp about the place willy-nilly in future.'

'And you think men like that will take notice? The law is run by and for the rich, Lord Mantaigne. It takes a dim view of those who're too poor to pay it to look the other way.'

'There are plenty of good magistrates,' Tom argued lamely.

'Luckily for us, Mr Strand is an indolent one. He'd turn a blind eye to anyone not robbing or murdering in front of his nose rather than leave his fireside on a night like this one.'

'Which must have been a good thing for you at times,' Tom pointed out absently, frowning at the notion any criminal who wanted to run tame about the area had a virtual *carte blanche* to do so if the local magistrate was as lazy as she claimed.

'True, and luckily he's terrified of Lady Wakebourne. A royal scold from her has saved us from eviction more than once.'

'I will let him know Dayspring is my business and who does or doesn't live here has nothing to do with him.'

'A nicely ambiguous reply—have you ever thought of taking up your seat in the House of Lords?'

'How do you know I haven't?'

He heard her snort of disbelief at the very idea and tried not to let her opinion of him as an idle and useless fool hurt. It was true he disliked politicians in general and avoided allying himself to the Whigs, Tories or Radicals, but he had a conscience and often voted on it. He even spoke out about causes close to his heart on occasions, for all the good it ever seemed to do. Since he had met Miss Polly Trethayne's incredible eyes earlier today, with that flash of contempt in them to make him wonder about himself more than was quite comfortable, he'd been wondering if it was time to stop taking life quite so lightly and properly espouse a few of those causes.

Since they exchanged that hasty kiss in the darkness her low opinion of him stung even more, and he fought off an urge to plead for her understanding and a better opinion of him. Her contempt was a useful shield between them, her scathing opinion of his morals and motives might keep him from falling on her like the ravening beasts he'd hated the very mention of when she spoke of the casual violence she'd met on the roads before she got to Dayspring and a sort of sanctuary. He sighed and wished her warmth at his shoulder and her scent on the air wasn't quite so intimate and endearing and that he wasn't quite so drawn to the prickly female. Begging sometimes seemed a fine idea if it would win her over and get her back in his arms for a lot longer than she had been tonight.

'What on earth have you two been doing in the dark all this time?' Lady Wakebourne demanded the instant they approached the still-burning lamp he had hung by the old steward's lodgings. She had obviously grown tired of waiting for Miss Trethayne to come in and was keeping watch for her ewe lamb to make sure she was safe from the big, bad wolf.

'Suddenly I know exactly how your Mr Strand feels,' he murmured and heard that delightful huff of feminine laughter again and felt the warmth of it to his toes.

'Terrifying, isn't she?' she whispered back, then stepped forward to greet her mentor with a serene smile. 'You did mean us to settle some differences and make everyone else less uncomfortable, didn't you, Lady W.? We had a lot of differences to sift through and it took some time, but I think we have finally agreed on a truce of sorts, have we not, Lord Mantaigne?'

'Indeed,' he said as solemnly as he could with the thoughts of what they had actually been about crowding into his mind. 'Miss Trethayne has agreed to take me and Peters on a tour of the closest parts of the estate, starting tomorrow,' he added.

It might test that truce to the limit, but she couldn't run round trying to find out more about tonight's unwanted visitors on her own if she was with them. With any luck it would take days to familiarise himself with his estates and in the meantime he and Peters could find out what the devil was going on here and do something about it while she was busy.

'You think you're so clever, don't you, my lord?' she spat so softly he was sure Lady Wakebourne had no idea how far from a truce they were.

'No, being clever is far too much effort. It must be

low cunning,' he muttered before bowing to her with such exquisite grace and wishing her a good night, so she had to curtsey back and return it with such over-done sweetness he knew she secretly wished him anything but a good night.

Polly had no choice but to follow her ladyship into the little entrance hall, but she went past the wretch without letting even a thread of her gown touch him. In the kindly shadows cast by the single candle he was as immaculate and exotic as he'd been at dinner. She told herself it was a timely reminder how far apart they truly were. Awareness of his subtly powerful body sent prickles of unease shivering across her skin like wild-fire and yet he looked calm and unaffected as if she had never fallen on top of him and felt the brilliant jag of attraction shock between them.

She took the lamp and held it lower to hide the flush that was making her cheeks glow and told herself it was as well if her ladyship didn't look too closely at his lordship's once-immaculate clothes. She'd kissed the man, for goodness' sake, sunk down and seized his mouth in a hasty snatched kiss that still sent shivers of awareness and want through her like a fever she couldn't seem to break.

'For heaven's sake, girl, I can hardly see a foot in front of me,' Lady Wakebourne chided so Polly had to raise their lantern to light the way after all.

Lord Mantaigne gave a warm and almost sleepy-sounding chuckle that made her think even more darkly sinful thoughts of rumpled bedsheets and sleepless nights of far too much intimacy. What had the wretched man done to her? She heard her own lips let out a muffled moan of denial as the thought of waking up beside him crept into her secret thoughts and settled in. No, he was an impostor—a rich and idle aristocrat, but not quite the harmless and noble gentleman he pretended to be. Nothing about his gaze—smoky with shadows as well as hungry and mysterious in this soft light— seemed either safe or gallant.

He knew he was a handsome and powerful man in his prime and she was painfully aware she was an awkward and gawky female, aware of him in every inch of her lanky body. All the time her head was trying to block him from her senses, she'd felt the power he could hold over her wilder senses, if she let him, and ordered herself to be very wary indeed.

He could walk right over a woman's most tender hopes and dreams and make them his before either of them realised it, then he'd walk away. Whatever else he was capable of, a deep-down sense of fairness told her he wouldn't inflict pain on another human being in pursuit of his own pleasure. She wondered about all the women who'd loved him, then watched him go without a backward look. The shudder that racked her at the very idea of being one of them was a powerful antidote. She imagined the desolation he'd leave in his wake when he left her and recoiled as if he'd brandished a lethal weapon instead of that rueful smile.

She raised her chin and met his eyes with as much indifference as she could summon. He stepped back and nodded as if to admit she couldn't take a lover of any sort and certainly not one like him. His bow said she might be right and he gently closed the door before either of them quite took in the fact he was gone.

'The boy has far too much charm for his own good,' her ladyship murmured and ignored Polly's sceptical snort with the queenly indifference of a true lady.

'If you say so,' Polly replied in as neutral a tone as she could after such a day and gave a weary sigh as she lit her ladyship back upstairs and whispered a soft goodnight before running up the next flight of steps to her own room.

She slept well only because she was exhausted by a day of toil and tension, but woke with a feeling of unease and the half memory of unquiet dreams. She scrambled into her work clothes, sparing a cursory glance as she brushed, then plaited, her hair. Once she was as ready to face the day as she would ever be she looked round her cosy room in the eaves, just in case this was the last time it was her home and not an old attic most would think old-fashioned and inconvenient. If they had to leave here, she would miss it more than her childhood home, but there was so much about Dayspring she had learnt to love and its owner obviously hated. This wasn't a significant part of the castle, but there was a wonderful view of orchards and parkland and a glimpse of the sea even from this side of the castle.

Going downstairs, Polly could almost sense the people she knew falling into places none of them had taken any notice of for years. A gap was yawning between those who had lived here as equals until yesterday. Soon she would have to don petticoats and whatever jumble of skirts they could put together out of the attics as a matter of course. She tried to picture herself looking clumsy and overgrown in the narrow skirts and high waist of the current mode and had to smile wryly at the very idea. Put ostrich feathers on any bonnet of hers and she'd make a sight to frighten small children and skittish horses.

Not that she could afford fashion, she reminded herself, and batted away the thought of Lord Mantaigne stunned speechless as she swept into the room dressed in a gown designed to make the best of her queenly height instead of the shabby and ill-fitting monstrosity of last night. Nonsense, of course. The most dazzling beauties of fashionable society must fawn on him like bees round honey and Miss Trethayne of nowhere at all still had too much pride to join in even if she could.

'Good morning, Miss Trethayne.' Mr Peters rose politely from the breakfast table to greet her, then looked significantly at her brothers until they stood as well.

'Good morning, sir, and a very fine morning it is too, but who are these polite young gentlemen? I can't say I recognise them.'

'It's us, Poll,' Henry told her wearily, as if wondering about her eyesight.

'May we sit down now, Sis? I'm hungry as a horse,' Toby asked.

'Of course you are, love, please carry on before you fade away in front of me,' she said, exchanging a rueful glance with Mr Peters that probably looked intimate to Lord Mantaigne when he strolled into the room.

'Good morning,' he said coolly, and she had to have imagined a flash of anger in his lazy gaze before it went unreadable again.

'It's going to be a lovely day,' she offered because she didn't want the boys to pick up on her worries about the future, or her jumbled feelings towards the marquis.

'Indeed, but the sea is still cold,' he said, helping himself from the pot of porridge set by the fire to keep warm.

'Don't say you've been for a swim, Mantaigne?' Mr Peters asked, seeming as startled as Polly that his employer would indulge in such bracing activity.

'I believe it's allowed if you have skill enough not to drown,' he said as if there was nothing unusual about a fashionable beau battling the full force of nature on such a bracing morning. Although the sun shone there was a lively breeze and taking on the waves must have been hard going.

'Don't even think about it,' his secretary said with a shudder, 'I can only imagine the fuss if you drown when I'm supposed to guard your back.'

'A task that should never have been set to you, my friend,' Lord Mantaigne drawled, but there was steel under all that careless élan.

Polly had spent years picturing the Marquis of Mantaigne as a spineless fool, ready to whistle his magnificent heritage down the wind on a whim. Under the expensive clothes and effortless elegance was a dangerous man, and last night proved how seductively the real Marquis of Mantaigne called to a wildness in Miss Paulina Trethayne she'd thought long gone. It would be as well if she avoided him as often as she could when this morning's ride about the estate was over.

'Prinny would take your land and fortune and give your title to one of his cronies,' Mr Peters mused. 'I'd have to tell the Winterleys how you met your end, though, so I'd really rather you didn't perish at sea during my time here.'

'Should your brothers need a schoolmaster I can recommend Peters as perfect for the role, when he's not too busy lecturing a fool of eight and twenty who's been going his own way far too long to listen.'

'About eight and twenty years of his life, by my reckoning,' Mr Peters murmured into his porridge, and Polly chuckled, then squirmed self-consciously under Lord Mantaigne's impassive scrutiny. She only just resisted the urge to put out her tongue and set the worst sort of example to her brothers.

'Thank you, but the vicar teaches Tobias, Henry and Jago. Josh and the younger boys have lessons with some of us here and I suspect Mr Peters has far too much to do already to join in with that thankless task,' she said to fill the silence.

'D'you think Mr Barker will tell us how he lost his leg today, Poll? He told Toby and I'll soon be as old as he is.'

'You're five years younger than your eldest brother, Joshua Trethayne, and some things have to wait until I say so,' Polly intervened before Toby and Henry could. 'And don't argue,' she added firmly.

'Why not? You're only a girl,' Josh muttered darkly.

'No, she's not, you ungrateful little toad,' Toby told him.

'No, for Miss Trethayne is your sister and for some odd reason she seems to like you,' Mr Peters said solemnly, and Josh grinned delightedly at the implication it took a doting gaze to see past his worst traits. Polly wondered why she couldn't be attracted to the man instead of his employer.

Oh, no, that was it, wasn't it? She was conscious of Lord Mantaigne on too many levels. Why did she have to feel a warm shiver of *perhaps* run over her skin at the very idea of being alone with a nobleman's secretary instead of the nobleman himself? Because she was a Trethayne, she supposed fatalistically, and they never did anything by halves. Falling headlong for the most unattainable man she'd ever come across would be a disaster bigger than any that had befallen her so far. There must be no more midnight adventures with him then and, after today, no daytime ones either.

'Still here, boys?' Lady Wakebourne asked from the doorway. 'Jago and Joe and Ben have already got their boots on.'

'And I expect Mr Partridge is waiting,' Polly prompted.

Some of the squatters had found work in the village of Little Spring, but Partridge had insisted on walking there and back with the boys ever since lights were first seen in the cove below Dayspring. Toby and Henry bolted the last of their breakfast and ran off to join their friends at a nod from Polly, and Josh dashed after them. Wishing she could do the same, she made herself eat in a suitably ladylike manner despite the sinking feeling in the pit of her stomach. Better to walk in Lady Wakebourne's shoes this morning, but the lady was so determined not to trade on her title that Polly was careful not to impinge on her self-imposed tasks.

'Shall we meet in the stable yard in half an hour for our tour of the estate, Miss Trethayne?' Lord Mantaigne asked.

'I'm ready now,' she said, because it seemed better to get it over with.

'Which of the spoilt beasts in your stable would you like saddled, then?'

'I always ride the black cob, but he won't let a stranger near him.'

'He must be a hard ride, and I dare say he's headstrong as the devil,' he remarked, trying not to call Beelzebub an unsuitable ride for a lady.

'He refuses to plough and I couldn't endure the thought of him being abused as a carriage horse.'

'Not to a coaching company or the mails, but I know a man who would treat him well and give you a good price. Can he be handled by anyone else?'

'Once he trusts you he's more amenable, but I found him wandering on the heath and he'd been beaten, so I could never let him go to someone who would try to break his spirit,' she said carefully, wondering if she could refuse a reasonable offer for her favourite when she would soon be homeless.

'I wouldn't suggest he might find a home with my friend if I doubted his ability to tell a rogue from a spirited beast with his worst masculine traits intact.'

'There's a lady present, Mantaigne,' Mr Peters protested, and Polly set him a little lower in her estimation and his master a little higher.

'Miss Trethayne doesn't want to discuss the latest fashions or how many fools crowded into Prinny's last squeeze at Carlton House, Peters.'

'I might,' Polly heard herself say as if someone else had taken over her tongue.

'I beg your pardon, ma'am. Then I must rack my brains for the details as best I can at this hour of the day.'

'You must know I have no knowledge of either subject,' she said gruffly. 'I would look ridiculous in London fashions and feel like a fish out of water at Carlton House, but a cat can still look at a king.'

'I know what you mean,' Mr Peters said with a wry look that won back some of Polly's respect and seemed to sink him in his employer's. 'I often wonder if Prinny wouldn't be happier if he'd been born on a fairground instead of in a royal bed.'

'It must make a fine spectacle, but I would hate to take part.'

'It's hot as Hades and noisier than a parliament of crows. I'd certainly give a good deal not to sit through another of Prinny's never-ending banquets,' the marquis said with what looked like genuine revulsion for all that show and waste Polly had read about in the discarded newspapers that sometimes came her way at third- or fourth-hand from the local squire.

'If your entrée to such places was withdrawn, I dare say you would feel the snub all the same,' Mr Peters said quietly.

'I expect you're right, but if we're all finished we might as well adjourn to the stable yard before the morning has gone, if you agree, Miss Trethayne? I hope you will ride one of my horses today. Although he will be nowhere near as fast or fiery as your own mount, you would be doing us a favour. A full stallion will never tolerate the presence of our hacks without a lot of fire and brimstone.'

He was right of course; Polly had been hoping Beelzebub's antics at the proximity of other males, even if they were geldings, would put a premature end to the tour. She resigned herself to hours in the disturbing man's company as both gentlemen stood back for her to lead the way, then carefully didn't look at anything less than six feet off the ground lest they be accused of ogling.

Dotty Hunslow was sitting on the granary steps, smoking a short pipe and exchanging flirtatious glances with a wizened little man who looked like a former jockey. He jumped to his feet and did his best to look as if he'd been busy all morning, and a warning glint sharpened Dotty's knowing gaze.

Unease prickled down Polly's spine as all the risks of having too much contact with a lord like this one ran through her mind screaming. No, he wouldn't give her a second glance if she was properly dressed and that was just as well. He could ruin her and her brothers' slender prospects in life if she wasn't very careful, and the throaty murmur of her inner wanton whispered it would be a very pleasurable descent, before sensible Paulina dismissed the idea as completely impossible.

No, she would have to find time to search the attics for skirts long enough to hide her legs from him and his fellow rakes so he would turn his hot blue eyes elsewhere.

'Please saddle the grey for Miss Trethayne, Dacre,' his lordship ordered as if it was an everyday occurrence for a lady to ride astride.

'He's feeling his oats,' the little man argued.

'Miss Trethayne usually rides the black cob, so Cloud will seem like a docile pony in comparison.'

'Cloud it is then, ma'am,' the small groom said with a nod of limited approval.

'Thank you,' she said, trying not to feel self-conscious in front of the stable lads while she waited for the animal to be saddled. 'Oh, you're a handsome lad and a true gentleman, aren't you, sirrah? I warrant you'd hunt all day if you had to,' she greeted the powerful-looking animal as he arched his neck at her like a circus horse and waited to be admired.

He was as big a rogue as his master from the look of him and her opinion of Lord Mantaigne rose as he laughed at the grey's antics and told him not to be such a commoner. He sobered as he cupped his hands to take her booted foot and boost her into the saddle.

'I don't hunt,' he said, eyes flicking in the direction of the tumbledown kennels Polly knew lay on the far side of the yard so as not to disturb anyone in the castle with the restless baying of the hounds.

'You don't enjoy the exercise then, my lord?' she asked a little breathlessly, trying not to be impressed as he boosted her into the saddle as easily as if she was a foot shorter and as slender as a fashion plate.

'Perhaps I pity the quarry,' he said lightly.

She was still wondering about that remark as they set off. She'd heard whispers that a miserable childhood had led to his hatred of Dayspring, but all that had mattered then was that he stayed away. Eyeing the powerful figure of the now very real Marquis of Mantaigne, Polly tried to see past it and wonder about the man under the careless elegance.

He was relaxed in the saddle of his fine horse as if he hadn't a care in the world, but she sensed wariness in him, an unwillingness to feel the appeal of this fine place on such a beautiful spring morning. Would a bright but abused boy learn to guard his thoughts and emotions from his persecutor? Yes, she decided, and any woman tempted to love him would have to fight her way past the shield wall he still kept them behind. She pitied her, whoever she turned out to be. To throw your bonnet that far over the windmill would mean being prepared to risk everything without any guarantee he would even want her once she'd done it.

Tom expected the parkland to be overgrown and small forests to blur the beautiful landscaped gardens his grandfather had paid Lancelot 'Capability' Brown to design for him. Instead the park was close-cropped by sheep and a herd of cows grazed the meadow by the lake that dreamed under the spring sun as he remembered it doing on days when he'd escaped his prison to wander his own land like a poacher in constant fear of discovery.

Not even that sense of such freedom being short and

forbidden spoiled the joy of a spring morning in this wide landscape then, but that was quite enough of the past. Today the trees looked as if they'd been kept tidy by foresters. He ought to ask Miss Trethayne how that could be when he didn't have any, but he let himself feel all the promise of spring about them instead and saved the argument for later.

'Where are we going?' Peters asked and saved him the trouble.

'To the Home Farm, through Cable Woods, then down into Days Magna,' Miss Trethayne said concisely.

'A neat slice across the closest parts of the estate,' Tom conceded and saw from the tightening of her lush mouth how his pompous reply annoyed her.

Since he couldn't make her his mistress, and she was nothing like any marchioness he'd ever come across, he told himself it was good to see the look of impatient contempt back in her fine eyes. He must do his best to keep it there for the next couple of weeks and then he could return to London or Derbyshire, leaving them both more or less unscathed.

'Who has the Home Farm?' Peters asked, and it was a reasonable enough question, so why did Tom feel jealous, as if he was the one who should be having easy conversations with Miss Trethayne and not Peters?

Perverse idiot, he condemned himself and urged his horse a little ahead, so he could leave them to talk while he watched this once-familiar landscape for changes. Yet he took in very little of it for listening to their conversation and keeping enough attention on the road in front of them to make sure he didn't fall in the dust and make himself even more of a fool than he already felt as he fought the need to have all her attention focused on him and him alone.

'The Allcotts have held it for generations,' he heard her answer Peters question obliquely and wondered why she was uneasy about it.

'And do I have a forester?' he turned in the saddle to ask.

'Several, my lord,' she said, and there was that sense she wasn't telling him the whole story again to pique his interest and let him convince himself his interest was nothing personal.

'Don't expect me to believe they come from the same family who felled trees here from the dark ages on, then. I well remember my guardian railing that he couldn't keep a male worker on the estate thanks to the press gangs and fishing boats and quarries robbing him of manpower.'

'I suppose those alternatives were more attractive,' she said so carefully he knew her thoughts were busy with all the rumours she'd probably discounted about him and Grably and how bad it had been at Dayspring once upon a time.

'Yet they came of their own free will once I ordered the place kept empty? Perhaps they fell my timber for nothing out of the goodness of their hearts,' he said blandly, and her gaze slid away from the challenge, as if she didn't want him to read secrets in them.

'Maybe they wanted to keep faith with the Banburghs?' she suggested.

'My father died, and I turned my back on them. I

can't see the locals feeling aught but contempt for the Banburghs,' he admitted harshly, conscious of Peters's shrewd gaze as well as her discomfort with the subject.

'Maybe they felt guilty?'

'I hope not; the fifth marquis is dead and I don't care.'

'No, of course you don't,' Peters said, and Tom sensed the two of them exchanging rueful glances behind his back and fought temper and something a little less straightforward—surely it couldn't be jealousy?

To be jealous he'd have to want Miss Trethayne as irrationally as Luke and Chloe Winterley had wanted each other during their decade of estrangement. So that meant he simply could not be jealous. He didn't want to ruin or marry her, so he must be immune to her smoky laugh and everything that made her unlike the pursuing pack of would-be marchionesses he dodged so carefully at *ton* functions.

'No, I don't,' he echoed as coolly as he could. 'So let's stop dawdling like a trio of dowagers and get on with our day,' he added to put an end to the conversation.

Chapter Eight

W hen they got to Home Farm he could see nothing wrong. Allcott was at the local market buying and selling cattle, but the neat-as-a-pin house and yard spoke of a diligent master. Yet Mrs Allcott didn't meet his eyes when he complimented her on her hen yard and the neat gardens and the thriving orchards surrounding the ancient stone house.

'Tell your husband I'm well content with his tenancy,' he tried to reassure her.

'Thank you, my lord, he'll be glad to hear it,' she said, her mouth in a tight line, as if it might say something it shouldn't if she let herself relax.

'Are you going to tell me why I might think Allcott an unsuitable tenant if I had actually managed to meet him, Miss Trethayne?' he asked when they were in open country again.

'He's a fine farmer and a good man,' she said defensively.

'And?'

'He was pressed into the navy as a lad and spent ten years at sea. They let him go after Trafalgar.'

'And the navy don't give up experienced seaman in times of war unless they can find no further use for them.'

'No, Allcott was blinded as well as lamed in the battle,' she replied as if she expected him to rescind the tenancy of Home Farm on the spot.

'Then he's an even more remarkable farmer than I thought,' he said tightly, angry that she thought him such a shallow fool.

'He knows more about soil and seed and weather with four senses than most men do with five,' she said as if she needed to defend the man anyway.

Squashing another of those nasty little worms of jealousy, he nodded at the outskirts of Cable Wood ahead of them. 'Is there anything I should know before I meet these woodsmen I've heard so little about?'

She couldn't mean anything to him, or he to her, he reminded himself, so it didn't matter that she thought him a hard-hearted monster. He only had to imagine the reception she'd get if he introduced her to the *ton* to shudder on her behalf. The fops and gossips would make her life a misery and the wolves would ogle her magnificent legs, raise their quizzing glasses to examine her lush breasts and tiny waist with leering attention, then pounce on her as soon as his back was turned.

He'd probably have to kill one or two to punish such disrespect, then flee to the Continent even though Bonaparte controlled most of it. No doubt she would follow, cursing his black soul while she lectured her brothers about the places they were seeing on their less-than-grand tour. No, the very idea of Miss Trethayne making the best of things at his side like that really wasn't as seductive as it seemed and he had plenty to keep him occupied here for the next three months without fantasising over a woman who would like to pretend he didn't exist.

'What are you doing your best not to tell me this time, Miss Trethayne?' he insisted wearily as she hesitated over answering his question honestly or leaving him to find out for himself.

'One or two of them are a touch impaired,' she said tightly.

'Can they do their job?'

'Of course, you only have to look around you to know that.'

'Then why expect me to turn off men who keep the rides neat and my woods just so?'

'Because they could get no work elsewhere.'

'Until today not even my worst enemies have accused me of following the crowd, yet you seem to have done so before we even met, Miss Trethayne.'

'You turned your back on a heritage most men would give their right arm to possess in a fit of pique. What did you expect the folk who depend on the castle and estate to think of you after that?'

A fit of pique? Oh, damnation take the dratted woman. Had she no idea what beatings and hardship the ragged little lord of all this had once endured? The old mess of rage and hurt pride and that feeling of being cut off from the good things in life threatened to spill out of him. If he let her, she'd wrench details out of him he hadn't even confided to Virginia. No, if his beloved godmother couldn't coax the details of his old life from him, he wasn't dredging them up for the amusement of a vagabond Amazon queen determined to think the very worst of him.

'How very tedious of me,' he drawled as indifferently as he could manage.

'Oh, why pretend? You watch every change here like a lover looking for changes in a beloved he hasn't seen for too long, yet you expect us all to believe you hate the place and don't care a tinker's curse what happens to it? No, my lord, I don't believe you and why should you stay untouched by life? You behave as if you are a summer butterfly; too gorgeous and empty to understand life isn't only made up of sunny days and nectar.'

Tom felt Peters try to meld into the quiet wood like a green man. Part of him admired the trick, but the rest was busy fighting a ludicrous idea this woman had the right to rage at him. Tall and magnificent in her man's saddle, she met his angry gaze as if it cost her nothing and if only life was different he might have agreed.

'I don't think I should care to start life as a caterpillar, or make a quick meal for a hungry bird or frog,' he managed with a careless smile and a shrug that made his horse sidle, as if it sensed the turmoil Tom was trying so hard to ignore.

'Perhaps you're right, my Lord Mantaigne should be eaten by something nobler than a slimy little creature with a harsh voice.'

'Aye, he ought, Miss Trethayne, but if it makes you feel any more charitable towards me, I'll admit I have missed the Mantaigne lands, if not the castle that goes with it.'

'I beg your pardon, my lord. I forgot our unequal stations and trespassed on your privacy,' she said as if he'd intended a subtle rebuke by reminding her he was a marquis and she was only here because he hadn't been for decades.

'I think I preferred you in a rage,' he said, her unexpected humility shocking the truth out of him.

'I don't suppose you'll have to wait long for that. I've never been very good at minding my tongue,' she admitted with an almost-smile even as her sharp eyes picked out the deep marks of a heavily laden cart on one of the cross-rides, and she veered off to examine them more closely.

'I don't think Miss Trethayne is concerned that your phantom woodsmen have been shirking their duties, do you?' Peters muttered as if Tom might not have noticed.

'No,' Tom agreed, frowning as an image of similar ones leading to the cove at Dayspring reminded him this could be a dangerous coast for more reasons than unexpected currents and powerful spring tides.

He wished he'd listened harder when the subject of evading hefty government duties on so many things arose. This was his place, his heritage, and it was time he took some responsibility for it. He wondered about quizzing Polly Trethayne about the so-called free-traders, but something about her closed expression told him she would evade his questions. He decided Partridge would be his best source of information. Even if the old rogue wasn't involved with the gangs who ran this stretch of coast, he wouldn't be able to help himself finding out as much as he could about them.

The woodsmen were working on a tangled mess of dead trees and brambles he supposed he should be ashamed of. Most had strong backs and put the arms they had left to good use. Did Miss Trethayne really think he'd dismiss them for having served their country, then been discarded when the enemy fought back? From the sharp and defensively hunched shoulders that came his way once they realised who he was, she wasn't alone in that view of him. Tom silently cursed his careless reputation and picked out the leader of the now-quiet foresters.

'Good day,' he said in a voice he knew would carry round the clearing.

'Good day, milord,' replied the giant who had been hefting a huge axe until he laid it down so carefully Tom knew he'd been tempted to swing it in his direction.

'Aye,' he said with a grin that acknowledged what a tempting target he made for an angry man, 'it certainly seems to be.'

'It's spring and the sun's shining.'

'It is now,' Tom said with a nod to the carefully cleared brambles and other brush waiting for the bonfire nearby. 'You have let light in on years of neglect, so I must thank you for doing a fine job here.'

'Must you, milord? That ain't the way I heard it.'

'I understand you doubt my intentions to the Dayspring estate, but I'm not used to having my words questioned when they're hardly out of my mouth,' Tom said evenly, holding the giant's remaining eye steadily and feeling as if the man would like to challenge him, but didn't quite dare.

He raised his voice so the other men could hear him clearly in the now-silent clearing. 'You have obviously worked hard and, if you continue to do so, I won't import my own woodsmen when they had far rather stay at home and do the job they know. Consider yourselves employed, gentlemen, and let me know honestly how many weeks' pay you have done without. I am home and things will be different at Dayspring from now on.'

'That's what I'm afraid of,' the leader said bravely, and Tom nodded at the reference to his boyhood determination to let the castle and estate go to rack and ruin.

'I'm man enough now to realise a pile of stones and its lands have no part in the cruelties of men. I shall take a proper interest in the Dayspring estates from now on, even when I have to be elsewhere.'

'Until yon castle falls into the sea?' the man said with a gesture in the direction of the distant towers visible over the top of the tallest trees in the woods that protected Spring Magna from the harshest of winds from the sea.

'Did you never say hasty things in your youth?' Tom replied. 'I'm not sure what I'll do about the castle yet, but I want the estate put in order and kept that way.'

'About time,' his disrespectful head forester informed him sternly, but luckily Tom preferred plain speaking to toadying.

'Aye, the Banburghs learn slowly, but do it well in the

end,' he admitted and thought he heard the odd murmur of approval. The man in front of him and Miss Trethayne seemed unconvinced, but Tom resisted an urge to demand what else they needed to hear, because he probably didn't want to know.

'Are you going to bring in a bailiff and outsiders to work the estate, my lord?' this doubter asked.

'I won't bring in my own woodsmen if that's what you mean. Why would I uproot men who want to stay at home and bring them here when they're not needed?'

'Because they've got all their arms and legs and everything else we left behind after we took the King's shilling.'

'I see work well done and, as long as you're content, I'm happy to have you carry on. Some of you might prefer work more suited to your skills and experience, but that's for a time when I've leisure to examine the fine details of how this estate should work in future.'

'With some fancy new man you'll bring in to run the Castle estate, my lord?'

'Perhaps, but for now if you have a problem you will have to come to me.'

'Where would I do that, then, milord?' the man asked warily.

'I'll be at the castle for a while yet and intend to find a suitable manager before I leave. An estate this size can't run well without someone at the helm.'

'We have a captain,' he said with a nod at Miss Trethayne that made her blush as no flowery compliment from a Bond Street Beau could.

'I said a *suitable* manager,' Tom said clumsily. She

would hear his words as lack of confidence in her rather than a statement that it was too dangerous for her to ride about alone. 'I'm very grateful to Miss Trethayne, but it's not a burden I can leave on her shoulders for ever. You can come to me if a new man wants to make changes you don't agree with and I'll always give you a fair hearing.'

'Sounds like paradise,' one of the men joked sceptically, but sly smiles and the odd laugh greeted his sally all the same.

Tom thought his battle largely won, but the leader wasn't convinced. Apart from the eye-patch over his damaged eye, it wasn't until he moved that the halt in his gait made it a wonder he'd managed to keep both legs. Tom decided he wouldn't want to be a naval surgeon who tried to take this man's leg off if he wanted to keep it as the big sailor-cum-woodsman sneaked a glance at Miss Trethayne, and what a fool he was not to have seen it straight away. Of course, the man was in love with her.

Now he was home the big woodsman could either take up the role of head forester or chance his luck with the smugglers, while as for Miss Trethayne…

Yes, and what *would* Miss Trethayne do with herself if she left Dayspring? Even if she didn't have her brothers to care for, Tom couldn't see her as a lady's companion or governess. He supposed she might catch a widower or a cit if he contrived a Season for her in one of the minor watering places, where her looks and goddess-like presence would eclipse her years, height and lack of fortune. Or he could shame Lord

Trethayne into meeting his obligations. He doubted Miss Trethayne would take a penny-piece from the selfish old dog now, though, and he hated the idea of her having to lower her pride if she decided it was too expensive a luxury for a woman with three little brothers to provide for.

So what the devil *was* he going to do? He could marry her, but picturing her towering over every other female in a set of court feathers when she was presented at a Court Drawing Room as the new Marchioness of Mantaigne made him shudder. Yet how else could he rescue the stubborn female from the impossible situation she was in simply because he'd come home and she had nowhere else to go?

Polly tried to pretend she wasn't there while Lord Mantaigne made the acquaintance of his woodsmen. She had no connection to the family who'd owned this land since the first Banburgh claimed it and built a stronghold. The truth was she was jealous of the current marquis's ownership and his right to neglect it, then turn up and take it back while she, who loved it, would have to leave. The injustice of it might have made a Jacobin of her, if it hadn't been for the memory of her French stepmother starting at shadows and paling whenever she recalled the Terror.

The rightful owner of Dayspring Castle had come into his own. That phrase had a ring to it she would have laughed over only yesterday, but today there was nothing funny about it. She could almost picture her father giving one of his careless shrugs and telling her blithely that nothing stayed the same for ever. He was probably right and she might not have been able to hold the castle and estate together for much longer. The late-night incursions into the castle had been troubling her for weeks, and she thought of last night with a shiver of mixed emotions that shot through her and sent poor Cloud dancing as he sensed her turmoil through the bit she forced herself to relax her grip on so she could at least conceal it from the fine animal she was riding and his equally fine master.

Now the wretch was climbing into his saddle with an easy word to his new employees and turning his chestnut gelding towards the ride where she and Mr Peters sat silently waiting. Lord Mantaigne had a knack for getting what he wanted, and she let herself wonder for all of a minute what he might want of her. A swift and trouble-free departure after she had explained how things stood here, she suspected. She slanted him a stern look as he followed in her wake, because she knew the way and he'd let himself forget it, and tried to behave like a rational woman.

'Do you think they'll stay?' he asked once they were out of earshot.

'Most have families to support. They don't have much alternative,' she told him as evenly as she could.

'It's thanks to you they're usefully employed though, is it not?'

'I'm sure someone would have suggested they could usefully tame your woodlands and perhaps sell the wood to make it worth their while sooner or later if I had not.'

'And a wild wood makes a fine hiding place for vagabonds and villains the local magistrates could well do without,' he said, and Polly wondered if he was remembering smugglers liked wild places and hidden tracks to hide the pony trains that carried goods away from the coast.

'And those who like to avoid *them* might resent the loss of cover,' Mr Peters said shrewdly.

'I doubt that would be seen as a bad thing in Days Magna,' she replied absently, wondering if he was right.

'Are you telling me the free-traders are unwelcome round here, Miss Trethayne?' his employer asked as if she was trying to muddy the waters.

She recalled how sharply his gaze had focused on a careless footprint left on one of the less-obvious tracks and how he'd frowned at the deeper-than-they-ought-to-be ruts on the road down to the sea. The man did his best to hide a rapier-sharp mind under that air of lazy indifference, but she was beginning to see through it to the real man underneath. She wondered if he knew how many of his talents and intelligence were wasted being the idle man of fashion he pretended he was.

He wouldn't think it a waste, she answered herself cynically. Gambling and carousing and defying the devil was a game to him, along with seducing other men's wives and charming anyone who wasn't yet convinced the Marquis of Mantaigne deserved all the treasures and comforts he'd been born to.

She only just managed to bite back a tirade on the subject of gentlemen who thought they had a right to anything they laid greedy eyes on and decided to want. No, that was just being lazy. Wrong to add him to the leering beast who had thought a penniless female like her was fair game, she knew he wouldn't dream of forcing himself on a woman without anyone having to say so. Yes, there was a hot glitter in his blue, blue eyes when they rested on her too long, but she felt a new excitement stir deep inside whenever that happened so she couldn't deny it was a mutual wanting. It left her wondering how she would feel if they satisfied it, but that was never going to happen.

'They are part of everyday life here, but sometimes it isn't comfortable to know they pass too close,' she replied to his question about the smugglers and hoped he thought her silence had been because she was considering her answer, not the chance of being anyone's lover, but more especially his. 'The villagers know they must either accept the fact the Trade runs through the area like a seam or leave it. Evading the duty on goods that puts them out of reach of all but the very rich is often seen as their God-given right as free-born Englishmen,' she managed to say coolly.

'So I've heard,' Peters said grimly, and she hoped he wasn't thinking of taking on the deeply rooted traditions of the whole area single-handed.

'Even if the customs officials manage to catch them, the magistrates round here wouldn't prosecute hard, and no jury would convict them if they did,' she warned them, then squirmed under Mr Peters's cool gaze and wished she'd held her tongue.

'It's not the Trade itself that vexes me, or even the

ruthless nature of the smuggling business for anyone who gets too close, but Bonaparte's use of his damned guinea boats to subvert our currency,' Lord Mantaigne argued.

'I doubt that's the only reason he winks at the smuggling trade,' Polly said and felt the tug of conflicting loyalties most people must, if they stopped to consider it as other than a local way of life that had been going on since anyone could remember. 'I wouldn't have wanted to live in the days when the Hawkhurst Gang and their like terrorised everyone for miles around, but I can't roundly condemn a trade that puts a few luxuries in the hands of folk who labour for a pittance while their masters enjoy every indulgence they can think up, however foolish it might seem to the rest of us.'

'You sound like a revolutionary, Miss Trethayne,' his lordship drawled.

'Do I, my lord? How very shocking of me,' she replied lightly.

'I know there is much that is unequal and unfair in this country and no wonder working folk look at what others have and want it for themselves, but consider how it would be if the French Emperor invaded us as he has so many others. For all their talk of liberty and equality they treat their conquered nations like vassals and plunder them of treasures and, worse, I should hate to be a young and attractive female under such a regime. Those who hail Bonaparte as a liberator and a lawmaker should take a closer look at Spain and see how it feels to live under his heel.'

Polly allowed herself a shudder and blessed the fact

she wasn't on her usual mount. Beelzebub would have bolted at the feel of her involuntary flash of terror as she thought of the fate so many women had met at the hands of victorious invading troops in this horrifying, never-ending war.

'I would not wish to be an enemy nobleman in such a world either,' she pointed out.

'No, I think I'd better arrange to expire on the barricades if the worst should ever come to pass. I don't relish the role of a craven captive, or trying to ransom myself at any cost while my tenants and workers look on with contempt.'

'For heaven's sake, will you stop joking about the things you care about the most, man?' his usually meek secretary snapped, clearly as close to the end of his tether with the foppish aristocrat Lord Mantaigne pretended to be as Polly was.

'It is deeply exasperating,' she agreed.

'My apologies, the last thing I ever set out to do was prove tedious. To relieve you both of the trouble of bearing with me any longer I will leave you and flit off on a selfish errand of my own. Why don't you take my conscience here into Spring Magna instead of my unworthy self and introduce him to anyone who is interested for me, Miss Trethayne? I'm sure you can assure them everything they least wanted to hear about me is true and they must hope I shall depart as unexpectedly as I came amongst them,' Lord Mantaigne said as coldly as if he truly wished the estate was desolate, his castle in ruins and himself a hundred miles away.

'Well, that put us properly in our place,' Mr Peters observed calmly as he watched the marquis ride away.

Polly couldn't help but admire his horsemanship as his powerful, supple figure adjusted to the pace of his galloping steed as if by second nature. He confused and angered her by turns, yet felt an odd tug of sympathy for him haunt her as she exchanged a rueful glance with Mr Peters and considered how they'd been ordered to spend their afternoon without him.

'It will put the local rumour mill in a fine spin if we go on together without him, Mr Peters. You could always ride on alone and introduce yourself to the folk of the Spring villages. They will be pleased with any sign the marquis is taking an interest in them and are sure to make you very welcome. I might as well return to the castle and help with the spring planting since I seem to be redundant here.'

'That was not well done. Lord Mantaigne is a man of more impulsive character than he wants us to know at times, but I cannot let you ride alone. I may not be a native of this place, but I do have eyes in my head and can see that large groups of men have been marching about this land all too recently for my comfort. You must not take risks with your personal safety, and only think how Lady Wakebourne and your brothers will feel if anything untoward happens whilst you're out alone.'

'I have been out alone, as you call it, for years.'

'Then it's a very good thing we arrived when we did,' the man argued, and Polly only just suppressed an unladylike grunt of disagreement.

'I could learn to dislike you nearly as much as I

should your employer if you insist on being right all the time, Mr Peters,' she said half-seriously.

'I fear it is a sad failing in my half of our species, Miss Trethayne,' he replied with a mournful shake of his head that disarmed her and made her feel a fishwife for taking her fury with the marquis out on this man all at the same time.

'And of mine to argue. You really are wrong this time as well, though, because for us squatters it isn't a good thing at all. With your coming, we must leave the castle and it is never a good thing to be rendered homeless twice.'

'However maddening his lordship might be, he won't turn you out to wander the roads with your family and friends like the lost tribe of the Israelites. I can see signs of an unknown number of people determined to invade your sanctuary, though, and well before we turned up. It could be a very good thing the owner of Dayspring Castle arrived before they could succeed, despite your mixed views on the matter.'

Polly noted how neatly the man had his own plans for the afternoon running as they retraced their route from the castle even as she had half her mind on arguing with him. She went along with him, though, because she was safer in his company and it gave her time to think. Soon she would catch herself thinking it a good thing they were here as well, if she wasn't careful.

If their lives were different, how would it feel to arrive at Dayspring as a guest of Lord Mantaigne with her stepmother and Papa? For all of a minute she indulged in an air dream of herself superbly dressed and elegantly coiffured, stepping down from the carriage to meet the warm blue gaze of an admiring Marquis of Mantaigne. In such circumstances it might be quite all right to feel the same rush of heat and wonder as when they actually did meet; in a stable, among the faded and patched up rags of Dayspring's glory days. Instead of being dressed in silks and finest muslins she'd looked more like a scruffy youth—sweaty and weary and windswept after another busy day trying to keep the wolf from the door.

The differences of how they really were fitted neatly into that one scene. He was rich and powerful and unforgivably handsome; she was poor, powerless and awkward as a heron in a hen yard. *That's how my life really is*, she told herself sternly, trying to focus on what her real and adoptive family were going to do now Lord Mantaigne was back in his castle after all these years. Or he would be if he hadn't just galloped away from it in a temper, and suddenly the unease she'd been feeling for the past few weeks left her worrying about his safety instead of her own or her family's.

He would make an irresistible target for a villain lurking in still-untamed parts of the woods, or he might stumble on one of the secluded coves the landsmen used to hide their illicit cargo until they could be carried inland under cover of darkness. Marquis or no, he might never be seen again if he was unlucky enough to come upon them taking goods inland by one of the hidden lanes that scored the remotest parts of this countryside. Sometimes a Revenue Cutter lurking offshore would spur men into taking unprecedented actions, like moving a cargo by day, or setting an armed guard over their most precious hiding places.

Even if he was simply set upon by a rogue on the lookout for an easy mark, he would yield a fine haul. His clothes and boots alone would bring in several months' wages for a labouring man, even at a fraction of their true value, then there was that fine gold fob-watch she'd seen him consult earlier today and his signet ring as well as the plain gold pin in his spotless muslin neckcloth.

Before she got to the end of a list of things about my Lord Mantaigne that could be profitably marketed by an attacker they were in sight of the castle and she had to put aside her horrifying inner picture of him lying naked and unconscious by some distant roadside. Maybe he would be held for ransom, and how on earth would they raise the enormous sum any sensible villain would demand for his safe return?

No! She must stop this nonsense; he was nothing to her, and it was up to Mr Peters to look out for his employer and answer the marquis's friends if he went missing, if he had any of course.

Once she was home again, Polly did her best to go about the normal business of her day as if she hadn't a care in the world, or a marquis who ought not to be allowed out without a suitable chaperon on her mind. By the time he rode into the stable yard as darkness was all but on them, looking as if he hadn't a care in the world, she had a thumping headache and decided to have an early night as Lady Wakebourne suggested with an anxious frown at Polly's tense and pallid face.

With any luck she wouldn't dream at all and could forget about an annoying aristocrat without a care for anyone in his handsome head as easily as he had about her and Mr Peters this afternoon.

Chapter Nine

That day set the pattern for the Marquis of Mantaigne's return to his primary country seat. Whenever it didn't pour with rain he spent his days exploring the estate and its villages, with or without his secretary at his side. If he stayed home he was polite and surprisingly easy with the interlopers at his once-grand mansion and they did their best not to ask what he intended to do about them as days grew into weeks. Polly felt like the outsider as her friends and family came to look on him as a genial and civilised gentleman. So why was she the only one who felt as if she was constantly waiting for the second shoe to fall?

Her life had narrowed to the park and gardens, and she supposed glumly that it would prepare her for a time when they must leave and patch together some sort of life elsewhere. One day she came home from working in the fields around Dayspring to find a beautiful riding habit draped across her bed. For a moment she enjoyed the sheer pleasure of seeing the richly dyed forest-green fabric lying there in the dappled sunlight slanting through the ancient leaded windows. There were depths and shifts in the folds that told her it was the work of a master weaver and she knew that colour would suit her to perfection, if she had any intention of wearing it.

Knowing she was being stubborn and ungrateful, she still felt her temper rise to dangerous heights at Lord Mantaigne's presumption. If the man didn't like her as she was he could tell her so; this was an attempt to force her into the role of a meek and properly dressed female without him having to point out her clothes were unladylike and shocking even to a rake like him.

She refused to fit into a neat little niche where spinster ladies with no prospects must live. She couldn't cram herself into such narrow confines even if she wanted to, she concluded, with a severe nod at the beautiful garment lying there like a false promise. How did he expect Miss Paulina Trethayne to force herself into the cramping styles of a proper lady when she hadn't a penny to her name she hadn't earned through working his land when his back was turned? Surely he didn't think local society would blink at such an unlikely spectacle and make space for her?

The very idea of the derision that would greet her if she tried to cramp her long limbs and unladylike lope into the mincing gait and quiet littleness of a spinster's day-to-day life made her cringe. He was setting her up to be a mockery, and she felt the sting of it, even as she slammed the door of her bedchamber and ran back down the stairs to find the wretched man and berate him for taking this latest chip out of her self-confidence.

He didn't need her to accompany him about the estate while he was visiting folk who only a few weeks ago had turned to her for help and advice. They had little choice but to ask her for what little help she could give them after years of neglect by their lord, but now they'd forgotten how long he'd left them leaderless and bewildered and she might not even exist for all the need they had of her now. She hoped they never came to regret relying on a man who might easily forget them for another decade.

Fighting her hurt at being forgotten in the dazzling presence of the latest Marquis of Mantaigne, Polly felt weariness pinch after her latest day of hard physical labour. She was driving herself and the men who worked the smallholding they'd made in the castle's vast kitchen garden too hard, but fear of being left with nothing again goaded her on. This was their last chance of a good harvest and it ought to be the best one they'd ever had. If they could make enough money from their crops this year, maybe they could sell the surplus and set up a small farm elsewhere. It wouldn't be Dayspring, of course—nothing could equal the noble old stronghold by the sea she had come to love so much—but they'd work hard to make it a different home.

As she strode across the inner bailey and looked for my Lord of Mantaigne instead of avoiding him, Polly wondered why nobody else worried about the future. The marquis was with a stranger when she tracked him down to the little parlour he had appropriated as a study-cum-estate office and the surprised-looking visitor, trying so hard not to look at her legs, made her more uncomfortable than if he had leered like an uncouth lout. She hung back impatiently while Lord Mantaigne escorted the man outside and bade him a cheery farewell without ever managing to say who he was and why he was here in the first place.

Anyone would think the lord was the land steward he had still not appointed, despite his fine promises, and not a noble fashion plate, Polly told herself scornfully. Yet even she had to admit he looked like a hero from Ancient Greece in the mellow evening light, the long shadows from the setting sun lending his features such stern definition even she couldn't accuse him of being a soft dandy. She saw him laugh at something the man said and once more felt the pull of attraction even as a frown pleated her brows and she shook her head impatiently.

At this distance he looked like a gilded lord out of a legend—a modern King Arthur about to unite his ravaged kingdom with daring deeds and the circle of charm such beings cast on their friends as well as their subjects. Except he was real. And here. Every female impulse in her felt the siren call of such a compelling and deeply masculine man, even when he didn't know he was making it.

She drew a picture for herself of the woman he would happily pull close to kiss and caress in the fading May twilight as their visitor rode away. She would stand no higher than his heart. His true mate would be an intensely feminine beauty with hair of a paler gold than his own, eyes as compellingly blue, but softer and a great deal more demure. There would be a special grace to her slender limbs that not even her detractors could deny and, as one of those detractors, Polly was quite sure she would try very hard to do so.

His ideal woman's voice would be soft and low, and Polly was horribly certain she would sing like an angel. She added a low-cut, narrow gown of gossamer and fairy-dust and knew the wretched female would have sensual curves and a lovely line to her slender limbs to hold him to her for life. Already she hated the smug creature and waved a hand in front of her eyes as if she could erase the differences between such a paragon and herself just by wishing.

She glanced down at the mud and dust-stained work boots she'd once seen as a necessity of life and now regarded as a mark of how little she had in common with the ladies she should have grown up with. Then came her ridiculously overgrown legs, encased in ancient breeches she had found in an attic, discarded by their original owner decades ago in the belief they were too shabby and threadbare to wear even for rough jobs about the castle and the poor probably weren't poor enough to want them.

When she was growing up she often felt a freak, her overlong limbs tangling in her skirts and tripping her up at the most awkward moments. Now she knew she was a female others would mark out as extraordinary for all the wrong reasons and why on earth should it matter to her if the marquis watched her every move or kept his distance as sternly as she'd told herself she wanted him to ever since that first day and night at Dayspring?

She remembered the titters of some other girls when she fell on her nose in church one Sunday not long after her sixteenth birthday. She had crushed the brim of the new bonnet she had longed for so passionately. The pretty delicacy of it hadn't suited her, as one of them unkindly pointed out when humiliated tears streamed down Polly's sore face and bloody nose. Her stepmother had loyally informed them such cattish remarks were neither pretty nor delicate and said more about them than they did about her daughter. Even so Polly had seen the worry in Claire's dark eyes when she hugged as much of her strapping stepchild as she could still reach and whispered one day she would grow into herself and be magnificent, but those commonplace little girls would just be little and commonplace for the rest of their lives.

Loss twisted in her gut as painfully as the day Claire had died when Josh was born. Something in Polly's father seemed to die with her and grief for both of them fought its way past the anger Papa's ruin and reckless death brought with it and she let herself see how deeply he'd loved Claire and how impossible he had found life without her at last. It didn't make the things he'd done to forget his terrible grief right, but suddenly they were more understandable.

The possibility of loving so passionately might trip her up as well, but maybe she had inherited too much sense from the first wife Papa had wed with his head for such a headlong risk of everything she was for love. *Idiotic woman*, she chided herself, *haven't you just con-*

gratulated yourself on being a prosaic female and now you're longing to be the exact opposite?

'He has me in such a spin that I don't know what I do want any more,' she said out loud this time and heard the soft murmur of her own voice sound round the little room with horror.

What if someone was close by when she gave away so much she wanted to keep to herself? Sneaking a look to see if she really had given herself away, she saw nobody and heard only the cool silence of a place with history in every shadow. Fanciful nonsense, of course, Polly decided with a wry smile for her sudden outbreak of lunacy. She touched one of the cool old pieces of glass in the leaded window that overlooked the yard where the marquis and his visitor were still talking earnestly. If she closed her eyes and pretended hard enough, the image she saw through that glass might be him. In another dimension she might reach through and touch the man's very soul instead of the far-off untouchable reality.

There now, at last the marquis had said his farewells and the stranger was riding away. No time like the present, she told herself, and braced her shoulders for the argument she'd been promising herself as she did her best to recall why she was so angry with him in the first place.

'Miss Trethayne, you must have found the habit your friends have worked on so diligently from the stern expression on your face,' he said genially, as if he'd been expecting the flare of temper in her eyes and was finding it a little too amusing.

'If they made it, how come the material is so fine?' she demanded, telling herself she felt so frustrated and suspicious because arguing with him was like trying to wrestle with a shadow; the moment you thought you had a grip on it, it faded and all you were left with was a mocking smile and frustration.

'I remembered seeing a trunk full of such lengths of cloth hidden away in a room tucked away under the eaves that you and your friends must have missed,' he said, a tension in his eyes she might have welcomed a few moments ago to remind her how distant they really were from one another. Now it made her uneasy, tugged at some connection between them she really didn't want to know about.

'Then it's rightfully yours,' she said and shot him a baleful look.

'Ah, but it's not my colour,' he quipped.

'Don't shrug me off and don't treat me like a charity case.'

'I would never be so rash or so rude, even if you were anything of the kind and you're not,' he said sternly, as if he thought the rest of the world spent too much time tiptoeing about her temper.

'You have no idea what it's like to have nothing,' she replied defensively.

'Do I not? If you'd seen the ragged boy who used to risk his life climbing out of the highest tower window up there and down the outside of his own castle in search of scraps to fill his hungry belly, you might change your mind about my ignorance.'

'But you didn't really have nothing,' she argued

weakly, pity for such a desperate boy causing a lump of sadness in her throat she knew he would hate.

'And neither do you. You have a family who adore you; friends who would walk barefoot to reach you if you were in trouble and the whole neighbourhood sings your praises at me until I'm almost sick of the sound of your name on their tongues.'

'None of them need me now you are here.'

'Just as well, since you've been hiding behind a set of harrows or pulling weeds out of turnips or whatever else you've been finding to do with yourself all the hours God sends these past few weeks in order to avoid me.'

'I wasn't hiding.'

'Were you not? If nobody else could have done any of those tasks, then I bow to your superior knowledge and must consider you sociable after all.'

'You know very well there was nothing uniquely skilled about any of the jobs I've done lately.'

'Perhaps you ought to let someone else do them then. I've offered anyone who wants work all the employment they could dream of in my sadly neglected pleasure gardens, woods and the acreage the castle once kept under its own management. Kingwood wants to retire and tells me he's only been farming the land you and your friends couldn't cope with because he felt he owed it to my father. You have no idea how humble I'm becoming under the goad of such words, Miss Trethayne. Everyone here thinks my father a much better man than I'll ever be, although I can't remember much to back that opinion up. In fairness, he could hardly be a worse master than I have been, so the competition is not fierce.'

'They want to admire you,' Polly heard herself say softly and wondered how he'd turned her from raging virago into his sympathetic champion in so short a time. 'Some would even love you, if you let them.'

'Love is the most unreliable of human emotions, Miss Trethayne. I do my best to avoid feeling it or asking for it from others.'

'Then I must feel sorry for you, my lord,' Polly said with a corrosive feeling of disappointment and pity nagging at her as she turned to walk away.

'Don't. I'm perfectly content with friendship and mutual respect.'

'I hope it keeps you warm in winter then,' she murmured and would have gone back to her eyrie to take a second look at the riding habit that now sounded like a gift of love, except he held her back with the lightest of touches on her arm.

'So do I,' he said far more seriously than usual. 'I also hope you'll accept Lady Wakebourne's scheme for your joint futures when she proposes it, Miss Trethayne. The lady has no family and those wild young rascals of hers to bring up on her own somehow. I don't think you'd want her to struggle on alone, even if the idea of me freezing to death on an Arctic ice-floe would probably cost you no qualms.'

'You're so wrong about that,' she told him, meeting his eyes for a long moment. 'It would cost me a great many.'

'But you have a tender heart, Miss Trethayne. I dare say you would make a push to rescue your worst enemy from such a chilly ending,' he said, and there was something in his gaze she dared not read, something that spoke of more than lust or mere liking for her and that simply couldn't be a possibility between them.

'Perhaps I would,' she agreed with a faint smile.

'And you will listen?'

'I would always give such a good friend a fair hearing and try my best to be reasonable about whatever it is she has to say.'

'If that's what it takes to render you open to reason, I must wish I was your friend then.'

'So must I, my lord,' she said rather sadly.

'Could we not try it?' he offered, and for a moment the chance of such an unlikely relationship tempted her to take the admiration in his gaze and warmth of his hand in hers to seal a bond between them.

'I don't think a marquis could be friends with a beggar,' she said and hated herself for being less democratic than he was as she made herself turn away.

'I don't think that so-called beggar can be friends with herself until she accepts we are each of us more than a rank or a piece of ignorant name-calling,' he said quietly as she went to walk away.

She hesitated, wishing so hard she dared accept his olive branch and see him in the same rosy light as the rest of the unofficial residents of Dayspring Castle did.

'I expect you're right,' she said tritely and made herself leave, before she swore undying devotion to him, or even blurted out some disaster of an emotion he would dislike even more.

Thinking back to his idea that she would be happy to hear he'd met such an awful end, she fought down a denial it almost hurt her not to voice. Of course she didn't want anything to happen to the arrogant lord of Dayspring Castle. The very idea of him enduring such hardship when she wasn't there to try to make it less hurt her. Tears blurred her vision before she blinked them back as she strode off to her room to find clean clothes to put on after the bath she so badly needed.

Half an hour later Polly sat back in her tub of hot water in the women's bath-house with a contented sigh, then reached for the soap Lord Mantaigne had insisted on sending for as a luxury he refused to live without. He wasn't the man she'd thought him at first sight of all that perfect tailoring and gilded splendour, but he wasn't the man he thought either. She'd done her best to pretend he was just a London dandy, but he was so much more. If he ever stopped keeping the rest of the world at arm's length, he would be an extraordinary and unforgettable man. It was the waste of such magnificent potential that made her want to cry, though, not a more personal sort of desolation that she wasn't the woman to unlock it.

Washing off the sweat and dirt of her labours, she did her best not to think of making love with the wretched man like this, with her limbs all smooth and warm and naked and her feminine curves undisguised by mannish clothes and rough labour. What would he make of her if he could see her naked? The very idea shot a hot quiver of anticipation through her like an arrow of molten gold, but that was a silly idea, wasn't it?

Gold was far too soft even for Cupid's arrows and

she didn't care to even consider being pierced by one of those. A knot of pure heat still clutched in her belly, though, and on down to whisper all sorts of impossible echoes of him and her at her deepest and most secret core. She considered what he might look like similarly naked and as curious about her as she was about him and blushed in places she didn't know she could blush. Would he want her if he saw her like this? Would his manhood betray the fact a vigorous and healthy male would always want a reasonably well-formed female, if the chance arose to be closeted with her hot and naked in a steamy room with a fire lit in the corner to make it cosy and intimate? Probably, but a cynical voice whispered in her head that it didn't mean she would be in any way special to him and he would be the sun and moon to her if she wasn't very careful.

She ran a speculative hand down the long sweep of her wet thigh and shuddered with feminine curiosity, longing for his hands to shadow hers there and admitting for once how very much she wanted him as her lover. Even the thought made her breasts grow heavier and tighter, and she cupped them to push them up and wonder. How would it feel to have my Lord of Mantaigne seize one hot, tight nipple in his knowing mouth and suckle, even as his long fingers played with the other so it didn't feel left out in the cold?

Polly gasped at where her wicked imagination was taking her, hastily snatched her hands away and reached for the rosemary-and-soapwort infusion Lady Wakebourne made up especially to clean the mud from her hair. She cleansed every lock until it squeaked, then poured the jugs of water over her head, adding the one of icy cold, drawn from the well lest any of the others proved too hot, for the last rinse of both her hair and her unruly body. There, that ought to chill the ardour out of her; shock her into seeing how impossible such a coupling was for both of them.

He would probably leave her with child and she would leave him with regrets and a duty to care for her and her by-blow for the rest of their lives. No, no and no. She would never do that to a man like him, one who would have to find a suitable marchioness one day. Pretend how he liked to be a care-for-nobody, he would suffer the guilt of the damned about any lady whose life he'd ruined in the eyes of the world, once the heady passion was spent and he woke up to find himself the other half of such an unlikely pairing with her.

Her tender smile wobbled at the thought of him arguing he hadn't a soul for her to concern herself with, as he surely would if he was here and knew what sinful wonders she was thinking about. He knew so little about himself it shocked her. It was as if the neglected and abused boy he'd once been had taken the hard things his obnoxious guardian threw at him and secretly owned up to them, as if every word was true. She was sure that was too simple a way to explain it, but she ached for the boy he had been and the man he really was.

Was the *ton* really so wilfully blind they only saw the gilded nobleman he offered up for them to wonder at? She supposed it was a brilliant act; his pose of shallow and vain aristocrat, more concerned about the knot in his cravat than the state of the world or the well-being of his fellow man. Perhaps he showed up less as the man he really was there than he did here, set as he would normally be amongst the brilliant but shallow pleasures of the *haut ton* and pretending to be as indifferent as the next care-for-nobody to the affairs of ordinary humanity.

He'd offered work to those who wanted it here though. That smile played about her mouth again and it was as well there was no mirror in the women's bath-house to show her how gentle it went at the thought of him pretending to be indifferent, even as he gave the local men a chance to wean themselves away from the smuggling trade or the sea, if they chose to take it.

If he really thought they would lose the chance of a night's work as tub-men and gain luxuries a working man couldn't dream of otherwise, he was probably doomed to disappointment. At least he was giving them a chance to earn an honest living, though, and it would be good to see the Banburgh estates worked as they should be once more, or at least it would be for everyone but the gangs who had used the neglected woods and byways as the ideal conduit from coast to warehouse.

There, she had got through roughly towelling the water from her heavy hanks of hair and drying her over-receptive body without longing for the impossible again, here with her, loving her as she secretly longed to be loved exclusively by him. Was that it? Was she afraid of falling in love with the marquis? Worse even than that disaster—was she already halfway there?

Well, if she was it was about as much use to her as a lunatic longing for the moon, so she had chosen a man who would do her no harm—since it would never even occur to him to love her back. She was nearly six feet tall with four and twenty years of life in her dish; had three beloved obligations who would need her until she was old and grey *and* she habitually wore breeches in preference to petticoats, for goodness' sake. How could he consider her as a potential lover when she was about as ineligible even as his bedmate as a woman could be?

Seizing the delicately carved comb she had felt guilty about taking from one of the bedchambers in the closed-up and neglected part of the house, she began tugging at the tangles in her hair as if it was their fault she was undesirable. Not only was that ridiculous, but it hurt, so, taking a deep breath, she made herself begin at the ends and work towards her crown until every tangle was banished. As it began to dry the firelight picked out red and gold and russet lights in the curls it sprang into wherever Jane had cut the full weight of her heavy locks away.

It was stupid to be vain of a mane of hair she often thought couldn't make up its mind how to be, but the weight of it on her naked shoulders felt silky and rich and sensual. Telling herself it was as well to be re-alistic about her own attractions, she unwrapped the bath towel, another of Lord Mantaigne's luxuries she couldn't bring herself to argue against using, and felt as if even her skin was more sensitive than it had been before he came here. She felt as if only his sigh against the softness of her shoulders, or the whisper of a finger-tip on her arm, might set a blaze of something sensual and irresistible running over her like wildfire.

You are a deluded idiot, she chided herself as a hot shudder of wanting probably made it a good idea to plunge back into the rapidly cooling water and wash away the very idea. She'd been in here far too long already, though, and what if anyone suspected she had been preening and dreaming and longing for impossible things, instead of simply scrubbing herself clean and getting ready to face his lordship's indifference once more with a mental shrug and roll of exasperated eyes?

For once Polly took some trouble about dressing for the evening ahead because she did have a certain amount of pride after all. She grimaced at the latest ill-fitting gown with its wide skirts and unfashionably long bodice. She'd snatched it from the usual attic as the only other one left that would be long enough for her without the wide hoops designed to make it the first stare of fashion decades ago when a fine Banburgh lady ordered it from her mantua-maker.

She looked a quiz, she decided as she fumbled her bare feet into the old-fashioned high-heeled shoes that added another few inches to her already impressive height. At this rate she would be given a torch and told to stand instead of a light on the headland to keep ships away in a storm. Well, this was the truth: Miss Paulina Trethayne in all her unadorned plainness. She felt a twinge of regret for the jewellery she'd been forced to sell to pay some of her father's debts and feed the boys until she could beg, borrow or steal enough to keep them all from starving. Her mother's gold locket or single row of pearls would have diverted one glance from the stark lack of style in anything she was wearing.

The magnificent diamond ring Claire had managed to keep hidden somehow throughout her frantic flight from the Terror in France was hidden safely away behind a neatly re-mortared stone in Polly's bedchamber to be sold to help her boys one day. So far Polly had managed to tell herself *not yet*, but soon it would have to be *now*.

'Ah, there you are, my dear,' Lady Wakebourne said absently when she slipped into the dining parlour at the last moment before Prue would tell her she was too late and must make do with whatever she could forage in the kitchen.

'I was too dirty to sit down to dinner without a bath,' she told whoever might be interested.

'You shouldn't be slaving in the fields like a peasant girl,' Prue said sternly, and her sister nodded a solemn agreement.

Toby frowned at the last of his rabbit stew as if it suddenly tasted less savoury and shot her a worried look. 'We should help you instead of idling at the Vicarage all day,' he told her as if he'd suddenly grown up and become the man of the household.

'I'm not idle,' Henry objected, 'I work hard.'

'No, but you're a natural scholar, Hal, and love your dusty old books. I don't see much point aping the little gentleman much longer and pretending I have the least bent for learning, though, because I haven't.'

'I doubt any of us struggled to provide you with an education in order for you to throw it in our faces, my lad,' Lady Wakebourne chided with a glare at her own protégés that Jago returned with a shrug that said he wasn't going to complain about a lack of hard work after his years spent cleaning chimneys from dawn until dusk.

'I don't think any of us could describe you as little gentlemen without being accused of stretching the truth mightily,' Lord Mantaigne intervened before Toby could dash out and sign on as cabin boy on the nearest merchant ship and his littlest brother as powder-monkey to a man o'war.

'I promised your mother I would raise you as gentlemen, so you're not getting out of your lessons that easily, young man. And you promised her you would do as I said until you were one and twenty. By my reckoning, I have another six years of blissful obedience to my every whim to look forward to,' Polly said with a steady look for her eldest brother, then a wistful glance at her dinner.

She had worked up a mighty appetite at her labours and was very sharp set, but her brothers took precedence over everything else until she'd convinced them there was no point setting out to see the world before it had an idea they were coming.

'Let your sister eat in peace, Tobias,' his lordship said quietly, and Polly waited for a protest, but none came.

Toby held his new friend's eyes with a steady challenge for a long moment, then seemed to accept some unspoken reassurance Lord Mantaigne was giving him and grinned like the schoolboy he still was.

'Can I have some more, then?' he asked Prue, who pretended to be shocked by his huge appetite, as usual, then helped him to another plateful and muttered about growing boys who grew cheekier by the moment.

'You know very well I'm your favourite,' he replied with a grin, and Polly had to fight a smile, because he was quite right. Prue loved the way Toby enjoyed her food so openly and he also had the easy charm of generations of piratical Trethayne males to call on when he chose to use it.

'You take no notice of him, young Henry,' Prue said and piled another helping on Hal's plate unasked.

He grinned and ploughed his way through it with nearly as fine an appetite as his elder brother, but he was more comfortable in his own shoes and accepted he was loved as easily as one of the mixed pack of dogs lying fast asleep in front of the fire seemed to do. Little Josh had worn himself out chasing about the countryside on some mischief and had already been packed off to bed before he went to sleep in his dinner. Polly took time to wonder at how different her brothers were. Each had a special place in her heart and she would lay down her life for them if she had to, but did she love them enough to lay pride aside and let Lord Mantaigne offer them some golden future she could not?

The hint of it was in the air, the promise of a different life for them all in his vague reference to a plan he and Lady Wakebourne had been hatching between them. She wondered at herself for not wanting to snatch hold of it with both hands. How would the boys feel in ten years' time if they lived on a rich man's charity? And how did Mr Peters feel about his lot in life now? She shot him a wary glance as she did her best to recall Claire's teaching that real ladies took small bites and chewed their food to stop herself gulping Prue's stew down as fast as she could before running out of the room to escape all these uncomfortable problems.

The answer was that Mr Peters seemed content enough to play second fiddle to his employer, most of the time. She frowned at the notion he also seemed braced for some long-expected burden to fall on his shoulders and that odd idea didn't answer any of her questions. All Toby and Henry and Josh needed to do was make a path for themselves through life, though, and she hoped it would lead them to happiness and middling prosperity. They had an honourable name, but nobody would expect them to shoulder the heavy weight the head of a noble family had to bear.

She ate her fill and drank a little of the wine so long left to age or even spoil in my lord's cellars and thought about that weight. The Marquis of Mantaigne carried such expectation, so many demands on those broad shoulders of his, so how could she let her brothers become one more? The long put-off notion of trying to get the head of her family to help her again surfaced. The mellow claret turned bitter on her tongue at the thought of asking the arrogant old man who'd looked down on her father for anything, after he'd thrown her and the boys out of his house as if they'd polluted it and ordered her never to come back. She gulped her wine so carelessly it went the wrong way and she demonstrated all too clearly why she'd never be any man's conformable wife by spluttering and going red as a beetroot at the dining table.

'Try to breathe slowly and evenly and you'll soon be right as ninepence again,' Lady Wakebourne urged comfortably as Polly did her best not to cough at the same time as she mentally pushed the imaginary Marchioness of Mantaigne out of the room and slammed the door in her smug face.

'Tea, Miss Polly, that's what you need,' Prue said sagely and went off to make some before she could argue.

It would take a lot more than a cup of smuggled Pekoe to right the trouble that ailed her, Polly decided. She let Lady Wakebourne lead her from the room and sit her down in the slip of a room she'd christened her drawing room, as if she was still the prosperous squire's daughter of her youth, though, and enjoyed being soothed and mothered for once. Tomorrow was soon enough to face the very adult problem she had been fighting not to admit she had since the moment her eyes first met Lord Mantaigne's across one of the Dayspring stables.

Chapter Ten

'What are you planning to do about them then, Mantaigne?' Peters asked when he found Tom on the old outer walls watching the moon rise over the sea.

'Schools for some, trades for others. Boys need to be busy and will get into trouble if they're not occupied, whatever Lady Wakebourne thinks about turning her urchins into little gentlemen. The adults must decide what they want out of life for themselves, since I can't do everything. There will be posts here if they want them, but not the sort of freedom they have had until I came back.'

'For some that was only freedom to starve, but what of the ladies?'

'Ah, yes, the ladies. Now they really are a conundrum.'

'One beyond your ability to solve?'

'It will take some thought and a measure of cunning,' Tom replied with a frown at the calm waters below and the cloudless twilight sky above them. 'At least there's no need to worry about smugglers tonight—it's far too bright a moon for them to risk being out and about,' he said, as they were a lesser problem than the one Miss Paulina Trethayne and Lady Wakebourne's presence here had set him.

'I don't worry about them much on any night. There's little point doing so when half the coast is actively involved in the trade and the other half wink at it.'

'Aye, it would be a bit like trying to keep water in a sieve,' Tom admitted with a frown at the calm scene that was so at odds with the turmoil inside him.

'Which is why you don't ride to certain coves or visit outlying farms at the wrong time of day, I suppose?'

'I've never been one for tilting at windmills,' Tom said with the uneasy feeling he might be lying.

'And there's trouble enough close to home.'

It was more of a statement than a question, and Tom didn't know if he least wanted to think about who was managing to invade his castle right under his nose, or what to do about a female unlike any other he'd ever encountered.

'You are a clever lawyer, Peters, but Rich Seaborne tells me you're an even wilier investigator of knotty problems certain rich and powerful men would rather you did not untangle.'

'Does he, my lord? I wouldn't have thought Mr Seaborne so ready to wag his tongue about the shady affairs of such men to anyone who asked him.'

'Oh, don't worry yourself on that head; I had the devil's own job prising even that much information out of him. He only admitted to knowing you as anything other than a lawyer when I told him of my mission from my godmother and the fact she had engaged you to come here with me to guard my back and investigate my enemies. He said she wouldn't have asked you to do so on a whim, nor would you have agreed to come here if it was as easy a task as it appeared.'

'These incursions into a near-ruinous castle don't have the feel of anything truly sinister about them to me,' Peters said as if he was a connoisseur of the worst sort of criminal mind and this one wasn't up to his mettle.

'No, I suspect it's a mean little affair, much like the rest my one-time guardian had running in his lifetime. His nephew seems even less effectual, if also slightly less mad, than he turned out to be.'

'Yes, he does seem to have been a bully of the worst sort, but a coward with it, I suspect,' Peters said as if that was all the world needed to remember of Philip Grably, and Tom wondered if he was right.

'He was a twisted and devious coward and bully, though. All the tales I hear of my father when I ride about the estate and villages have made me realise he knew this place like the back of his hand. I can't help remembering how Grably used to rave he loved my mother better than any other man and how dared my father lay his filthy hands on such a perfect and fragile woman when he wasn't fit to black her boots? I suspect he might have murdered my father, for all the good that could do him when my mother was already dead. Perhaps he thought he was avenging her, or who knows what he thought when he pitched his supposed best friend down a two-hundred-foot drop onto the rocks below five years after she died?'

'That's a grim suspicion to live with, Mantaigne,' Peters said with sympathy Tom would have felt uncomfortable with only weeks ago.

'Aye, but it could explain how my father stumbled so close to the edge of a cliff-path he walked every morning and knew better than anyone.'

'It could, but if so it's a secret Grably took to his grave,' Peters agreed quietly.

'True,' Tom replied with a frown at a certain window in the old part of the castle where the women had their quarters. 'And the Trethaynes are alive and under my roof. Their welfare trumps old sins.'

'Indeed,' Peters agreed so blandly that Tom decided he didn't care if the man thought he was a besotted fool or not.

'Don't *you* think it strange even a junior branch of such an old and powerful family was left to beg, borrow or steal their daily bread?'

'Profligacy has brought many a rich man to ruin,' Peters said with such austerity Tom wondered if that was a reason a clever and devious man might become a lawyer and whatever else the man was when he wasn't busy.

'I know, but Lord Trethayne's fortune seems intact. I don't know how the man could leave those children to starve when he should feel a moral duty to look after his nephew's family, even if the idiot didn't leave them to his care until they were grown. That seems the logical step for the nephew of a lord to take when he began to breed so many boys with his second wife, don't you think?'

'The late Mr Trethayne doesn't sound like a sensible man.'

'No, but his second wife fled to this country after the revolution in France. She must have known first-hand how it felt to lose everything and would have pushed the idiot to make some provisions for her children, however feckless he was otherwise,' Tom confided the unease he'd felt about that destitution ever since he found the family here scraping a living on his land.

'I believe his ruin began after the lady died, but it happened nearly a decade ago and I can't recall any details. Nobody mentioned he had children when the tale of his rash dealings and sad end went the rounds, so I didn't think it remarkable Lord Trethayne disclaimed all responsibility at the time. Now I can see that you're right; it's odd and needs looking into, if only to find out why he didn't help them. I expect I will find out more in London at this time of year than I could at Trethayne's country seat, so I'd best arrange to be summoned there urgently before the week is out if you truly wish me to take this any further.'

'Aye, I do, and I'm sure the place is teeming with crimes and misdemeanours awaiting your attention by now,' Tom said with a mocking grin to offset Peters's knowing smile that he cared enough about the Trethaynes to go to so much trouble on their behalf.

'At least I'll be spared the tension in any room when you and Miss Trethayne are in it for the next few days. I half expect crockery or candlesticks to start flying round the room whenever you meet without one of Miss Trethayne's brothers or Lady Wakebourne there to make you guard your tongues and tempers,' Peters replied with a look that told Tom he also wondered if he was about to be punched in the nose.

'Well, don't, Miss Trethayne is too much of a lady to vent her temper on innocent bystanders. If I can remind Lord Trethayne of his duty to his family and the fact she and her brothers are his responsibility, at least they might be able to go home and excuse the rest of you such a state of civil war at the breakfast table.'

'She will never agree to go anywhere near the old vulture after he left her to tramp the roads with three little boys when her father died,' Peters cautioned as if warning him not to get his hopes up.

'The trick will be to present things to her in the right terms,' Tom said with a feeling finding those words wasn't going to be as easy as he made out, especially as his best words seemed to desert him in Miss Trethayne's company and all sorts of wrong-headed ideas took their place.

'I doubt a poet could come up with those,' Peters cautioned.

'I can't let her leave Dayspring with nothing in her pockets and an easy mark for any rogue who might threaten or exploit her and her band of fellow vagrants.'

'If I were you, Mantaigne, I'd look a little deeper into that particular charitable impulse before you lose something precious without ever realising you had it.'

Tom felt his way along that sentence and found knots in it. There was a deep sadness in Peters's expression he'd never thought he'd be allowed to see, and Tom fumbled to pretend he hadn't seen that glimpse of the man's private self Peters wouldn't relish sharing with the likes of him.

'Just as well you're not me then,' he said facetiously and saw Peters's frown at his refusal to be counselled.

He might have learned to love his childhood home again, had even let the sad old house and grounds and the folk on the estate into his life as far as he could, but he wasn't ready to give up everything he'd learnt about surviving in a hostile world. If he let himself care about everyone within his orbit he'd collapse. Too many people depended on him for him to risk burdening himself with a wife and a ready-made family and hadn't he decided on his way here he had true friends in Luke and his family? So he should be able to look forward to the end of Virginia's three months with the lightest of hearts.

Yet, despite her poverty and unconventional life, Polly Trethayne wasn't a female he could stow in a neat little corner of his life labelled 'mistress' and forget the rest of the time. She wouldn't fit, for one thing; for another he didn't want to leave her less than she was now and embittered by his betrayal into the bargain. He wanted her with a passion he couldn't recall being this fierce even as a spotty youth desperate to find out about sex and any female who'd let him have some with her. What he felt was a freakishly heated physical attraction that would burn out as soon as he got her out of his castle and as far away as he could put her. Even a few miles away would be good enough for now, though.

He felt the gap in his heart and mind at the idea of being a stranger to her and hers again. He licked his suddenly dry lips and tasted her on them, as if her lush mouth had only just parted from his instead of the gap of *impossible* that stretched between them. He was the one who walked away; he'd made that gap and would always have to make it.

Haunted by the idea he might look back on this time with the bitter regret Peters seemed to feel about some lost chance at love he regretted, he made himself remember where and what he was. With Peters probably noting the reminiscent smile Tom found himself giving at the thought of creeping through a dark and dusty mausoleum with Polly Trethayne's hand in his, it was high time he remembered the Marquis of Mantaigne cared for nobody again, especially not for a female he'd never be able to ignore as so many of his peers did their wives once they'd got their obligatory heir and spare. And when had he jumped from mistress into marriage, even in his head? Heavens, but he'd been right after all; the woman was a danger to herself and everyone else and the sooner she left the better.

'Anyway, we must make sure the felons plaguing my castle are run to earth,' he said. 'Neither of us can leave until we find out what the devil they're up to.'

'Until we catch them in the act again as you so nearly managed to that first night, or find out why they want to explore this dusty barrack of yours at any time of day, you would seem to be stuck here then, my lord,'

Peters said with a lack of respect Tom was beginning to admire. If the man ever did treat him with some, at least he'd know he'd earned it.

'Hell's teeth,' he exploded with frustrated rage.

'You have nigh on a month left on your slate, my lord,' Peters pointed out less than helpfully.

'And you know just what you can do with that happy reminder, don't you?' Tom asked sarcastically and decided he'd been tried enough for one day. 'I'm going for a walk,' he told the man with a glare that dared him to say it was nearly midnight and he needed to have a care until their night visitors were unmasked.

'I hope your groom can put up with your moods better than I can whilst I'm in London, my lord, since it seems to me you need a bodyguard more than you do a lawyer at the moment.'

'At least I'll be able to cheer myself up with the thought of you ploughing through piles of dry and dusty documents and listening to tedious old gossip while I'm here and you're in London though, Peters.'

'I could ask Miss Trethayne for the details, I suppose and persuade her to confide her sad tale to me. It would save us both a great deal of time and trouble.'

'Only if you don't like the way your head currently sits on your shoulders, Peters,' Tom told him grimly, an image of Peters and Polly Trethayne discussing her life so far as rain beat intimately on the mullioned windows and the outside world seemed far away punching into his gut like a fist.

'I do. Lovely, spirited and unique though I think she is, Miss Trethayne is not for me and nor am I for her.'

'Just as well,' Tom said, 'I'll see if I can find out if anyone on the estate knows where Grably went when they removed him from Daybreak while you're gone. Someone else might have heard him raving about his treasure and the most precious things at Daybreak he'd make sure I never got to lay my filthy little hands on.'

'You're sure that's what he said all those years ago?'

'He bellowed it loudly enough for half the village to hear him when Virgil demanded he returned everything he'd taken from me, but I'm in no humour to think of him right now. Get on with delving into the Trethayne family fortunes and tomorrow I'll go through that mountain of rolls and boxes in the Muniment Room myself.'

'It's a full moon tonight and your villains won't even need a lantern,' Peters warned him as if he knew there were a pack of wild ideas skittering about in Tom's head, but somehow the Trethaynes' well-being seemed far more important than a few dusty *objets d'art* and mementos of a mother he had no memory of.

'I'll watch my step,' Tom said as patiently as he could manage as he set off to reacquaint himself with Dayspring by moonlight.

At least the exercise might improve his temper and allow him a few hours of sleep uninterrupted by fantasies of a softly warm and satiated Polly Trethayne asleep at his side and tangled round him with sleepy-eyed ardour when they awoke together. Sometimes he couldn't get her out of his head long enough to relax into oblivion for a few hours, but even when he could, waking up alone felt stark and lonely. Thinking about his light-hearted affairs of the past, he shook his head and wondered why this woman threatened to be essential as breathing to him.

He strode on through the silvered landscape and vividly remembered how magical this place was to the small boy he'd been when night and the moonlight offered him escape from his guardian's thugs and mood swings and invited him to explore a new world. At night the place was alive in a very different way and Tom hoped the poachers and landers were staying home tonight in deference to the power of the nearly full moon.

Which thought brought him right back to where he started and the heady fantasy of returning to his own bed to find a sleepy-eyed goddess in it all warm and welcoming and murmuring unlikely promises. Drat the wretched woman, would she never give him a moment's respite? Thinking of such impossible and significant souls as Polly Trethayne, he realised now why Virgil had never seemed quite content when Virginia was out of sight and sighed at the idea both of them would be highly amused by the sight of him acting the fool over a woman like this.

Once he'd sworn never to dance at another being's bidding and here he was back at Dayspring on Virginia's orders and pining for a woman he couldn't have. At least he was trying to make peace with the past as Virginia must have intended when she sent him and Peters here to find out what had gone amiss at Dayspring. That ought to be enough even for his ever-interfering godmother, and at last Tom saw the joke was on him as he paused by the lake to moodily skim stones across its otherwise mirror-like stillness.

A moorhen shrieked a protest, then hastily fell silent as a hunting barn owl scoped the edge of the trees on silent wings and a vixen barked to her cubs to behave themselves and come away from somewhere close by. They were noises of the night he'd been so familiar with once upon a time he marvelled that he'd forgotten how good it felt to enjoy the freedom of his own land in the dark, when nobody else but smugglers and poachers and creatures of the night wanted it and a forlorn boy could feel free of all that made his days hideous. Even though he'd hated the castle back then because his guardian lived in it, he'd loved the land and still did. Another lesson learnt, he decided with a resigned sigh as he wondered if that was another reason for his godmother's demand he spend a season here and never mind all those childish oaths never to set foot in the place again.

'Damn it, Virginia, I'm here, aren't I? Shouldn't that be enough for you when I swore I'd never set foot in the place again until you went and died on me and left that confounded list of things to do behind you,' he murmured into the night air. He could have deceived himself into thinking he heard her argue less than the best was never good enough for her godson, thank you very much. 'God, I miss you so much,' he whispered to the now-still lake and the moonlit shadows and decided restlessly wandering the cliff-paths all night wouldn't do anyone much good and he couldn't avoid his bed for ever because there was no Polly Trethayne in it, waiting for him to come home and make love to her in the heady shadows of my lord's currently humble bedchamber.

Polly had been out of sorts for the rest of the evening. When the fire was burning low and conversation lulled to a sleepy murmur she looked up from a reverie about what lords and their secretaries talked about when nobody else was listening and caught Lady Wakebourne's eyes resting on her. For a while she tried to join in the relaxed chatter after the day's work until her thoughts took over and she lapsed into silence again.

If Mantaigne was here, no doubt he'd manage to annoy her in all sorts of subtle ways. And yet… And yet nothing; he was just a man and much like any other. Under his fine clothes and fastidious grooming he was still only another son of Adam. For a supposedly idle man he had a set of very powerful muscles on that lean body of his, though, and she had a feeling he was as impressive without a stitch on as he was with all that fine tailoring and spotless linen not doing a very good job of concealing his manly perfections from the eyes of the world.

He swam in the sea every morning whatever the weather, just for the sheer pleasure of pitting himself against the elements so far as she could tell. Then there were all those long hours spent in the saddle and it really wasn't quite right for her to long for an excuse to ride at his side and simply watch the play of his well-honed muscles over that long body of his as he moved as one with his horse. He might have helped her out in her quest to find fault with him, she decided crossly, but, just when she was ready to find him as idle and frivolous as he wanted her to, he would do something that showed how unlike the image he worked so hard to portray he was underneath those fine clothes.

She recalled him on that first day, dust and ancient cobwebs clinging to his sweat-sheened skin until she'd challenge his fashionable friends to even recognise him under the grime. Heat rushed through her at the memory of him so utterly male and yet so endearingly boyish in all his dirt. That hot bolt of what must be carnal desire unnerved her.

She'd spent years thinking herself a freak for *not* feeling the wanton urges some women seemed to be brought so low by. Now she was yearning like a schoolgirl for a man who very likely wished she didn't exist. Horrified to catch herself sitting among her friends, a dreamy smile on her face, she tried to make sense of the various strands of conversation and join in, but it was like trying to weave cloth out of cobwebs and the chatter faded into the background again as sorting out her feelings towards the lord of Dayspring Castle took centre stage once more.

The man was a walking conundrum, she concluded, frowning at the empty fireplace. If she understood him a little better, maybe she could put him out of her head and get on with her life. At first sight he'd looked almost too perfect, like a hero out of a myth rather than a real man. She supposed she'd been as taken in by his surface polish and glamour as everyone else after that first bolt of heady shock that here was the man she'd never let herself dream of, standing there watching her with whole worlds of promise in his blue eyes. Something told her that shield was part of a game he played with his fellow man even then and perhaps that accounted for her irritation with him as soon as she realised he wasn't put on this earth to make her feel unique and feminine and *found*.

Could such a self-contained man let anyone see him as he really was? She doubted it, but if he did she hoped she wasn't here to see it. There, she had admitted it, even if only in her thoughts. She wanted to be his special female, the one to unlock his guarded heart and make herself uniquely at home in his arms. Well, she could want as much as she liked, it would never happen. How could it when she was herself and he was Marquis of Mantaigne?

'Woolgathering again, my dear?' Lady Wakebourne asked softly.

Polly realised the others had said goodnight and gone to their own quarters without her even noticing. 'Apparently,' she admitted, finding her gaze hard to meet.

'High time you got some sleep if you're planning more relentless toil in the morning, my dear,' her ladyship told her, and Polly meekly got to her feet and took a last look round the now shadowy parlour.

How much longer would they be able to sit together so sociably at the end of a day's work like this? The question added another layer to her discomfort as she followed her ladyship down the grand stone stairway and outside into the twilight. So much was changing here and Polly knew her driven urge to work hard stemmed from a need to fight those changes and pretend all would be well again. That was obviously impossible; they lived in a different place and time now and she should accept it and plan her next move.

'Did Lord Mantaigne really find that lovely cloth for my new habit in an attic we managed not to discover somehow?' she asked as they made their way across the courtyard and she did her best to curb her long stride to her ladyship's shorter pace.

'Yes, he thinks the box must have been thrown in a dark corner when his grandmother died and the fabrics she planned to have her London dressmaker make up for her were forgotten. Lucky for us, since if they had been turned into clothes we'd have had to look at you dressed like a scarecrow for evermore.'

'I shall ignore that comment as best I can, but it must have taken a deal of work to make it up so beautifully.'

'We love you, my dear,' the lady said simply, and Polly battled tears.

'It's so long since anyone said so,' she admitted huskily, 'and I love you too.'

'Thank you. After Greville shot himself I thought I was too bitter and twisted up with fury and grief to love anyone again, but you and your brothers and the unlikely friends we've gathered along the way taught me otherwise. You have made a lot of difference to a good many lives, Polly. I hope you'll see how special you are one day and how very lucky those boys of yours are to have such a sister.'

'I only did what any sister would,' Polly protested uncomfortably.

'Most would have sent their brothers to a charitable

institution and done whatever they had to in order to make their own way in the world. Not many would put their half-brothers before their reputations and any prospect of a decent marriage. I would not have done what you did at seventeen; I was far too selfish and pleased with myself for such a sacrifice back then.'

'You would have done exactly as I did. The boys had done nothing to deserve what happened to us and I couldn't let Papa's folly cost them a future.'

'At the price of your own,' her friend pointed out gently.

Polly paused before she spoke, wondering why they'd never talked this freely in all the years they had known each other. 'I was too young to see that then and now my brothers' needs outweigh mine.'

'You are still human, child—you can't rule passions and emotions out of your life because your father seems to have indulged in far too many of them. If you ever need a listener, I'm an older and wiser woman than I was once,' Lady Wakebourne offered as if she thought Polly might stand in need of a confidante before too long.

'Finding a new home and some sort of future for Toby and Henry and Josh is more important than my little worries,' she said as if that was all that mattered in her life, as indeed it had to be.

'You're still too young to shoulder such responsibility. I really hope your father was properly ashamed of himself for leaving you in such dire straits.'

'He always thought we would come about.'

'When that last ill-considered venture took every penny he had?'

'It could have worked,' Polly defended her feckless father.

'And you should have had a life of your own, instead of being provider and protector to those heedless boys before you were out of the schoolroom.'

'They're not heedless, and I'm happy here—or I was until we were found out,' Polly argued. 'Anyway, I would never have taken in polite society.'

'Nonsense, you may be taller than the average, but the polite world would be well pleased by the sight of you if you'd ever had a Season in town.'

'There we must differ, so shall we forget building castles in Spain and go to bed, my lady?'

'Aye, although whether you'll sleep when you get there is a very different matter,' Lady Wakebourne said as if she knew a little bit too much about Polly's restless nights and disturbing dreams for comfort.

Chapter Eleven

'Someone was skulking about the castle again last night, my lord,' Partridge the gatekeeper informed Tom about a week after Peters left for London and Miss Trethayne resumed her petticoats.

The idea he measured out his days by her actions disturbed him more than any rogues ambling about the disused wings of the castle in the dark. Unluckily for him, she looked even more magnificent in skirts than she did in breeches. Lady Wakebourne was obviously intent on torturing him, since each garment produced out of that accurst trunk in the rafters suited her protégée better than the last.

First there was that dratted habit, draped so delightfully about her long limbs and feminine curves he could hardly concentrate on staying in his own saddle whenever she was wearing it, let alone any of the places he was supposed to be taking such an interest in. Then there was a dark-crimson monstrosity, made from finest silk velvet with such a sneakily modest bodice he was certain its wearer had no idea how immodest it truly was. The colour suited her and the fine stuff clung to every sleek and lovely line of her and when she moved he badly wanted to know how it felt between his touch and the warm woman underneath.

He only just suppressed a groan at the very thought of her hips swaying gracefully in front of him as she'd preceded him into the makeshift dining room last night. As if that wasn't bad enough, this morning she was wearing a deep-sapphire abomination of the very finest wool, made up into a morning gown, of all things, with a lawn fichu gathered almost to the neck that ought to be just what he'd been longing for last night, but was more of a disaster than the last instead. He was learning the magic of the hinted-at rather than the blatant whilst he tried to eat his breakfast now and he really hadn't wanted to know how well a fashionably high waistline showed off her firm, high breasts and magnificent length of leg.

Had he groaned out loud at the shattering memory of her sitting at the breakfast table, greeting him as if not quite sure he was the urbane gentlemen everyone around her seemed to think him? Wise woman, he told himself distractedly, as he met Partridge's speculative gaze with a rueful grin. He doubted much about his ridiculous preoccupation with Miss Trethayne's artfully designed new wardrobe had escaped the shrewd scrutiny of yet another man outside his natural orbit. There were so many of them at Dayspring he almost added himself to the list, but a terrible feeling of belonging was creeping up on him unwanted.

A good job this man knew how to keep secrets then;

Tom decided to ignore any minor crimes he'd committed in his hot youth and trust he hadn't brought them with him from London. Partridge was the main reason the odd assortment of people living in his castle had gone unmolested for so long, so Tom could trust him where they were concerned, even if he was less certain about the man's relationship to the free-traders and his supposed lord and master.

'You're quite certain this business has nothing to do with guinea boats or smuggling spies in and out of the country? I might wink at the Trade for the sake of my tenants and half the inhabitants of the south coast, but I won't look the other way if they run traitors or Boney's guineas in and out of Castle Cove.'

'They wouldn't do it now you're here anyhow. Folk round here are more loyal than you deserve and they'd never tell the landers you don't go in that part of the castle if you can help it.'

'I'd hoped nobody would notice.'

'I've lived a lot longer than you, my lord, and not much passes me by.'

'Which would make you a good gatekeeper.'

'So I'm told.'

'Ah, so there *is* a lady in the case. I thought so somehow.'

'Love gets to us all in the end, if we're lucky enough. The real trick is to recognise it when it hits you between the eyes, my lord,' the man said blandly.

'And to know it for the passing joy it is,' he muttered grumpily.

'But then it wouldn't be love in the first place, would it, my lord?'

'No, damnation take it, it wouldn't and it isn't. We were talking about intruders and thieves, Partridge, not fairy stories.'

'So we were, my lord. Then it's high time we found out who's getting into your castle and why they keep coming now you're here and busy at long last.'

'Perhaps we'd best find out what they're looking for, then,' Tom said, resigned to searching the part of the house he'd managed to avoid since his first day back.

'Stands to reason they wouldn't keep coming if there was enough of them to search properly in the first place.'

'So it won't take many of us to catch them.'

'You want this kept quiet, milord?'

'Yes, the place is all but empty and no sane felon would bother to break in.'

'Aye, most everything was taken away years ago. They certainly ain't busy picking apart state beds and all that fancy stuff you lords have built into your palaces. Folk round here are good at not seeing things, but they'd notice if the old place was being emptied bit by bit and the pickings trundled past their windows of a bright night when everyone's at home where they ought to be for once.'

'Or they'd have to get it past you,' Tom said thinking that the most difficult part of the whole unlikely business.

'True, so how many of your men can you trust, my lord?'

'All of them, but they're grooms and coachmen, not redbreasts or hedge creepers. I'd rather keep this to ourselves and plan a surprise my unexpected guests won't be able to refuse.'

A couple more weeks crept by with the skies overcast and dull and sometimes a heavy shower of rain before the sun came out for a few brief moments to show how spring ought to be, in a more settled country. Polly wondered if the local smugglers were the only ones happy at the sight of dull skies as the Preventatives stayed by their fires even when the moon hid in the clouds. She stared out of the rain-soaked window one morning after breakfast and wondered why she was still here, almost a season on from Lord Mantaigne's arrival at his castle and what should be her cue to leave.

The boys had gone to their lessons, and Polly didn't know what to do unless the rain let up enough for her to go outside. She didn't know what to do most of the time even when she was out nowadays anyway.

It was nearly June now and long past the usual time for spring cleaning, but Lord Mantaigne still wouldn't let her hire a small army to sweep away the dust and grime of decades from the newer parts of this vast place. She didn't know how he resisted the need to have the past purged from his castle, but somehow he still did and why it should matter to her was an even bigger mystery. Once he was free of the dust and shadows of the past, the marquis would be able to raise his family here. She could think of no better cure for the harsh memories of his childhood than a pack of well-loved and well-fed boys of his own to make him forget the deprived and resentful one he had once been himself.

Lady Wakebourne stubbornly refused to tell her what plans were being hatched for their futures, but part of her knew they needed to go. It was time for new beginnings, and she must be banished too, she decided, still with a huff of annoyance at them both for being so secretive. Apparently several of the middling houses in Castle Magna were being refurbished, and Polly wondered if the marquis had it in mind to put them in one of them. Close to the woods and with miles of coves and dunes to explore nearby, it would be ideal for the boys, but she really didn't want to live so close to the castle. She would have to smile and be grateful and pretend she didn't care when Lord Mantaigne wed a suitable lady and made her the mother of the children who would run wild at the castle instead of her brothers and their friends.

For weeks she'd been trying to come up with a plan to allow the boys to stay under Lady Wakebourne's benign wing while she somehow found a place for herself with no carelessly irresistible marquises close by to make her feel a stranger in her own skin. In her opinion the marquis should be kept in Mayfair for the good of the female population of Dorset. It was ridiculous to feel uniquely drawn to him, to know no other man would ever touch the hidden feminine depths of her as he had done. Well, it might be ludicrous and on the edge of dangerous as well, but that didn't mean she was going to stop feeling it because they no longer lived under the same roof.

She had hoped it was a silly infatuation she could get over as swiftly as it came, like a spring cold or a fever, but he'd been here nearly two months now and she longed for him more ridiculously with every day that passed. It was time she began to plan a life without him, more than time. If they shared a house much longer she'd let herself fall in love with the dratted man and that would be an even bigger disaster.

She was young and healthy as a horse; she knew more about running a large estate than a lady ought to and was capable of anything her sex allowed her to do. The fact that was such a pitifully small number of things could not stop her making plans. It hadn't taken her long to realise she wouldn't be a very good companion to the sort of nervous and fainting lady who usually needed one. Now Polly made up an ideal employer in her head and started her on a series of fanciful and raffish adventures that would keep them both well entertained without any need of tatting or reading sermons to snoring invalids. She was in the midst of planning her escape from the amorous attentions of her imaginary lady's discarded lovers when Lord Mantaigne came in and found her staring out of the rain-soaked window as if spellbound by the dismal view.

'Not even a Revenue Cutter would brave the Channel on such a day, so you can't be staring at one of those,' he remarked genially, but she refused to look at him.

'Even I am permitted the occasional daydream, Lord Mantaigne,' she told him as distantly as she could manage when his very presence in a room could make her heart race like Ariel after a rabbit.

'Really? I wonder you find the time,' he said with a long look that told her he'd noticed she went in the opposite direction to any he took of late.

'They don't take long,' she lied, 'and this rain give me an excuse to sit and twiddle my thumbs with a clear conscience.'

'How would we English manage without the weather as our favourite topic of conversation, I wonder?'

'Very ill, I should think. In better climates people must have to put so much more effort into the niceties of everyday life, don't you think?'

'On topics such as that one, I do my best not to think at all,' he said with an impatience that made her look him in the face out of sheer surprise he could dismiss the very small talk he'd been using to fend off the rest of them since he got here.

She blinked at the shock of seeing him anew. Every time he was out of her sight she dearly hoped her memory had exaggerated the impact of his looks and personality and every time he came back into it she knew what a vain hope it was.

I really want to kiss you, she heard a wild and reckless part of herself long to murmur to him like a siren, as if there could ever be anything more than tolerance between them. Thank heavens her sensible side had control of her tongue today. She could just imagine the horror with which he'd hear such a blatant invitation.

What if another Thomas Banburgh from this honourable idiot replied, *And I want to do more than just kiss you back, Paulina*—would she let him? Probably, so it was as well she hadn't put either of them to the test.

'Was there something you wanted, my lord?' she made herself ask with such distant politeness he ought to take it as a hint and leave her alone again.

Always, it felt like a whisper on the air as he met her gaze with more than she'd ever thought to see in the hot blue of his clear irises. Had he said it? Or was it wishful thinking? She heard a pair of masculine boots stamp outside the quiet room as silence stretched between them inside, and she cursed heartily under her breath. One kiss would not have made her into a wanton and it seemed a small comfort for all the years she would probably have to spend seeing my lord and his lady go by her new home, like a stray cat watching a king and queen.

'Partridge wants to know where my guardian went after he left here, although why he can't come in and ask you if you know himself is beyond me,' the marquis said loudly. 'Virgil told me it was best I didn't know and he didn't want to lest he be tempted to ride over and strangle him one dark night.'

'Virgil was your new guardian?'

'Yes, his wife was my godmother and they took me into their home and civilised me as best they could when they found out what a poor thing I'd become.'

Polly's heart ached for that small, vulnerable version of him. 'My godmother sent me a book of stern sermons for my confirmation and I never heard from her again. Why worry about your guardian now, though?'

'Not to wring the man's neck—he's already dead, so I couldn't if I wanted to,' he replied and raised his voice a little. 'For pity's sake, stop stamping about out there as if Miss Trethayne and I are discussing state secrets, man.'

'It was my idea, see?' Partridge told her when he finally sidled into the room as if she might bite.

'What was?'

'Folk here'll talk to you as they won't to his lordship or me,' the man said awkwardly, and Polly was intrigued by an unspoken dialogue between the master of the house and his self-appointed gatekeeper they thought she didn't know about.

'So you're taking all this trouble to find out where a lunatic spent the last few years of his life?' she asked, and her old friend shifted and look uneasy, but neither attempted to answer her question. 'Nobody ever mentions him anyway.'

'I'd like to forget he existed myself,' the marquis muttered, 'but we need to know something now and it's like trying to pin down a wraith.'

'Old Mrs Allcott might be able to remember where he was taken, if she's having one of her better days, or your lawyers would seem to be a safe bet to know where the man who did you and yours so much harm was put, don't you think? What a shame Mr Peters is absent at the very moment you need to find out so urgently.'

'Of course, her daughter-in-law said she was housekeeper here once and knew the place inside out,' the marquis said with an impatient frown, as if he now felt a fool for trailing that question so temptingly in front of her on a rainy day when she'd just admitted to being bored.

Then there was her niggling suspicion that Mr Peters had gone to London to find out anything he could about herself and Lady Wakebourne. She understood their past might affect Lord Mantaigne's future wife's tolerance of his dependents, but it felt intrusive and rude of them to delve about in the catastrophes that had overtaken them and led them to Dayspring when it was perfectly plain he didn't want to set foot in the place himself.

'What a shame you didn't think of her before you asked me, my lord,' she said blandly, a challenge in her eyes as she made herself meet his.

She felt a fool for not realising that, while the smugglers moved on as soon as they knew he was back at Dayspring, the feeling they were not always alone here hadn't gone with them. Adding that to her unease about the future and whatever he might stir up from her past, she was amazed at herself for being so wrapped up in trying not to want the man she'd almost forgotten how much depended on her being awake and alert for any threat that might hurt her brothers.

'Yes,' he agreed tersely, doing a very good job of concealing his thoughts from her so she felt more shut out of the real life of Dayspring than ever. 'I can't find the plans drawn up for improvements to the public rooms, which were due to be made just before my father died. Needless to say they never happened afterwards and I began to wonder if Grably took them away. I want the roof repaired this summer and it would save a lot of time if I had those drawings.'

'True, and Partridge is going to be your clerk of the works, is he? How very sensible. I'm sure everything will go on splendidly with or without those plans,' she said as if she almost believed them. 'I don't suppose the people left here when your former guardian was taken away would have let him take more than the shirt on his back. He may have burnt some of the estate papers before he went, of course.'

'True, so that settles it then,' Lord Mantaigne said with a heavy sigh.

'It does?' she said brightly, wondering what unlikely tale they'd invent next.

'Yes, I'll have Peters search the Muniment Room one last time when he gets back, but it seems likely the job must be done again.'

'No reason I can't look, is there, m'lord? I can read,' Partridge offered.

'I'm sure Peters would be delighted if you did.'

'Least I don't mind getting my hands dirty,' Partridge said and stumped out to begin a task none of them quite believed in.

Polly suspected they were looking for any secret ways in and out of the castle. The newer parts were built after a bloody civil war and a wary lord could well have ordered an escape route built to the sea in case it happened again.

'We've offended him now,' Lord Mantaigne said ruefully.

'I expect so, but you do it so well, don't you?'

'I do, don't I?'

'One more way of keeping us lesser mortals at a distance, I suspect.'

'Then it doesn't appear to be working since I came here.'

'You do yourself an injustice, milord, I feel I might as well be in the next county right now. Do you let anyone past that wall you keep round your heart?'

'Not very often,' he said with a shrug that said that was a good thing.

He also looked as if he had a hundred places he'd rather be, and Polly concluded he was only staying here because he wanted to distract her from the subject they had been discussing. He was doing quite a good job just by being here, but probably not the one he intended. She ought to be finding out what he and Partridge were really up to, but all she could think about was him. Silence stretched as he struggled not to tell her to mind her own business, and what right had a beggar like her to enquire into the state of a marquis's heart in the first place?

He wasn't going to admit he kept his essential self as shut up in that tower room as his guardian had the rest of him as a boy. Nor would he own up to the need that felt so strong she could almost touch it. And why would he when they were about as far apart as two people could be?

Yet only her presence had stopped him facing down those intruders that first night and, if she let him do as he wanted and keep her out of the way next time, he would take risks she couldn't seem to think of without a chance the bottom might drop out of her world if he got himself murdered, just because he was such a stubborn great idiot. He would certainly take on the rogues himself rather than trust anyone else to do it for him.

'Then you should,' she argued with his determination to always walk alone. 'You will never be truly alive if you don't.'

'Why, for Heaven's sake? I'm perfectly happy as I am.'

Polly found his ignorance of all he might be more touching than any conscious attempt to garner sympathy, but my Lord Mantaigne didn't need sympathy, did he? He didn't need anything he couldn't buy or charm out of those who only wanted to be charmed or bought, or so he obviously believed.

'I suppose you'll never know unless you try,' she said huskily.

'Don't even think about it,' he ground out as if denying what was there in the room with them and pushing them to explore a lot more than a mere friendship hurt him physically yet he couldn't stop doing it. 'Just don't.'

'All right then, I won't,' she whispered back, hoping Partridge really had gone to search through dusty piles of documents the lawyers hadn't thought worth taking away. It was as well to only lose one man's good opinion at a time, and she was very fond of the gatekeeper of Dayspring Castle.

'I've tried so hard not to touch you or kiss you again, you do know that, don't you?' Lord Mantaigne said with a feverish glint in his eyes that confirmed it and made her feel a lot better about the brazen course of action she was about to take.

'Be quiet, rattle-pate,' she chided him gently and took it.

Well, she would regret it for ever if she didn't, so she

kissed him, since he was being such a gallant marquis they might be in their dotage before he got round to it. Wanting him so badly made her ache in places she hadn't known a woman could ache for a man and she really had a lot of experience to make up in a hurry. Even so, this was playing with fire and it flashed and roared into a blaze even as he met her kiss for kiss. He tasted of rain and fresh air and himself and it was like all her birthdays as a child piling into a whirlpool of excitement and promise and hope all mixed together.

Then he took over the kiss and made it deeper; more sensual; unique. She had known, but not known. He was experienced and compelling and he knew how to make that fire slide under her skin and speak to the same force in him as they stood, mouth to mouth. Who needed words when there was such a use to put their tongues to? He slowed the pace, showed her how to enjoy the scenery on the way to a destination she'd never visited or expected to visit. It was subtle and somehow beautiful and how could he think himself isolated and unlovable when he had all this magic in him?

He gave a soft groan against her lips, and she felt the shake in his mighty body. Despite all that fine control of his, he needed her and that sucked her into another layer of wanting him altogether. He licked the swollen line of her lips with sensuous little darts of his tongue where they almost met, and she sighed with pleasure so he had a way to dart inside. This was so much more than a kiss now—more of a pagan dance he was showing her true, wild inner self as they explored and deepened and fed the heated delight that was taking over every inch of her body.

Even dancing wasn't close enough now. Mind and body united; touch and thought all wrapped up in needing this one man as she never would any other. His arousing, worshipping hands explored her narrow waist, down over the lithe curve of her hip and rested on the neat softness of her feminine buttocks, and she wriggled shamelessly until the urgent evidence of his need of her rose emphatically against her hot, wet core even through his gentlemanly breeches. Her soft, clinging and light-as-air skirts were a fragile barrier between them now. She appreciated them as she never dreamed she could when she put them on this morning.

It would take only one flip of the fine-spun stuff and the gossamer petticoats underneath to leave her open to such pleasure it made her breath catch at the very idea of it. One more fiery impulse and he'd be there, inside her—doing something about the delightful pain that was winding her so tight it hurt not to have him there. Instead of held back and still apart, they could have everything, right now. They could soar into sweet, hot darkness together; dizzying and brilliant as racing up to the moon. It was there; on their tongues, in their reaching, exploring hands, in their lips; as if they had to take all there was to take and love every second.

A surge of heat and pleasure sang though Polly. She wanted to meld with the pure essence of Thomas Banburgh and forget he was a lord and she was a pauper. She swayed into their kiss to deepen it even further, because she knew he wasn't going to let that happen and she desperately wanted him to spin beyond thought, beyond restraint with her. He was who he was and she was who she was and she felt him clamp fearsome self-control on the rigid need she could feel through his fine clothes and hers as well.

'Noble idiot,' she muttered reproachfully.

'If I was that, I'd never have got so close to losing control,' he said unsteadily, leaning his head against her bowed forehead as if he didn't want to break contact, but being kissable and not beddable was an agony she wouldn't share.

'You didn't, I did,' she said wearily and heard the jag in her voice as she said goodbye to so much they could have been and faced reality.

'I'd only harm you in the end and I'm not worth it.'

'Don't try to hide the truth behind your imaginary shortcomings. I am a nobody; less than that even as far as your kind are concerned. I was born a lady, but now I'm less than a beggar because I've fallen so far. Tell me I'm not a suitable mistress if you have to, but don't hide it behind polite lies.'

'How can I when it's not true? You're as good as any other woman I've ever met and I wouldn't offer you so little,' he told her with a fierce frown.

'Damned with faint praise,' she managed to say as his words sank in and she couldn't find even a trace of lover-like adoration in them.

'I lose any smooth words and easy compliments I ever had the use of when I'm with you. Maybe I left them at the castle gate the day I arrived and ogled at you like a looby,' he admitted with a flush of colour across his hard cheekbones that made her hope he had been a little bit besotted with her after all, even if it was only at first glance and seemed to have worn off.

'I'm not sure if I'm delighted or insulted by that lack.'

'Neither am I,' he said with a wry grin.

She felt a tug of temptation to smile back at him and pretend it didn't hurt, but it did. 'Don't expect me to interpret your lack of a glib answer, I obviously have no idea what makes you lords of creation tick along to your own tune,' she said as coolly as she could manage. She wanted to rage at him for rejecting what they could be to one another—and that was little enough, in all conscience—but she wasn't going to give him an excuse to sidle away from her as if he'd been right not to trust her with much of himself.

'And I really didn't draw back because I wanted to insult you, but more because I didn't, you know?'

'Yet somehow you managed to without trying.'

'Aye, well, clearly I'm a rogue of the worst kind.'

'Are you, my lord? I wonder.'

'Don't, but you do make me wish myself otherwise,' he said, so perhaps she'd made a small dent in his mighty defences.

His hand shook when he cupped the back of her head and drew her closer so gently she felt breakable. She looked up to meet his brilliant blue gaze defiantly and saw so many questions in it tears stung her eyes instead. No, she had her pride and made herself gaze back at him with desire bold and brazen and bare for him to see what she might have been with him, and what he could be with her, if he wasn't denying all that made them right together in defiance of all the wrongs the world would whisper.

'You're not the man you think you are,' she told him firmly.

'And you're not quite who you believe either, have you thought of that?'

'No, but Partridge might be back any moment and the rain is stopping, so it's clearly time for us to consider other things besides there not being a you and me for anyone to worry about, my lord.'

'I will, if you will,' he murmured and kissed her so gently it hurt.

'Go away,' she said unsteadily, the thought of a day spent dancing round each other as if nothing untoward had happened tearing at her like a battle wound.

'Will you be all right?'

'I'm always all right,' she said, 'it's what I do best.'

'There I have to argue, even with a lady,' he told her with the ghost of his wicked smile.

'Go and find your plans, my lord—even Partridge doesn't deserve to search through some endless piles of documents alone for much longer.'

She thought she heard him mutter something uncomplimentary about the family archives, but went back to her window until he stamped out of the room in a show of masculine bad temper, as if she was the one who had put a stop to what could have been a glorious lovemaking and not him.

The great blundering idiot would probably ride himself and his unfortunate horse to a stand-still in the rain now and all because he wouldn't admit he was subject to the same needs and emotions as the rest of humanity. Never mind what he felt or didn't feel for her, he was grieving deeply for his beloved godmother and wouldn't even admit it to himself.

Would a man who felt nothing for his own kind spend so much of his time finding out all he had omitted to do in the past two decades and do his best to put it right? Would he put himself out to find work for her mixed bag of fellow squatters if he was the care-for-nobody he did his best to pretend he was? No, and he wouldn't try to find a place for Lady Wakebourne and herself to go to when they left either.

Sure enough, there he was, racing his beautiful bay gelding through the park as if the devil was on their heels. So much of her wanted to be out there with him, full of life and strength and risk, that she turned away from the last glimpse of them tearing into the rain-soaked landscape she had come to love so much with tears blinding her to anything closer by until she blinked them away and reminded herself she wasn't the sort of female who sat indoors and cried for no reason on rainy days when the whole of nature seemed ready to weep with her.

Chapter Twelve

'Has it ever struck you that the intruders we thought were prowling round the Stuart wing of the castle could be choosing moonlit nights to avoid the free-traders, Lady W.?' Polly asked Lady Wakebourne over the luncheon Prue insisted they took in the 'Drawing Room' while the rest of the self-appointed staff had theirs in the kitchen.

For a while Polly had tried to insist nothing had changed with the marquis's homecoming, but the air of restraint and discomfort in the otherwise cosy kitchen had soon defeated her. Now she reluctantly bowed to the divisions that seemed to have grown up between gentry and working folk once more. It was tempting to blame his lordship, but fairness made her admit he'd done nothing to put those barriers up, he had given in to the fact they existed much as she had herself.

'I do my best not to think about the smugglers who infest this coast, or anyone else who might be wandering about in the night when I'm in bed. And don't call me Lady W. in that vulgar fashion.'

'If you really mean to adopt me as well as your mixed quantity of urchins so Lord Mantaigne can get us out of his castle, then you'll have to let me to call you something other than "your ladyship".'

'As if you ever did treat me with much respect,' Lady Wakebourne scoffed.

'Yet I still respect you and might even have admitted to loving you now and again, if you recall?'

'You know it's mutual,' Lady Wakebourne said. Polly felt her own smile wobble as it occurred to her it wasn't only Lord Mantaigne who had held back his feelings these past few years.

'I also know you stood with me when the rest of the world turned its back and without you I would have been so lonely I can't even bring myself to think about it. Besides that, who else can understand the things that concern me most? I love my brothers far more than they like me to admit now they're so grown up and manly, but they aren't interested in where their next pair of breeches is coming from or how to keep them well and happy on nothing a week.'

'You're far too young for that to be the beginning and end of your ambitions now, my dear, so at seventeen you were unforgivably youthful to be left to bring them up without a penny to bless yourself with. I would be a very hard-hearted female if I'd turned my back on you and those three little boys then.'

'And you're certainly not one of those, are you? Do you ever intend to tell Lord Mantaigne how your great-aunt somehow contrived to interfere in his young life, my lady? No, don't try pretending she had nothing to do with his timely rescue from his awful guardian because I know you as well as anyone can by now. Hearing how it was done might help him live here and not see that monster around every corner when the rest of us must leave.'

'And you take a humane interest in the man's welfare, I suppose? Do you really take me for such a fool, Paulina?'

'No, but you know as well as I do it's all I will ever share with him.'

Lady Wakebourne gave Polly a steady look as if she would like to argue, then sighed and shrugged her agreement that there was no future for a lady of no means at all and a rich and powerful marquis. 'Nevertheless, I am always here if you need to talk to someone about it. Carrying your burdens alone as you have had to all these years has made you both older than your years and at the same time as inexperienced as a débutante at her first ball. Promise me you'll come to me if you need a woman's advice or even a sympathetic ear?'

'If I ever come up against a problem Lord Mantaigne doesn't resolve before I have a chance to make my own decisions, I will,' Polly said bitterly and knew how much she had betrayed when she saw the look in her acute friend's dark eyes.

'How very ham-fisted of him,' the lady said with a glint of unholy satisfaction in her gaze that left Polly torn between agreeing and feeling even more hurt.

'We are better having as little to do with each other as possible when we must live under the same roof.'

'If you say so, my dear,' Lady Wakebourne said so equably Polly gave her a suspicious glare.

'Anyway we were not talking about me and the lord and master of this poor old place, we were discussing how your relative came to intervene in his childhood.'

'Well, no, we were not if we intend to be strictly accurate. You made an unsubstantiated observation and I didn't deny it.'

'That's splitting hairs.'

'No, I once made a promise and I don't easily go back on one of those.'

'But I was right, wasn't I?'

'If you make your own connections, I suppose it wouldn't break the letter of any agreement we might have made to keep quiet about Lord Mantaigne's early life for his own sake.'

'Cunning of you.'

'Yes, isn't it?'

'And you didn't recall this place was empty by an inspired chance either, I suppose?'

'No, and I made Virginia no promises on that front. She made sure the right backs were turned when I appealed to her for a chance for us to make some sort of a life for ourselves here since we had nothing. It wasn't as if his lordship wanted anything to do with the place and she agreed we were better than some villainous gang of rascals taking the place over.'

'Rather than the rascals who live here now?'

'Aye, we are something of a mixed bag, are we not?'

'At times I can't help feeling sorry for Lord Mantaigne for having to endure our ramshackle company,' Polly admitted ruefully.

'Don't waste your pity; he's enjoyed it, for the most part, and it distracted him from brooding on things he'd rather forget.'

'I suppose he does like the boys and seems to get on remarkably well with Barker and Partridge and one or two of the others. You could be right.'

'Of course I am; it's one of the privileges of middle age. Another is noticing it isn't only the boys and those two rogues he likes.'

'He does get on well with Jane and Prue and I'm sure if Dotty was twenty years younger he'd like her far too much.'

'If you say so, my dear.'

'She must have been lovely in her prime, don't you think?'

'Not if I can help it, for goodness knows what she got up to back then.'

'I hate to think.'

'Best if you don't, but you have so little grasp of your own attractions it might be dangerous if your marquis wasn't nearly as bad. I never came across two people more genuinely ignorant of their own qualities that sometimes I feel as if I'm in the midst of one of Shakespeare's comedies.'

'Except it's not very funny.'

'If I had charge of the ending, it would be,' Lady Wakebourne said with the happy ending she would write onto their sad little tale in the almost-smile she gave Polly as their eyes met in an admission it was nigh impossible.

Polly looked away to try to tell them both it wasn't even worth speaking of and tried to recall what had got them on to this dangerous ground in the first place. 'You still haven't answered my original question,' she said as she retraced their steps and remembered her theory about those moonlight nights.

'Which was?'

'If those intruders you have always done your best to pretend you didn't believe in come here at the best times to avoid being spotted by the smugglers? I suppose that says either they are afraid of them or think they'd be recognised.'

'Either I suppose, if they exist at all outside your fancy, my dear.'

'Oh, they do, Lord Mantaigne and I heard them inside the closed-up wing the first night he was here, so at least now I know my ears do not deceive me.'

'And I know you two are reckless and headstrong as a pair of runaway horses.'

'Don't change the subject, although while we're on the subject of who knows what and when, did you really contrive to get word to Lady Virginia there was something wrong here before she died?'

'I'm sure she had her sources in the area. The late Lady Farenze had a wide circle of friends.'

'If she was half as all-knowing and infuriating as you, she could have run a spy ring for all anyone else would have known about it.'

'Lady Virginia was far more of everything than I

am, Paulina. Such a shame you never knew her, for you have much in common.'

'I think not,' Polly said stiffly, horrified at the image of a formidable lady looking down her aristocratic nose at her.

'If nothing else, you could have compared notes on Lord Mantaigne, since you both dote on him.'

'I certainly do not dote on that stiff-necked idiot of a man,' Polly ground out gruffly and wished her ladyship a brusque farewell until later so she could go and watch out for him to return from his afternoon of avoiding her in peace.

Later that afternoon Mr Peters rode back up the drive in time to meet his employer coming the other way. Polly wasn't watching for either of them by then, of course, but she happened to glance out of the a window overlooking the coast road and wondered how two gentlemen could be so wet and muddied and yet so vital she longed to be out there with them just to find out what they were talking about. Whatever it was that kept them out there longer than any sensible creature should be on such an inclement evening, it must be of absorbing interest, or so confidential they didn't wish to be overheard.

How might it feel if she happened to be the true lady of this ancient castle? Perhaps one of the previous ladies of Mantaigne had stood at this very window, watching for her lord to return from court or some foreign war and seen him at last on the horizon. She could have waited with breathless longing for it to be really him, this time, at last. Imagine how that lady would feel knowing he was safe and back with her again, joy surging through her at the sight of him, breathless with longing to lie in his arms all night again, desperate to be held close and told how deeply he had missed her every moment they were apart and she had held his fortress for him in his absence.

It seemed that dreaming of another time and different ways of being lords and ladies had let her think of herself as his lady as she never had in the here and now. The how she might have been as Lady Paulina of Mantaigne was queenly and proud instead of beggarly and defiant, her carriage fluid and assured as she swept down the stone stairway from the Great Parlour to greet her lord. She knew he adored her just as she was; that he knew she would defend his lands and his people and their children like a she-wolf protecting her cubs. A mighty lord needed an independent lady then, for how else could he know his lands and people were safe when he was not at home?

She shook her head and told herself not to be a fool. Not only was that then and this now, but here and now was real and there and then was not. Something about Peters's and his lordship's earnest conversation told her they believed some important problem had been solved by that mysterious trip to London, and it made her shiver to think that would be that. Now his lordship would leave and perhaps never come back. Even that phantom lady of his queening it over the neighbourhood seemed better than never setting eyes on the wretched man again, or only once in a long and weary decade when he might come back to see if his castle had fallen into the sea quite yet. Lady Wakebourne was right to accuse her of doting on the man and knowing it at least gave her the sense to distance herself from him.

If it was in any way mutual, he wouldn't have been able to turn his back on her and ride away from her this morning. She had offered herself to him so blatantly and he had all but blushed and said a polite 'no, thank you'. Shame rushed into her cheeks in a hot flood of colour, and she leant one on the cold window pane to cool it and saw with horror his lordship's rain-dark head raise as he caught sight of her. Gasping a denial she had been watching for his return like some faithful hound, she jumped away and refused to look back, but it was too late—the image of him soaked to the skin and his fine clothes plastered to his body as if they couldn't love him enough was stamped on her mind's eye.

Even from so far away she'd seen the intensity in his blue gaze as if not even that much rain would douse the heat in it. Drat the man, but he called to the wild instincts and hot blood in her. Her heart was pounding, her body roused and eager and her breath coming short through parted lips. She caught sight of herself in a watery old Venetian glass mirror almost too old to do its work any more and put suddenly cold hands to her hot cheeks. She looked wanton and, worse, enchanted; like a silly maiden in a fairy story put under a spell by the very sight of the handsome prince who had come to rescue someone else. Well, she wouldn't be the bereft spectator on his life. She was her own person and that was that. Easy enough to think it, but telling her body to let go of all those seductive images of her curled about him all loved and sated against that mighty, muscular body proved much more difficult.

'I wish a lady like that one would look at me as Miss Trethayne just did at you,' Peters joked down below in the stable yard as he and his latest employer led their tired horses through the stable doors Dacre had flung open as if he'd been waiting for his lordship to come home too.

'If I ever catch you watching her with that glint in your eyes again, I'll black at least one of them for you,' Tom told him brusquely and for once couldn't have cared less what his supposed secretary thought his feelings for Miss Polly Trethayne might be.

'No need, I have the sense to see when a woman has hardly noticed I live on the same planet, even if you are wilfully blind about your feelings for her.'

'A little less of both than I was when you left for London,' Tom said softly as the image of her, warm and dry and wistful as she gazed out of that window like a princess in her tower wishing she had a prince on the way, replayed through his mind.

'Less wilful, or less blind?'

'How plain do I have to be? I know she is like no other woman I ever met, that any man who could call her his would need to thank his maker on his knees for her every morning and work hard to deserve her for the rest of the day and into the night.'

'A delightful pastime, no doubt, but why does there

seem to be a "but" running under all that promising infatuation?'

'You have the devil of a sharp tongue, man; are you related to the Winterleys by any chance?'

'Not that I know of,' Peters said as soberly as any judge, but Tom was beginning to know him well enough to be certain he was laughing at both of them for some reason best known to himself. 'And the "but"?'

'But I'm hardly the sort of man who deserves the love of a good woman.'

'If we all had to wait to be worthy of that, the human race would have died out long ago.'

'Yet if what you say is true, Miss Trethayne will soon have the chance to meet a man who can offer her so much that I cannot.'

'A castle, perhaps? A comfortable lifestyle at the heart of the *ton*? Or do you think she might prefer a fortune not even laying out funds to support half the countryside can make a dent in?'

'Please don't think accusing her of being a gold-digger will make me furious enough to give away some phantom truth about my feelings for Miss Trethayne, Peters. I'm not some naive young fool up from the country.'

'It might be better if you were.'

'Better for whom?'

'For you of course, my lord,' the man said abruptly and made way for one of the grooms to take over caring for his tired horse as if he couldn't endure the company of such an idiot for very much longer.

'He's right, lad,' Dacre informed him.

'Not you as well,' Tom mumbled with a tight frown he hoped would put the man off one of his homilies.

'Me more than anyone, m'lord. Her ladyship trusted me to keep you from riding straight to the devil when you was younger than Master Josh and I ain't done yet.'

'Thank you,' Tom said as the fury died out of him at the sight of genuine concern in the old groom's eyes. 'You always were more patient with me than I deserved.'

'High time someone was,' Dacre said gruffly, as uneasy with speaking of his feelings as Tom had ever been, but doing it all the same.

How humbling to know his old friend had more courage than he did, but perhaps this was his day for being humble.

'Any woman worth her salt wants to make her own choice, boy, and that one's worth a lot more,' Dacre told him with a severe nod and went to fetch the warm mash he had ready for the unlucky gelding who had gone so hard for him all afternoon.

'Anything to say?' he challenged the weary animal as he finished grooming it and stopped to pet him. 'No? You must be the only one who hasn't today,' he murmured in the gelding's responsive ears and even his own weariness wasn't enough to blot out the feeling he'd done the most stupid day's work he'd ever done by walking away from all he could be as Miss Paulina Trethayne's grateful lover.

Polly refused to go across the courtyard to dinner that night and sat in her lofty room, staring into the fire that would never have been lit on a soaking May evening before the marquis came home. She sighed at the thought of how much had changed here since she saw him that first time, like some gilded god come down from Olympus to play stable hand for a day.

Feeling sad and forsaken and thoroughly out of sorts with herself and the rest of the world, she tried hard not to turn into a watering pot when Toby came up the stairs with a plate carefully covered to keep it warm and insisted on watching over her while she ate. How could she refuse to do so like some fine lady in a fit of pique when he had taken so much trouble to look after her? Luckily he was also old and wise enough to know she didn't want to talk about what was upsetting her, but a little later Hal and Josh tapped on her door and sidled in, looking as if they thought it was their fault she was blue-devilled.

It was no good, she decided with despair eating even deeper into her than it had before. She couldn't do it. Not even for the sake of loving Lord Mantaigne as she so badly wanted him to let her love him could she cut herself off from her brothers. Since her stepmother had died when Josh was a baby, Polly had tried to fill the gaping holes in his little life as best she could. Then there was her usually serious and studious middle brother, who sometimes lost himself in a book as determinedly as Lord Mantaigne did in his life of hedonistic pleasure.

Did Hal hide the same sort of sensitivity behind a front of self-sufficiency as his lordship did then? Unlikely, Polly decided as Hal's own character trumped the fear he was deeply damaged by the loss of parents he barely remembered. Her Hal was a natural scholar, a thinker who would find a comfortable corner of life somehow and settle into it with a genuine pleasure few outside his own world would ever understand. Worry as she might about Toby and his adventurous spirit and Josh's sometimes wild imagination, she knew Hal would be happy as long as he was able to keep following clues and trails only he could read in some dusty old tome.

So now she could worry about Toby instead. He knew how it felt to have two loving parents and a comfortable life because he'd been eight years old when his whole world fell apart. Those first years were nothing like the past seven had been and now she thought she could rob him of the small security he had with Lady Wakebourne and all their other friends and fellow travellers? No, not even for Lord Mantaigne. There wasn't a man on earth she could love enough to risk throwing away her brothers' happiness for.

So, that was that. She would do whatever it took to keep these boys as happy and secure as they could be without a penny to their names but what she could earn or accept from a man who felt guilty about them for some reason. Once upon a time she had been too proud to accept charity, but could any woman who stared destitution in the face afford pride? It might be charity, but it would do. They would go to the Dower House of Spring Magna Manor House when it was ready if Lord Mantaigne offered it to them. The man had houses enough to quarter an army in and was hardly likely to miss one he admitted he'd forgotten about until he stumbled on it on one of his lone rides and asked who owned it.

If he intended to salve his conscience by allowing her and her friends to live in the Dower House, then so be it. She would watch that fine and suitable marchioness of his playing lady bountiful in the villages and smile. Polly might hate the pity and puzzlement in such a fine lady's eyes whenever she encountered the oddest of her husband's dependents, but she would be polite and deferential to the devil himself if it kept her brothers safe and happy.

'I know you don't want to hear it, but I do love you all, you know?' she said and watched them roll their eyes at each other and pretend to be sick with a feeling her real world had just slotted back into place.

Anything else was only a dream, yet wasn't the pain supposed to stop if you told it not to be real? How could something as insubstantial as a dream still hurt as if part of her had fallen off a cliff and been bruised and battered half to death?

'We know, and we do you too,' Toby said as if to get it out of the way in as few words as he could on behalf of all of them.

'We decided to show you our secret to make you feel better about whatever it is you feel miserable about, Poll,' Hal informed her solemnly, and the parent she had tried to be for the past seven years pricked up her ears and worried about what that might be. 'It's all right, it's nothing bad. We didn't want to tell anyone about it, but since a man's going to come and set the castle right very soon, or at least so Lord Mantaigne says, you might as well know about it before everyone else does.'

'I agree,' Josh said solemnly, and Polly wondered if letting them sleep in the men's quarters in the ancient castle keep had been such a good idea after all. It might have made them more independent, but apparently it had also left them free to wander about the rest of the empty and maybe dangerous old house whenever they felt like it.

'Where is it then?' she asked warily.

'We'll have to show you or you won't understand properly,' Hal said with a look that said it wouldn't be much of a surprise if they told her where it was and Polly concluded her middle brother could sometimes be a bit too clever for his own good.

'Come on, Poll, the doors will be locked and everyone supposed to be in bed if we don't hurry and we need to know what to do about it anyway,' Josh said with a defiant look for his bigger brother as if that was an argument they had long been having with each other.

'Very well,' she said, for they might as well get it out of the way so she could tell Mr Peters who would inform his employer about whatever small niche the two of them had found in this once-great fortress.

'It's as well you aren't wearing skirts tonight,' Hal said with an approving glance at the breeches and jacket she'd put back on for some obscure reason even she couldn't understand when she came up here to brood alone over what was and what ought to be and wasn't.

'Most brothers would be glad to see their sister ape the lady.'

'We're not most brothers and you're not most sisters,' Hal said, and Josh just looked puzzled by the whole idea she could be anything else but what she was— their big sister.

Chapter Thirteen

'Got them at last,' Peters murmured as soon as he caught the sound of a latch snick very softly into place somewhere on the other side of the wide hall he might have admitted finding echoing and ghostly in the last dying rays of daylight under threat of torture.

'Quiet,' Tom cautioned him and went back to waiting for whoever was haunting his dusty mansion to walk into his trap. 'What the devil?' he muttered a few moments later when unexpectedly light footsteps walked down the hallway as if they had no great need to hide their presence and a right to be here.

'Who goes there?' Peters allowed himself to challenge them as some boyhood part of him must have longed to all his life.

'We do,' Josh Trethayne's voice sang happily back at them, 'and what are you doing sitting here in the dark all alone like Polly was until we went and got her, Mr Peters?' he asked as brightly as if they'd met at a summer picnic.

'Confound it,' Tom cursed quietly to Peters because it was either that or bellow at them like a choleric squire. 'Why the devil must they choose tonight to roam about my house in the dark?' he added and opened up the shutter on his dark lantern to light up the three young Trethaynes nearest to them, then raised it to inspect their sister by directing the beam of candle on her unconventional breeches and spencer jacket.

'Lost something?' he drawled as if he had the right, but how could she simply stroll in here with her little brothers in tow as if that fiasco his first night here had never happened?

'No, have you?' she asked with a dignified lift of her chin Peters seemed to admire rather more than he did just at the moment.

'My patience,' Tom muttered under his breath, racking his brains for a way of getting them back into the older and safer part of the castle without giving away the fact he and Peters were here for a purpose. 'But it's getting darker by the minute and surely those two urchins of yours ought to be in bed by now?' he made himself say as lightly as if they had met in the everyday rooms as a matter of course. He'd never thought himself much of an actor until that moment and was even quite proud of his unexpected skill, until she sniffed as if to inform him she wasn't a fool and anyway, she was the one who decided when and where her brothers went and not him.

'We've come to show Polly the secret room to cheer her up,' Josh said happily.

'What secret room?' Tom made himself ask casually.

'Unfair, my lord,' Polly Trethayne rebuked him, 'Josh is seven years old and not yet up to playing your games.'

'Yes, I am, Poll, and anyway I'm nearly eight.'

'Do you think you could postpone this particular argument until another day or take it somewhere else?' Peters asked wearily, nodding at the uncovered window of the lantern to remind Tom they were lying in wait for villains, not four people they already knew were at Dayspring and probably knew it better than either of them.

'Aye, will you please return to your part of the castle if I promise to tell you exactly what happens here afterwards?' he heard himself plead and wondered where the occasionally haughty Marquis of Mantaigne had disappeared to for a fleeting moment, then found he didn't much regret him.

'No,' all four Trethaynes replied at the same time.

'Then we must abandon the hunt, Peters,' he said, straightening up and scowling at Peters as if it was his fault, since he could hardly take his fury out on three boys and a militantly oblivious female, however richly they deserved it.

'That you must not,' Polly said with an offended glare he ought to have learnt to expect by now. 'Hal will make sure Josh keeps quiet and Toby and I can mind our own tongues, thank you very much,' she told him and folded her arms across her chest to make it doubly clear to him she wasn't going anywhere.

Tom bit back a full-blooded curse for the benefit of her brothers rather than Polly Trethayne and let himself admit he admired her daring nearly as much as he wanted to curse her for putting so much as a hair on her head in danger. How the devil had that happened? He eyed her through the gloom and ran a series of images of her through his head, from the moment he first looked up to see her looming in the stable-doorway to the delicious, delirious experience of kissing her with every inch of him one long agonised scream of frustrated arousal this afternoon.

Was it even possible Thomas Banburgh had fallen in love? And with possibly the least suitable potential marchioness he could find in the entire kingdom while he was about it? Clearly it was impossible, yet somehow or another there it still was, as real and alive as if he'd written it all over the walls of his own castle and advertised it in the Strand.

Stunned by the certainty that if he never set eyes on her again after today his life would be lived in twilight, he felt as if he was floundering in the face of the storm of powerful emotions running through him like a natural disaster. He loved her? Yes, he did love her. Tom Banburgh, who didn't want to either love or be loved, loved Polly Trethayne with all the hope and joy he hadn't dared feel so fully since he was a boy surging through him like a spring tide.

What was more, he loved a magnificent, delightful, grumpy and unconventional female who would never bore him or make him wish for his clubs or the sophisticated lovers he'd enjoyed before he met her. She was glaring back at him now; daring him to treat her like some delicate little gently bred female and send her back to her bed to cower there in safety. It would be a wild ride, loving her for the rest of his life, he decided with a hot look for her at the thought of starting it.

Meeting it seemed to make her forget her impression of an angry goddess confronted by a human she intended turning into a toad. Seeing puzzlement and a fine seasoning of curiosity in her gaze, he felt even more tempted to kiss that lush, doubtful mouth of hers. He'd better provoke her back into a fury before he lost all credibility with her and her brothers and Peters for life by kissing her in front of them and blurting out his shocked feelings.

'There's no excuse for putting your brothers in danger, even if you're reckless enough to forget how much they depend on you for love and support, and put yourself in danger,' he said in the hope she might be persuaded to worry about her brothers' safety as she didn't seem ready to about her own.

It occurred to Tom that one of the hardest parts of loving this woman might be enduring fear for her when she didn't seem to have any for herself.

'You were right, then, Hal, there really are pirates looking for our treasure here at night?' Josh asked wide-eyed and ready to believe almost anything. Tom could almost feel his sister being torn between a need to take her littlest brother out of here and a belief he would immediately find a way back, or make such a noise the intruders might be scared into shooting someone out of sheer shock.

'This isn't the Spanish Main, Josh, and I think we'd best get you to bed after all,' she said softly, then froze in her tracks as that soft thud she had puzzled over before silenced them all.

As if Tom had said what he was thinking, that she should give up trying to find out who was breaking in herself, she shook her head emphatically at him and glared as if he'd told her to go and drown some kittens. He supposed she knew her brothers a lot better than he did and waved a resigned hand as if to concede they probably had a right to know who was coming in and out of here at will as well. He resolved to put a stop to the whole business if there was even the sniff of real danger, but for now he'd just have to trust his own judgement that Grably's nephew and his partner in crime were neither habitual criminals nor natural murderers.

'You four can have the cupboard over there and Peters and I will watch the door from the basement, then,' he told her with what he hoped was steely enough purpose to tell her she had others to care about her even if she was thinking of rushing headfirst into action. 'It's not too late for us to make so much noise they will run off and never come back,' he added as the only threat he could think of to make them agree to stay out of the line of fire.

'Josh, are you sure you can keep quiet and not get hurt if the men have to fight?' Polly asked as if her littlest brother was at least ten years older.

'I'm very good at not getting hurt when the others fight,' he said matter-of-factly, and his sister nodded an admissions he was right.

'You are that, so pray continue to be so and promise me you'll run and get help if it looks as if we're going to be outnumbered?'

'I promise,' Josh said and crossed his heart for good measure.

Tom felt as proud of the boy as if he'd been his own little brother, or even his son, and the very thought of the tribe of potential giants he and Polly Trethayne might make one day threatened to turn his brain to a mush of besotted daydreams.

'You're all as mad as each other,' Peters muttered as if he thought Tom the worst lunatic of all for not abandoning their attempt to trap the intruders on the spot, or somehow make the rackety Trethayne family leave them to spring it alone. He clearly didn't know any of them as well as Tom did, then, or he wouldn't even consider it a real possibility.

'Maybe, but at least in there they'll be relatively safe,' Tom whispered so low so that the intrepid quartet now piling into the broom cupboard as if it was the only place they would dream of being on a June night wouldn't hear him.

He wanted to laugh at the same time as he felt oddly proud of them for being who they were. He also longed to get Polly alone so he could persuade her to trust herself and them to him for as long as they might need him. There was no question of him ever not needing her now, but one day her brothers would want to live their own lives. Until then they would be his as truly as if they really did carry Banburgh blood in their veins instead of the unique Trethayne kind he was longing to see zing through his own children mingled with his.

He half-believed they'd made enough noise and fuss to warn anyone within half a mile, but a mechanism behind the panelling in the room that had once been used as a butler's pantry clicked and opened even as he drew breath to call the whole thing off. He scented something he remembered from long ago on the air with a real sense of dread and wished too late he'd managed to send them away. Of course they would then lay in wait farther away from him and be at even more risk, so he stopped cursing himself for a dozen different sorts of a fool and listened for what came next with a fast beating heart instead.

'I told you we shouldn't come back here no more,' a half-familiar voice whispered as he followed a dimly lit and burlier figure into the hall.

'Stow your rattle,' the one he recalled a little too well from that first night here ordered impatiently, and Tom heard the smoothed-out tones of an educated man and raised his eyebrows in the darkness of their hiding place.

'If we can't find it after all these months, it ain't here to be found, Ollie.'

'Hold your tongue, you fool, of course it is.'

So what the devil was Grably's nephew doing back at Dayspring? Searching for something his lunatic uncle left behind when he was carted off to the private asylum by his embarrassed brother-in-law all those years ago, Tom supposed, hearing the two men argue about where they had left to look. Was this the moment to let them know they'd been discovered and it was time this wild goose chase came to an end? Probably, but the fools were between him and the Trethaynes' hiding place and he didn't trust Polly or her little brothers not to leap out and put themselves in danger just because it was there.

'He said there was a priceless treasure hidden between the moon and the earth and in the same part of the castle as he lived in when he ruled it and that idiot of a boy was kept in his proper place,' the nephew said with the same fixed stubbornness Tom recalled hearing in his guardian's voice all those years ago and only just managed to suppress a shudder.

He ran over their clue to the hiding place of whatever it was again in his head and this time had to bite back a laugh. There was an ancient carving of the moon and the sun orbiting the earth in a mantelpiece in one of the bedchambers Tom decided now had been reused from one of the older parts of the castle when the new wing was built. It must have seemed a shame to waste even such a quaint old masterpiece on a servant and so the fireplace had been moved. The fools had probably walked past it dozens of times and not even realised what they sought was right under their noses, but why they would be looking for it in the first place was beyond him.

Still, he heard a muffled grunt from the cupboard and shrugged in the darkness as he resigned himself to springing his trap a little before time. He hadn't much stomach for hearing more and at least they'd given any accomplices time to crawl out of whatever worm-hole they used to enter the castle without being seen. These two were alone and he doubted very much they would put up much of a fight.

'You've been deceived,' he drawled as he stood upright.

Two more dark lanterns were hastily added to the total as the intruders felt the need to find out who was challenging them. Tom hoped the Trethaynes would realise the Mantons in his and Peters's hands were primed and loaded and have the sense to stay where they were.

'Mantaigne, what the hell are you doing here?' the taller of the two asked as if he was the one with every right to ask questions.

'Funnily enough, I thought I owned the place,' Tom said lightly, circling the petrified figures to put himself between them and Polly, who saw what he was about and emerged from her hiding place to startle the intruders into stunned silence.

'He does,' she said with an emphatic nod that defied anyone to argue.

'I heard about a giant doxy in breeches who lived here behind Mantaigne's back, but I never thought you'd stay and warm his bed for him now he's found courage to come back after all these years of cowering away in town.'

'You take that back, she's my sister and she's not a doxy,' Henry Trethayne ordered, in a fine brotherly fury Tom hadn't thought the scholarly boy had in him.

'Ladies don't wear breeches or carry pistols,' the nephew pointed out with a sneer, and Tom wondered if *he* had found some courage over the past two decades, until he reminded himself the fool probably didn't believe she would actually shoot him, his mistake.

'Yet still I have the pistol and you have a great deal

of explaining to do,' she said as coolly as most ladies of Tom's acquaintance might if they were wielding a teapot and asking if an unwanted visitor would like more tea rather than brandishing a pistol he hadn't even known she possessed.

'I suggest you start now before one of us decides to shoot you for the hell of it,' he said coolly, despite this mad impulse to grin like a fool because he'd suddenly realised exactly how complex and how simple his life was going to be from now on.

Arrogant of him to believe he would win her when Polly was about as predictable as the north wind, but something told him the chance was right here, ready to be seized and gloated over, and he really didn't intend to waste it.

'I, for one, am getting very bored,' Peters said laconically and Tom had never liked the fellow better.

'And I just wish someone would let me have a go,' Hal said with an aggrieved look at his sister, who narrowed her incredible eyes and straightened her arm as if getting ready to pick which bit of villain to shoot first.

'All right,' the smaller of the two men said with a look of terror on his face. 'I'll tell you everything if you all promise not to shoot.'

'I'm not set on it, at least not in your case,' Tom said reasonably enough to his way of thinking.

'I really don't like the idea of them invading your house whenever they feel like it,' Polly said calmly, and Peters just grinned and cocked his pistol as if he didn't have to dislike a man to take a potshot at him.

'Our house,' Tom corrected as patiently as he could manage.

It was possibly the oddest proposal ever made, but she read it for what it was and let her gun arm waver for a breath-stealing moment. It was as well Peters seemed so deadly calm neither man moved an inch as he watched them with chilling indifference, since Tom was more interested in her response than their unwanted visitors.

'Do you remember all those seaman's knots Sam Barker has been teaching you to tie, Hal?' Peters asked casually.

'Of course I do. I'm not dexterous like Toby, but once I learn something I don't forget it.'

'Then tie one or two in these and make sure neither can get free. There's a good chap.'

'I can help,' Josh said crossly, for being seven was clearly no excuse for missing out on anything interesting for the Trethayne clan.

'You can keep your sister's gun steady on the fat one, my friend,' Peters said as if he didn't think so either. 'And I truly hope the sight of Josh Trethayne with a gun terrifies you as deeply as it does me, whoever you are,' Peters said as he held his own aim rock steady and made sure neither man had any thoughts about seizing Hal and using him as a hostage against their own escape.

Luckily it seemed to do so and they kept still as statues. Tom and Polly were far too preoccupied with not looking at each other to be much use, although Tom always swore afterwards if he hadn't had such an able pack of helpers he might have taken a much more active role in subduing the prisoners himself.

'Deal with them, would you, Peters?' he said absently as he took his eyes off Polly long enough to nod sagely at the others and let them leave without him.

'Will they be all right?' Polly asked as if she only had half her mind on the supposed business of the night as well.

'I should imagine so. I know your pistol wasn't loaded, even if Josh and that poor man he's driving along like a cow to market have no idea,' Tom replied.

'What do you mean "ours"?' she demanded in the semi-darkness from the single lantern the others had left them to light up a whole cavernous hallway and half an empty house.

'I mean marry me, live with me, love me,' Tom said a little desperately, for suddenly it didn't seem quite so certain she would believe him after that ridiculous scene this morning when he made it very plain he wasn't going to ask her to be anything in his life.

'Why?'

'Because I want you to?'

'Not enough.'

'Then do it because I think you the most extraordinary woman I ever met, because I can't imagine how tedious my life would be without you and your brothers and your oddly assorted band of friends and because I love you more than I thought I had it in me to love anyone. Be everything to me that I always thought I couldn't have, Paulina Trethayne. Please? Before I beg and embarrass us both.'

'I can't be meek and conventional and there's no point trying to make me into a proper marchioness. I'm more suited to be your mistress, but I can't do it. I can't abandon my family.'

'And if anything happened to me you would fight the devil himself back into hell to see that our whelps were safe. If I'm ever to have a wife and gamble on making children with her, she will just have to be you. I couldn't dare the fates and risk making them with anyone else, Polly. No other woman on God's earth has your courage and loyalty and that lioness's heart of yours and at last I've had the good sense to realise I don't want to live without you.'

So far they had faced each other like adversaries, but now he moved closer. She eyed him sceptically and he could sense her going through his list of reasons with a fine-toothed comb, but they had been enchanted on a more sensual level from the very first moment they set eyes on each other and he intended to take advantage of the fact right now.

'And you're sure you love me? It seems to have come upon you suddenly, considering you rejected me earlier today.'

'It crept up on me inch by inch from the first day on, but having the sense to know it did ambush me tonight. Now I wonder it took me so long to realise why I felt as if I was living in the wrong skin, why I lay awake in the middle of a howling gale, in the barest and most draughty room I've slept in since I was eight years old, night after night and longed for you to be lying in that bed next to me, even if you were fast asleep. If you'll promise to lie by my side for the rest of our lives, I'll put up with living in this old wreck while it's made fit for a marchioness to live in once again. If you tell me you can't endure the idea, I don't think I shall even be able to come back to Dayspring again, however, for I truly couldn't endure it without you now, Polly. I can't stand the thought of anything much about my life without you in it now I've come to see sense at last.'

'Put like that, I almost believe you mean it,' she allowed, and neither of them took much notice when the pallid light suddenly went out, as if the candle had been snuffed by some mischievous ghost.

'Believe it, my darling Amazon,' he whispered and the darkness seemed to unleash everything they felt together this morning and something more as well.

'Convince me,' she breathed as his eager hands reached for her and found no resistance at all, so he did so as thoroughly and emphatically as he could at such short notice.

Hours later Polly lay at her lover's side in that draughty bedchamber he'd complained about earlier and watched the moon set as he slept. She treasured every snuffle and snort as he lay there prone and deeply asleep, without any of the barriers my Lord Mantaigne usually put between himself and the rest of the world. Speaking for herself, she felt too energised, too loved and needed to sleep. A smile of remembered satisfaction curled her lips in a smile that felt as if it might never leave her lips, and she rolled over onto her front so she could watch him even more closely.

She had no doubt Tom was a peerless lover of beautiful women and part of her might thank some of them
for teaching him how to rouse and then satisfy a woman
until every inch and sense she had sang; on the other
hand she might not, since they were so beautiful and
had been so satisfied.

With awe and wonder and a residual heat she should
probably be ashamed of, she recalled how it felt to be
taken over by love, washed under by it, carried along
yet robustly active in the timeless dance of lovers she
had only just learned so it itched against her fingertips
to start up all over again. She couldn't resist smoothing
a hand down her bare thigh in a sensuous line of pleasures beyond her wildest dreams until today, couldn't
repress a wriggle of delight against the fine linen sheets
his finicky valet insisted my lord had on his bed, even
if everything else about his makeshift chamber was
beneath the dignity of a marquis and lowered the consequence of his personal servant.

'It's like sleeping with an eel,' Tom murmured a
sleepy protest, and she reached out and traced his smile
with an exploring finger, because she couldn't resist
knowing she had the right, or almost had it until they
were wed and she was sure of it. Here was everything
she had never thought to have with any man, let alone
this one, and how terrible it would have been never to
feel even a shadow of such glory.

'You will have to get used to it then, my lord,' she
murmured as another of those delight-soaked quivers
shot through her body, but this time a little less lazy

appreciation and a lot more eagerness for more shot through her in its wake.

'I dare say I might, although it's obviously going to be a sacrifice,' he said and promptly went from sleepy to demanding between one breath and the next.

'I admire a man willing to make those for the sake of the woman he loves,' she joked, still hardly able to believe it could be her.

'You are worth it, my Polly, worth every last long, elegant inch of sacrifice I'm making by sharing this very hard and narrow bed with you. You do know that you're perfectly designed to fulfil a man's wildest fantasies, don't you? I don't think I ever saw such long and lovely legs or felt the way I feel about you, here, and here and especially…here,' he whispered into the sensitised curve of her kiss-swollen lower lip and played with it between his own. 'Then there's all the way down here,' he husked as he ran kisses down her throat in a long and lovely line of hot licks that made her pulse race and her insides hot and wet and ready for him all over again.

She writhed under him as he reared up to appreciate that curve fully, then track even more intimately down and cup her waiting breast for them both to marvel at. She looked down and saw what she already knew. Fire stirred ever hotter in her belly as she craned her neck back to watch him nuzzle at the frantic nub of one of her tightly needy nipples, then seize it in his mouth to drive her nigh mad with clenched need. Even after he'd taken her so gently earlier tonight that they soared into an awesome new world she hadn't let herself believe in even in her wildest dreams until then, she couldn't quite believe even he could satiate the heavy need burning and demanding at her most intimate core right now.

He raised his head and sucked in a deep breath, seemed to draw in gentlemanly good manners along with the cool pre-dawn air, and tried to shift her so he could give her almost heaven with his gentle yet wickedly knowing touch alone.

'No, you or nothing,' she argued boldly.

'You will be sore, love, and I might get you with child,' he murmured a protest back. How could she not love him when he looked by the tight expression on his dear face in the last glance of moonlight as if his good manners were costing him dearer than even she knew?

'Since you might have done that already, and even you have to admit it takes two people to make one of those, you had best marry me out of hand then, my lord,' she told him, smoothing one of her unsteady hands over his set mouth to make him loosen the hold he had himself under so determinedly it was eating her up inside.

'It will take three days, according to Peters, who seems to know more than most about hasty marriages. I'm not risking a long courtship or a seven-month child with you, love, since you'd never let me hear the last of it if we happen to set the world by the ears in nine months' time.'

'I wouldn't dare reproach you, since it would be half my fault, but I want to be your wife, Tom, more than I've wanted anything in my life until today.'

'As far as I'm concerned you already are, but we'd best get the formalities out of the way as soon as can be,' he said and since he had been caressing her so intimately she had to pinch herself to realise this was really happening to her, Polly Trethayne of nowhere, then she writhed under his inflammatory touch, demand in every inch of her body as she wound as much of it as she could against as much of him as she could reach.

'Love me all the way through, then,' she whispered and ran a fingertip down his supple backbone and felt him quiver like a greyhound with sensual excitement. 'I need you far too much,' she added huskily.

'No,' he argued fiercely with her, 'you need me just enough. Enough to meet the desperation I have for you, the ache in my gut I've lived with since the first time I set eyes on you and wanted you so badly it felt as if I was being ripped apart by it at times. I thought I could never have you lie like this, feel you take me inside you like this…' He paused, and she opened to him, felt him drive within the slick, hot tightness of her most intimate core and shivered with sheer joy and exultation. 'I thought I could never rock and ride with you all the way to the heart of the sun,' he gasped as he took up the race again, and now she had the measure of it she felt the drive into something wonderful as well, as he rode hard and high inside her, and she wrapped her long and slender legs about his neat buttocks and rode with him.

She felt hot and greedy for everything he had to give her and deep and generous with all she had to offer in return. She wound her ankles together over his striving thighs and felt his whole body gasp at the feel of her wholly with him, completely engaged in the lovely flight into somewhere nobody else could ever go but them, together. Now the race was frantic and even more intense than it had been last time. She felt almost as if the full force of Mother Nature herself flowed through her as she threw back her head and felt the life of it shoot through her until even her toes and fingertips seemed to glow with it. 'Oh, my love,' she gasped as she writhed against him, and his thrusts deepened and seemed to take her even further away from her day-to-day self. There was that forlorn moment of wondering if the journey was all there was and their destination just tantalisingly out of reach and then they were there and how could she have doubted they would be?

'I love, love, love you,' she murmured on a keening whisper that turned into a satiated sigh that deferred to the fact her brothers were asleep only a floor below with the windows open.

Still their bodies soared together and the climax of that frantic ride seemed to promise eternity as they lay locked and mindless and yet so deeply mindful of each other all at the same time. Polly felt quivers of ecstasy rock her all the way down to her toes and wondered how rapidly he'd made her proud of her lanky inches instead of always half-ashamed to be so tall and supposedly unfeminine.

'Aren't you glad you came?' she asked innocently as the fire finally sank to a dearly remembered spark and the odd magical shiver of ecstasy still shook her.

To her surprise he seemed to find that comment irresistibly amusing and buried a bark of male laughter against her hair, where it spilled in a wild silky cloud against the down pillows of my lord's makeshift bed.

'What?' she demanded, almost managing to feel cross with the great puzzle of a man as he groaned with suppressed laughter, then finally made himself disengage from her sated body as reluctantly as she made herself admit it was near dawn and about time she resorted to her own part of the castle.

'I'm delighted I came back to my own and to you this spring, my love. Even more delighted that the next fool on my beloved godmother's list can now take over his part in her Machiavellian schemes and deliriously happy that I'll very shortly be marrying a marchioness after all my protests that I never would. Will that do?'

'Possibly, but why were you laughing at me so hard you nearly gave us both away just now?'

'I will tell you another time.'

'Will you now?' she asked as if she had the least intention of staying out of his bed anytime it could be avoided for the next forty or fifty years.

'It will give you something to look forward to,' he teased her with a wicked glint in his eyes and since she was beginning to be able to see the colour of them as the sun thought hard about rising on a fine June morning, she shot him a challenging look before she sprang out of bed and began to resume her scandalous breeches and best coat.

'Maybe, but today I'm looking forward to the boys showing us this phantom treasure that sounds like the little details of your mother's life nobody seemed to recall seeing for the past two decades. Then you should probably show me the lord and lady's private quarters of your soon-to-be-refurbished mansion, my lord,' she said with a jaunty smile and saw shadows steal into his gaze as he contemplated whether he could live with her in that part of the house after all.

She held her breath even as she pretended to be serenely convinced there was nothing out of the way in her plans for their morning and reached for my lord's fine set of hair brushes to smooth the tumbling mass of her hair into her usual plait to at least start the day halfway to being tame. 'My valet will be as shocked as a maiden lady if he comes in and catches you sitting on the end of my bed combing out your witchy hair for my very personal delight,' he warned her lazily.

'He'd better learn to live with me or find another job, because I'm not going to spend any more nights in my room across the courtyard to save his blushes or anyone else's,' she warned.

Chapter Fourteen

'Ah, Farenze, can't say I expected you to come since you're supposed to be busy with that ramshackle old place you bought off your brother-in-law. Is this your viscountess? Good evening, my dear. Delighted you could join us after all the invitations your husband has refused on your behalf. I dare say he wanted to keep you to himself.' The Earl of Trethayne bowed to the mystery lady the *ton* had been so eager to meet all Season and preened himself that they'd had to wait until his granddaughter's ball to do it.

The latest Trethayne chit and this grand waste of money his daughter-in-law had forced on him would be the talk of the town after tonight and for once he didn't begrudge the money all this show and frivolity was costing him. His gaze drifted onward to gauge what effect this social triumph was having on whoever was next in the receiving line, then sharpened abruptly, as if he'd been replaced by a statue of a grumpy old cheese-paring aristocrat instead of the real thing.

'The chit must know she ain't welcome here, I told

her last time she was here never to bother me or mine again,' he managed to stutter out between stiff lips as the statuesque lady dressed in the first stare of fashion reached him and looked as if she wasn't quite sure why she had bothered.

'I'm not a chit any longer, if I ever was, and I don't know why you imagine I need your welcome now, sir—I found none when I came to you and begged for help when I was seventeen and alone in the world but for three little brothers.'

'French whelps,' he almost spat at her as if she had suggested he helped her to look after a litter of un-wanted puppies rather than three then very small chil-dren.

'Half-French,' the stripling at her side informed him with nearly as much brass-faced impudence as his sister.

'I can assure you the other half is pure Trethayne,' the next gentleman in line said with his usual casual impudence and Earl of Trethayne frowned at the Mar-quis of Mantaigne and wondered why he'd never told the idle fool exactly what he thought of him before tonight.

'What the devil do they have to do with you or the Farenze connection?'

'Lord Farenze and I were brought up together, so we share a lot of family feeling, Trethayne. I'm sure you know the ones I mean—love, loyalty and caring for the welfare of others even when you don't always want to? I hope you don't expect Lord Farenze and I to ignore each other as our wives make their first forays into the *ton* tonight. That would be downright unnatural for such close connections, don't you think?' Tom asked silkily.

His host paled and flashed a glance from one to the other of the striking group taking up so much of his guests' attention there was near silence in the overcrowded ballroom. For a moment he seemed about to admit that the unlikely group of people in front of him were indeed connected in some way he didn't understand, then he gathered his senses and his long-standing conviction he was right and they were all wrong and fought back.

'What's that sentimental rigmarole got to do with them?' he said with a dismissive wave of his hand at Polly and Toby Trethayne, who stood surveying the glittering ballroom as if they were far more interested in the spectacle of the *ton* at play than anything their reluctant host might have to say about them.

'Firstly there is the fact we all value the company of your great-niece and great-nephew and would not go anywhere they are not welcomed. Secondly—'

'Thank you, my lord, but we are quite capable of speaking for ourselves, are we not, Tobias?' His bean-pole of a great-niece had the effrontery to interrupt an even more important nobleman than his lordship knew himself to be. 'Pray don't splutter like that, sir, it isn't becoming and since we're related it won't reflect well on us for it to be known our great-uncle cannot string two words together without recourse to cursing or roaring and ranting like a lunatic.'

'I don't know how you got in here...'

'No, I'm quite sure you don't, since you have done your best to make sure we all went straight to the devil. I may have begged you for help and been turned away time after time seven years ago, but I didn't have to walk here with a babe in arms and two little brothers at my heels this time. Nor do I need to plead with you to help me put food in their bellies, because I have somehow managed to do that myself for the past seven years, since you threw us out of your house as if we carried plague. You don't need to worry, my lord, we're not here to beg for help you have no intention of giving us tonight. I know from past experience it would not be forthcoming.'

Now the silence that had greeted the delightful surprise of Lady Farenze making her first public appearance at this débutante ball was giving way to a flurry of delighted speculation, and Lord Trethayne didn't have to turn round to know whispers that he'd let such youthful members of his own family all but starve were sweeping about the ballroom as the witch paused for a moment, as if selecting the best spot to slip in the killing knife blow.

'What do you want?' he managed to grab enough presence of mind to ask, before any further revelations could fall from the giant female's mouth and ruin the night he'd paid out so much to bring about.

'An apology would do nicely to begin with,' she told him softly. By now his guests were straining so hard to hear her he was surprised they didn't just pitch up and form a circle.

'I'm sorry,' he murmured with a furious glance at his open-mouthed daughter-in-law and that wispy little chit he'd gone to so much trouble to get off their hands.

'I didn't quite catch that, Trethayne,' Mantaigne very

nearly bellowed with that almost-an-idiot grin of his that Lord Trethayne suddenly realised he'd always found so damnably irritating.

'Sorry,' he barked more loudly.

'Such a gracious manner as you've always had with us, don't you agree, Tobias?' the woman murmured and had a dowager or two reaching for their ear trumpets.

'I remember,' the boy said, and Lord Trethayne could see he did from the hot glitter in those green-and-blue Trethayne eyes he'd managed not to notice when he scouted the French hussy's brats out of his house and slammed the door behind them for the last time.

'I very much wish you could not, but how could a boy of eight forget such a harsh dismissal from this very house and the life of beggary you condemned us all to seven years ago?' his sister said as if all this was for the boy's sake and not her own.

'Come to force me to frank a Season for you, have you, m'dear?' he made himself ask as if he was a genial uncle to a niece whom the very idea of a Season and presentation at court would make a hardened match-maker blench. Make a joke out of the girl and the polite world would laugh with him and forget he'd rid himself of her so hastily last time she dared darken his doors.

'I wouldn't dream of asking you for anything, but my friends and my husband requested my company, so I agreed to come here tonight very much against my better judgement,' Paulina the Pauper had the brass-faced cheek to drawl as if she'd been taking lessons in being elegantly annoying from Mantaigne.

'Ah, so you persuaded some fool to wed a girl who

will always make a fool out of him by overtopping him at every turn, have you?' He forgot his audience long enough to gloat. If the awkward filly was already wed, there was nothing for him to do but shrug and make it obvious he pitied the poor idiot his mistake.

'No, I laid siege so determinedly that in the end Miss Trethayne gave in and agreed to wed me out of sheer boredom at having to say me nay one more time,' Tom lied with a smile for his gallant love that ignored the apoplectic-looking peer and everyone else in the room but her and their friends and family.

'You?' the old fool barked out at the top of his voice.

'Me,' Tom replied with infinite satisfaction and a long, hot look for his bride that made her blush delightfully, despite the presence of her brother and the small matter of around three hundred of his lordship's closest acquaintances.

'She's a marchioness?'

'My wife is a marchioness, something I expect she will forgive me for one day if we both live long enough. That's what happens when a woman weds a marquis, you know, Trethayne? Whether she wants to or not, she becomes his marchioness.'

'Wants to? Of course she wanted to, that's why she married you, isn't it? Can't think any sane female would want to unless you had some strawberry leaves on your coronet.'

'I do have one or two more of them than you, though, don't I? Ah, well, never mind, I'm sure my lady will resign herself to them in time.'

A titter or two greeted that outrageous piece of play-acting, except Tom knew they were wrong and he meant it. Had he been a commoner it would have been a lot easier to persuade Polly to marry him, then come to London and grasp her right to a certain position in the social world, if only for the sake of the boys. As he was thinking of that, his eyes hardened on the steely old bruiser in front of him.

'My friend here acts for me on matters of delicate family business. You might have done well to employ him in your long and frustrating search for your nephews and niece after you let them think you would not help them upon their father's death, Trethayne. I hate to imagine how hard you must have looked for them after Tobias's godfather died and left most of his fortune to the boy, with you to hold it all in trust until he came of age. One can only imagine how ill at ease you must have felt at knowing you let them leave after one of those heated family arguments we've all heard so much about once you held such a fortune in hand for them and no heir anywhere in sight. Not being able to track them down to explain their abrupt change of fortunes must have galled you to your very soul.'

'Er…yes, distraught, weren't we, Robina?' the old fox picked up his cue as Tom fixed him with a cold stare that dared him to refute Polly or Toby again.

'I have often heard you speak of it with great sorrow for your loss of temper, Papa-in-law. Such a shame Miss Trethayne took your hasty words so much to heart that she and her brothers were gone before you could calm down and tell her you didn't mean them,' the lady said smoothly enough, but something about the glint in her eye told Tom a corner had been turned in her relationship with the miserly old hypocrite as well and he would not dominate the rest of his family so easily from now on.

'Knowing you as we all do, I'm sure you will have taken the utmost care of Tobias's fortune, Trethayne. Peters here will be visiting you tomorrow to discuss all the wise investments I'm sure you've made on the boy's behalf while he was too young to manage his fortune for himself.'

'That will be delightful, but tonight I'm sure you came here to renew your connections with your family, then dance and enjoy being with us on such a joyous occasion, Cousin Paulina?' Lady Robina said with a lot more conviction than accuracy, and Tom stepped back and let his wife meet the woman on her own terms.

It was how she lived her life after all, and she had done such a fine job of it up to now he didn't see any need to interfere, even if she would let him.

Chapter Fifteen

Tom watched and assisted his wife and brother-in-law whenever they needed it for the rest of the hour they had agreed to spend at the Trethayne ball before going on to another society ball to show the world they had come to town to do more than just challenge the old vulture at the head of his wife's family tree on his home ground.

'My thanks, Lady Chloe, Winterley,' he said as soon as he'd handed his lady up into the vast old town chariot Virginia had insisted was far more comfortable than more modern and less accommodating vehicles.

'Not at all. It was far better entertainment than I expected of my first appearance in London society,' Chloe Winterley said, 'and now I'm no longer the prime target of all the gossips. I swear I would like you for that, Polly, even if I didn't love you already for marrying Tom and preventing my lord here from worrying himself to flinders about his well-being and peace of mind when I would far rather he was intent on mine instead.'

'Then I'm pleased to have been of service,' his Polly

said lightly enough, but Tom knew she was a lot less relaxed than she was so gallantly pretending to be all the same.

'I wonder who the next one is,' he remarked to divert their attention from the strains of taking on the Earl of Trethayne and the most conservative part of polite society all in one evening.

'What next one?' Toby piped up, and Tom felt Polly's interest stir despite her weariness with this whole wretched business of claiming back Toby's fortune from the money-grabbing old villain who'd appropriated it as his own and blessed the topic of conversation he'd found so appallingly unamusing at the outset of his season at Virginia's beck and call.

Satisfied? he asked silently, as if his godmother could somehow hear him.

You'll do now seemed to come back to him as if she'd whispered it in his ear, but the laughter and satisfaction in it felt so much like her that his breath caught with love and loss. It was almost easy when you got the hang of it, this love business, and he realised he'd had a flying start at it by being taken in and loved despite himself by Virgil and Virginia all those years ago.

'My godmother's next victim,' he explained with an apologetic nod at the corner of the carriage he knew very well only held Toby and a silk cushion, even if it had been her favourite seat when she was alive.

'Victim?' Toby asked sleepily, and Tom wondered if they really needed to drag him across London for another interminable party, but Luke and Peters had insisted and he suspected they knew more about staying on the right side of the dowagers than he did.

'My great-aunt, being a great deal more fun and loving us as dearly as your own great-uncle clearly only loves himself, decreed four of her closest relatives and friends spend a quarter each of the year after her death carrying out errands on her behalf. This quarter was Tom's and the next… Well, only my darling wife and Peters' senior partner know who the next one on her list is and they are not telling us.'

'First I had to inform the person who will be expected to carry out her wishes, Luke,' Chloe told him, and Tom thought he knew what his friend had meant at the beginning of all this about enjoying watching the next on the list dance about at Virginia's bidding because he knew his task was safely over.

He felt Polly next to him and the enormity of the changes in his own life caught him up in wonder, that he should be so other than how he had thought he was back then and that Polly should love him anyway.

'So who is he?'

'That is not for me to reveal.'

'Me,' Peters's voice rasped from his own dark corner of the vast old vehicle as it rumbled to a stop, and the flares and noise of another great rout spilled out on to the streets around it. 'Confound it, but she picked me for some reason best known to herself.'

'I'm quite sure she had a good one,' Chloe said soothingly, and Tom felt his Polly lean forward to ask more and ran a distracting hand over her pert *derrière* now shadows and the flurry of disembarking covered up his need to touch her as often as he could get away with it.

'Enough, love, it's his job to work through the next few months as best he can. We have our own lives to work on for our next fifty or sixty years together.'

'True, but I can never thank your godmama enough for sending you back to Dayspring Castle this spring, Tom,' Polly said with such certainty in her voice he had to swallow back an unmanly lump in his throat.

She had done so much damage to the Marquis of Mantaigne's light-hearted indifference to the rest of the world he hardly recognised himself in Polly Trethayne's besotted husband, but the very thought of having missed out on this new life of theirs made him realise how deeply indebted he was to Virginia for making him return to the castle he'd sworn never to set foot in again as long as he lived.

'True, and if I hadn't loved her before I would have to now, love, for she's turned all I ever swore not to do on its head. If only I'd come back when I came of age instead of ordering the place to fall down without me, we could have been happy for years by now.'

'If you hadn't left Dayspring empty, we would never have gone to live there in your absence, you idiot,' his loving wife chided as Tom sprang out of the carriage to hand down his lady before any other rogue could do it for him.

'There you are, you see, Peters? I have a lifetime of scolds and humility to look forward to,' he said smugly as he stood back for Luke to echo his own determination not to let any other man lay a hand on his wife tonight and hand Chloe down from the grand old coach.

'I look forward to observing it from afar, my lord,' the supposedly quiet young lawyer told him solemnly.

'If you think you can get away from Farenze that easily you're about to discover your error. Fellow's like a limpet. Polly and I will call our first son after you, then you won't be able to deny our acquaintance either.'

'Frederick, wasn't it?' Polly asked, looking as if she was trying hard to like the idea, and Tom considered the notion with apparent seriousness.

'Peter?' he suggested, thinking that sounded a fair enough name for a future marquis and the son he'd once sworn never to have. He caressed Polly's long fingers as they walked up the steps to the next grand town house on their list unashamedly hand-locked. 'It would keep the boy's feet on the ground to have a good solid name to remind him he's not one of the lords of Creation.'

'He will have me for that,' Polly reminded him with a radiant smile as they joined the tail of guests waiting to be introduced to their host and hostess for the next hour or so and yet another blushing daughter recently launched on the marriage mart.

'How true,' Tom replied with a mock grimace at the idea of being humbled for his own good for the next fifty years or so. 'Perhaps we'd best call him after a great warrior after all then. It sounds as if the poor lad could need encouragement.'

'Even if I thought you were serious, my lord, there's no need to do either on my account,' Peters told him with an uncomfortable glance around another glittering ballroom that told Tom he would rather be almost anywhere else, but he'd been drawn into that Farenze Connection old Trethayne had referred to so scornfully against his will and felt some sort of obligation to support the rest of them tonight. 'Those are not my real names,' he added as drily as if discussing some obscure point of law with his fellow lawyers.

'An alias?' Tom asked with raised eyebrows and tried to ignore his wife's frown and shushing gesture as he challenged his latest brother-in-arms.

'We all sail under false colours in some ways, don't you agree, my lord?' the man challenged him back, and Tom looked at himself at the beginning of his quest and decided the man was right.

'Perhaps, but some of us not quite as deliberately as others. Are you the black sheep of the family then, cast adrift for some youthful sin I'm quite certain you won't tell us about?'

'I could be,' not-Peters said tightly as they approached the head of the receiving line, and delighted whispers began to break out in another overcrowded ballroom like ripe corn chattering together on a stir of summer hot air. 'I could be their worst nightmare,' he added so low nobody else but Tom and Polly could hear.

'Or their favourite dream,' Polly argued. 'You never know what the next three months might bring you, but I'm very glad Tom's brought him to me. Perhaps you should go back to them and find out if they really think themselves better off without you rather than deciding for them?'

'And perhaps I should do the decent thing and stay

away,' he replied with a bleak certainty even Tom found rather chilling for a man he'd come to respect and like, if he could get through the rigid self-control Peters used to fend off the world.

'Whatever you should or shouldn't do, you're at Virginia's mercy for the next season and I wish you joy of it,' Luke put in with a grin after they had got through the surprised greetings and hasty congratulations of their hosts and moved out into the ballroom beyond. 'I certainly intend to enjoy the fruits of my labours to the full,' he added with a wicked smile at Chloe.

'Cocksure braggart,' she chided softly enough so only they could hear her, despite the stars in her eyes.

'Guilty,' he admitted brazenly and whisked her into the next dance to show the polite world he only had eyes for his wife and intended to ignore all those dreadful rumours that the Farenze curse had struck again.

Dark and dangerous Lord Farenze himself had been captured and spellbound beyond diversion and now, horror of horrors, there was a rumour going about the ballroom that the Marquis of Mantaigne had wed the magnificent creature he refused to let go long enough to even be introduced. Society, or at least the young and hopeful female part of it, let out a long sigh of disappointment and readjusted its expectations of making a brilliant marriage or taking a dazzlingly handsome lover with that particular gentleman.

'So you see, Peters, for I don't imagine you're about to gift us with the use of your real name, you are in danger of being made happy despite your best intentions to be miserable,' Tom told him and dragged his own lady onto the dance-floor in his friend's wake before Polly could protest at leaving her brother to be guided through the avidly curious throng by Virginia's next hero.

'He'll guard your eldest lamb as if he's the only heir to a kingdom, never fear, love,' Tom whispered as Polly watched her eldest brother grin at the neatly dressed lawyer and follow him to the groaning refreshment table.

'I don't. Mr Peters has a very safe pair of hands and Toby is far more grown up than any of the pampered sons and heirs these people are accustomed to. If they try to pump him for details, he'll very likely to tell them some wild and improbable story just for the fun of it.'

'Aye, and I can't help liking him for it.'

'Neither can I,' Polly admitted with a chuckle that did something very drastic indeed to Tom's heart and sent him into a state of complete desire between one second and the next.

'I much prefer his big sister though,' he admitted huskily as they came back together for the next part of the dance and even a brisk measure with a very disapproving matron hadn't been enough to restore him to a fit state to inhabit a lady's ballroom. 'You couldn't manage a bit of a stumble, or perhaps even a faint, could you, love? I want to bed you even more urgently than I did this afternoon and I don't think there's any way I can conceal the fact from the rest of the world for much longer.'

'It would take half a dozen footmen to carry me out,' she said with a wry smile and a huff of laughter as she looked down at the evidence of his rampant need for her. 'Hmm, I do see what you mean, though,' she added with a delighted smile that only made it worse.

'I won't have you traduce yourself, or me for that matter, my love. You are just as tall as you need to be and I wouldn't have you even half an inch less and at least if I'm carrying you I can hide behind your skirts, for once.'

'You couldn't,' she gasped a little less certainly as the music finally wound down, and she looked as if she felt ready to melt from the inside out as well.

'I'm impressive, Polly, my darling, but not even I am too huge not to be able to hide what you do to me behind that delightful but highly unnecessary wisp of silk and nonsense,' he said with a dismissive glance at the finest gown in a whole wardrobe of them that the Bond Street modiste had rushed through her workroom in time for Lady Mantaigne to make her début in polite society at the advanced age of four and twenty.

'It is very necessary,' she argued absent-mindedly as she flitted through scenarios for getting out of this ballroom in double-quick time and without her lord making a scandal of them both mere days into their marriage.

'Not as far as I'm concerned it's not,' he argued as his intensely blue eyes met hers with a wealth of hot promises that made her shiver with anticipation. 'I want you in it, out of it and any other way I can have you, my lovely witchy Polly. From the first moment I laid eyes on you I've been racked with need and I don't intend either of us to be denied satiating that need again for much longer.'

'We sated it all afternoon, Tom,' she protested half-heartedly, but there was as much heat in her grey-green-blue eyes as in his, and her breath was coming so short his fascinated gaze was fixed on her décolletage as her breasts rose magnificently, begging for his attentions as soon as possible under the promise of all he'd taught her to expect these past few days since they married in haste. 'I suppose I am very hot,' she managed to say rather breathily.

'You most certainly are,' he drawled, with the Tom-cat smile that had once made her hackles rise and hot shivers of desire plague her dreams and now made her long to share them with him even more than she had a second ago.

'I love you, Tom,' she breathed, and to the devil with anyone who might be listening.

'And I love you, my darling, but any minute now I might have to beg you to get us out of here, because I can't seem to string two thoughts together than aren't of making love to you as soon and as long as I can find an excuse to.'

'Oh, very well then,' she said with a tight little sigh that told him more than a hundred words of how much she loved and wanted him back, because she obligingly drooped as if quite overcome by the heat and excite-ment of her first night amongst the *ton* and trusted him absolutely to catch her and get them out of here as fast as he could order his host to lend them the nearest carriage and throw guineas at the coachman to get them back to Mantaigne House faster than he could say knife.

* * *

Polly stayed totally limp against him for a long moment, savouring the mighty strength of her lover and revelling in being needed and wanted by the man she wanted and needed so desperately back.

'I never dreamed I would marry at all, you know?' she whispered as he held her even closer to shield her from the rocking carriage as it swept across Mayfair.

'I know it,' he said rather grimly, considering he had interrupted kissing his way up her throat to do so. 'I deplore it and yet… Oh, love, I'm so glad you were safe at Dayspring and away from the wolves all the time I was strutting about the *ton* pretending I didn't care a damn for anyone. I have no right to be so proud to be your first lover, but I am and fully intend to be your last as well, if God will grant us the time to glory in each other like this for life.'

'Idiot,' she muttered on a blissful haze of joy that almost went beyond words. 'Of course I'm glad it was only ever you and always will be. There's nothing wrong with being all in all to each other, nothing wrong with being glad we love and live and want each other so immoderately. Do you truly think Toby will be all right with Mr Peters, though?' she added as remembrance of the rest of her family impinged on the desire he was feeding so shamelessly she wondered if they would make it home and into his splendid marquis's bed before they fell on each other like ravenous tigers.

'Why else to you think the man agreed to come with us tonight?' Tom said and gasped in a huge breath as the brush of her thigh against his mightily aroused manhood made him grip his fists tight in his determination not to make love to his marchioness in a stranger's carriage. 'He's no fool and knew neither we nor Luke and Chloe would be able to keep cool in the company of our lovers. I dare say he would rather have teeth pulled than enter a Mayfair ballroom of his own accord.'

'Then he's a good man,' she said with a nod that said it confirmed her conclusions about her new husband's lawyer and perhaps friend. 'I hope your godmother hasn't bitten off more than she could chew this time, though, for I would dearly like to see your Mr Peters happy.'

'He's neither mine nor Mr Peters, love, but I have learnt to have even more faith in Virginia over the past three months than I had before, so I expect he'll end up wherever it is he thinks he has no right to be. However, my interest in the man is lukewarm at best when I have my Lady Mantaigne available to distract me with her many and varied charms,' he said as the carriage finally lurched to its destination.

'No,' she ordered him brusquely as he jumped out of the carriage and turned to lift her in his arms again. 'You will just have to carry this,' she declared, handing him her cloak as a mask for the state they had done nothing to diminish during the drive. 'I refuse to have you winded and exhausted when we finally manage to get ourselves upstairs,' she added with a haughty sniff as he eyed her with lordly determination and made a grab for her.

'She-wolf,' he accused as she dodged him and reminded him he'd agreed to pay the coachman another two guineas if he got them here before the clock finished chiming midnight.

'Tomcat,' she shot back over her shoulder as she gathered up her silken skirts and frothy petticoats in one hand and ran up the steps as if the devil was on her heels.

'Hand over the keys to the wine-cellar, marry him to your eldest daughter or just pay the man for me, would you?' Tom asked his butler distractedly before he set off up the steps to his once-stately and echoing mansion without a second thought for his lost reputation as an elegantly bored and sophisticated man about town.

'Yes, my lord,' the butler said with a glare for the grinning coachman. 'Breathe a word of this and I'll make sure you ain't up to marrying any man's daughter, let alone mine,' he threatened the man as he handed over the extortionate fee his master had promised him.

'Even the nobs will know by now he can't keep his hands off her, cocky, so that's a horse as has already bolted,' the man said cheerfully and went off to tell his tale to whoever was the most eager to listen to it.

'And ain't that just how it ought to be between a man and his wife?' the butler asked the sparkling June night, lit by stars so bright they even managed to outshine the man-made glitter of Mayfair in full fig.

'Hurry,' Tom gritted between clenched teeth as Polly streaked up the stairs ahead of him and he could see enough of her slender legs and the long, sleek lines of her hips and bottom outlined by that wicked provocation of a gown to drive him nigh demented. 'I hope your maid isn't waiting up,' he managed as she got to the door only one step ahead of him and fumbled it open before turning to snap a hasty denial.

'Of course not. Jane has far more sense,' she told him as if he was an idiot to even mention it.

'Silly me,' he said with a predator's grin and shut the door behind them with a contented sigh. 'Alone at last, my love,' he whispered and set about the laces of her gown with hands clumsy with too much haste even as he devoured her temptation of a mouth with a driven groan.

'Ah, love, quiet,' she soothed even as her still slightly calloused fingers raced to undo as much of Lord Mantaigne as she could while he was doing the same for Lady Mantaigne in his ham-fisted fashion. 'We have all night,' she promised even as she hastily shrugged out of her loosened gown and gave a crow of triumph as she pushed his roughly unbuttoned waistcoat and tightly fitting evening coat off his shoulders.

He dipped his head to feast on her roused nipples even as she moaned with pent-up need and haste and caressed his wildly disordered locks with such tenderness he raised his head and snatched another of those hasty, open-mouthed kisses before pulling far enough away to fumble off his cravat and tug his shirt over his head. Any last trace of ladylike restraint vanished as she eyed his hard-muscled torso and lean waist with a heavy-eyed smile.

'Evening breeches are a cursed nuisance,' she informed him as he bent to unbutton them at the knee and heel off his elegant shoes before impatiently stripping away his stockings.

'Oh, I don't know, they have their uses,' he said huskily as she attacked the buttons at his waist with more haste than skill.

'Not for hiding this,' she told him with would-be severity, but her eyes glittered hotly in the light of the candle Jane had left on the nightstand, so they might at least try not to ruin another set of expensive raiment and cause her and his lordship's valet even more trouble.

'Did you want to?' he asked with a wicked grin.

'Not from us, from all those other women,' she admitted rather painfully.

'None of them matter. I didn't love anyone until I met you, remember?'

'Oh, you man, you. You have always had it there deep within you, Tom, but you wouldn't let yourself know it. How else could you have made a family of the heart when your real one faded? How did you win a legion of friends and lovers who put you at the centre of their circle and had the sense to know you made them more than they were without you? You are so much more than you ever let yourself know, but what if you learn that for yourself one day and don't need me any more?'

'Now who's the idiot?' he asked with a catch in his deep voice. 'I will never not need you, Polly. I found pleasure with other women before I met you and if that makes you sad and uncertain of me, I'm sorry for it and wish it otherwise, but it was nothing like this. I've never needed to make love to another woman so desperately it feels as if I might expire of sheer need without you. Does it look as if I could ever stop wanting you, my love? Because if it does, I think we'd better get you fitted for some eyeglasses as soon as the spectacle makers are open in the morning.'

'I don't think there's anything wrong with my eyesight,' she said with a hiccup of laughter as she let her gaze linger on the very evident need he had of her. 'You're beautiful,' she told him, quite forgetting to be insecure at the sight of him so openly and proudly wanting her to the finest fibre of his being.

'Ah, love, come here and let me show you how breathtakingly lovely you are,' he said in reply and he actually blushed at her wide-eyed appreciation of his muscular body and rampantly aroused manhood. 'I love you, Polly Trethayne,' he told her as he held her eyes and parted her legs so he could thrust into the hot wet heat of her and unite them once more.

'Polly Banburgh,' she corrected breathlessly and opened wholeheartedly to him, sparing a moment to marvel anew that Polly Trethayne had found herself a husband, and such a fine and rampant husband as the Marquis of Mantaigne as well. 'I love you, Tom. With every last inconvenient inch of me, I love you.'

'Every last magnificent and delightful inch of you I hope you mean. Every bit of you is precious to me,' he said as he met her dazed eyes with his blazing hot, blue gaze so full of conviction she had to believe him. 'I wouldn't have you an inch less, my Polly, and don't let anyone make you feel awkward or overgrown ever again.'

'Very well, I won't,' she said meekly and let her inner muscles ripple around his hard member in delighted encouragement. 'There are so many parts of me in need of reassurance that you love right now, husband,' she murmured with wanton encouragement as she sneaked a suggestive hand over her own hard-peaked nipples and down the smooth line of her narrow waist and the curve of her hips before she reached their joined bodies and found his more fascinating than her own.

'Oh, I love you all right, so get ready to be reassured to your heart's content, Lady Mantaigne,' he said huskily as he silenced her with a long, hard kiss as if they'd been parted for weeks instead of hours and proceeded to show his wife he loved and appreciated and wanted every last fine inch of silky skin and every hair on her head.

* * * * *

REQUEST YOUR FREE BOOKS!

2 FREE NOVELS PLUS 2 FREE GIFTS!

HARLEQUIN

American ★ Romance®

LOVE, HOME & HAPPINESS

YES! Please send me 2 FREE Harlequin® American Romance® novels and my 2 FREE gifts (gifts are worth about $10). After receiving them, if I don't wish to receive any more books, I can return the shipping statement marked "cancel." If I don't cancel, I will receive 4 brand-new novels every month and be billed just $4.74 per book in the U.S. or $5.24 per book in Canada. That's a savings of at least 14% off the cover price! It's quite a bargain! Shipping and handling is just 50¢ per book in the U.S. and 75¢ per book in Canada.* I understand that accepting the 2 free books and gifts places me under no obligation to buy anything. I can always return a shipment and cancel at any time. Even if I never buy another book, the two free books and gifts are mine to keep forever.

154/354 HDN F4YY

Name   (PLEASE PRINT)

Address   Apt. #

City   State/Prov.   Zip/Postal Code

Signature (if under 18, a parent or guardian must sign)

Mail to the **Harlequin® Reader Service:**
IN U.S.A.: P.O. Box 1867, Buffalo, NY 14240-1867
IN CANADA: P.O. Box 609, Fort Erie, Ontario L2A 5X3

Want to try two free books from another line?
Call 1-800-873-8635 or visit www.ReaderService.com.

* Terms and prices subject to change without notice. Prices do not include applicable taxes. Sales tax applicable in N.Y. Canadian residents will be charged applicable taxes. Offer not valid in Quebec. This offer is limited to one order per household. Not valid for current subscribers to Harlequin American Romance books. All orders subject to credit approval. Credit or debit balances in a customer's account(s) may be offset by any other outstanding balance owed by or to the customer. Please allow 4 to 6 weeks for delivery. Offer available while quantities last.

Your Privacy—The Harlequin® Reader Service is committed to protecting your privacy. Our Privacy Policy is available online at www.ReaderService.com or upon request from the Harlequin Reader Service.

We make a portion of our mailing list available to reputable third parties that offer products we believe may interest you. If you prefer that we not exchange your name with third parties, or if you wish to clarify or modify your communication preferences, please visit us at www.ReaderService.com/consumerschoice or write to us at Harlequin Reader Service Preference Service, P.O. Box 9062, Buffalo, NY 14269. Include your complete name and address.

REQUEST YOUR
FREE BOOKS!

HARLEQUIN™ *Presents*~

PASSION GUARANTEED SEDUCTION

2 FREE NOVELS PLUS
2 FREE GIFTS!

YES! Please send me 2 FREE Harlequin Presents® novels and my 2 FREE gifts (gifts are worth about $10). After receiving them, if I don't wish to receive any more books, I can return the shipping statement marked "cancel." If I don't cancel, I will receive 6 brand-new novels every month and be billed just $4.30 per book in the U.S. or $4.99 per book in Canada. That's a savings of at least 14% off the cover price! It's quite a bargain! Shipping and handling is just 50¢ per book in the U.S. and 75¢ per book in Canada.* I understand that accepting the 2 free books and gifts places me under no obligation to buy anything. I can always return a shipment and cancel at any time. Even if I never buy another book, the two free books and gifts are mine to keep forever.

106/306 HDN FV3K

Name	(PLEASE PRINT)

Address	Apt. #

City	State/Prov.	Zip/Postal Code

Signature (if under 18, a parent or guardian must sign)

Mail to the Harlequin® Reader Service:
IN U.S.A.: P.O. Box 1867, Buffalo, NY 14240-1867
IN CANADA: P.O. Box 609, Fort Erie, Ontario L2A 5X3

Are you a current subscriber to Harlequin Presents books
and want to receive the larger-print edition?
Call 1-800-873-8635 or visit www.ReaderService.com.

* Terms and prices subject to change without notice. Prices do not include applicable taxes. Sales tax applicable in N.Y. Canadian residents will be charged applicable taxes. Offer not valid in Quebec. This offer is limited to one order per household. Not valid for current subscribers to Harlequin Presents books. All orders subject to credit approval. Credit or debit balances in a customer's account(s) may be offset by any other outstanding balance owed by or to the customer. Please allow 4 to 6 weeks for delivery. Offer available while quantities last.

Your Privacy—The Harlequin® Reader Service is committed to protecting your privacy. Our Privacy Policy is available online at www.ReaderService.com or upon request from the Harlequin Reader Service.

We make a portion of our mailing list available to reputable third parties that offer products we believe may interest you. If you prefer that we not exchange your name with third parties, or if you wish to clarify or modify your communication preferences, please visit us at www.ReaderService.com/consumerchoice or write to us at Harlequin Reader Service Preference Service, P.O. Box 9062, Buffalo, NY 14269. Include your complete name and address.

HPDIR13

REQUEST YOUR FREE BOOKS!

2 FREE INSPIRATIONAL NOVELS
PLUS 2
FREE
MYSTERY GIFTS

Love Inspired
HISTORICAL
INSPIRATIONAL HISTORICAL ROMANCE

YES! Please send me 2 FREE Love Inspired® Historical novels and my 2 FREE mystery gifts (gifts are worth about $10). After receiving them, if I don't wish to receive any more books, I can return the shipping statement marked "cancel." If I don't cancel, I will receive 4 brand-new novels every month and be billed just $4.74 per book in the U.S. or $5.24 per book in Canada. That's a savings of at least 21% off the cover price. It's quite a bargain! Shipping and handling is just 50¢ per book in the U.S. and 75¢ per book in Canada.* I understand that accepting the 2 free books and gifts places me under no obligation to buy anything. I can always return a shipment and cancel at any time. Even if I never buy another book, the two free books and gifts are mine to keep forever.

102/302 IDN F5CY

Name	(PLEASE PRINT)

Address	Apt. #

City	State/Prov.	Zip/Postal Code

Signature (if under 18, a parent or guardian must sign)

Mail to the Harlequin® Reader Service:
IN U.S.A.: P.O. Box 1867, Buffalo, NY 14240-1867
IN CANADA: P.O. Box 609, Fort Erie, Ontario L2A 5X3

Want to try two free books from another series?
Call 1-800-873-8635 or visit www.ReaderService.com.

* Terms and prices subject to change without notice. Prices do not include applicable taxes. Sales tax applicable in N.Y. Canadian residents will be charged applicable taxes. Offer not valid in Quebec. This offer is limited to one order per household. Not valid for current subscribers to Love Inspired Historical books. All orders subject to credit approval. Credit or debit balances in a customer's account(s) may be offset by any other outstanding balance owed by or to the customer. Please allow 4 to 6 weeks for delivery. Offer available while quantities last.

Your Privacy—The Harlequin® Reader Service is committed to protecting your privacy. Our Privacy Policy is available online at www.ReaderService.com or upon request from the Harlequin Reader Service.

We make a portion of our mailing list available to reputable third parties that offer products we believe may interest you. If you prefer that we not exchange your name with third parties, or if you wish to clarify or modify your communication preferences, please visit us at www.ReaderService.com/consumerchoice or write to us at Harlequin Reader Service Preference Service, P.O. Box 9062, Buffalo, NY 14269. Include your complete name and address.

LIHDIR13R